In the Serpent's Coils

By Venom's Sweet Sting

Between Golden Jaws

Maiden of the Wolf
May 2008

Queen of the Masquerade
August 2008

Oracle of the Morrigan
November 2008

The Marsh King's Daughter
March 2009

Snake Dancer
May 2009

Redemption
November 2009

Ouroborus Undone
Spring 2010

HALLOWMERE™

Volume Three

Between Golden Jaws

TIFFANY TRENT

MIRRORSTONE

Hallowmere
Between Golden Jaws

©2008 Wizards of the Coast, Inc.

Cover design by Trish Yochum
Cover Art © Jörg Steffens/zefa/image100/Corbis
First Printing: March 2008

Cataloging-in-Publication Data is available from the Library of Congress

9 8 7 6 5 4 3 2 1

ISBN: 978-0-7869-4797-3
620-21645740-001-EN

U.S., CANADA,
ASIA, PACIFIC, & LATIN AMERICA
Wizards of the Coast, Inc.
P.O. Box 707
Renton, WA 98057-0707
+1-800-324-6496

EUROPEAN HEADQUARTERS
Hasbro UK Ltd
Caswell Way
Newport, Gwent NP9 0YH
GREAT BRITAIN
Save this address for your records.

Visit our Web site at www.mirrorstonebooks.com

To Kimlet

PROLOGUE

[*Translation note: Spotted with dark stains, as of blood*]

June 1373

Frater Josephus—

I write in haste to inform you that word has reached us of the disappearance of Mary Rose. There has been no rumor of her since early April, and our watchers at court confirm that she is no longer to be seen in the company of Lord Huntingdon. Whether she has hidden her child away, or the girl was taken with her, remains to be discovered. We believe she may have been taken around the time of Beltane.

Naturally, we fear the worst. The Council feels that you should depart from Albion, until such time as we have need of you. The Father and Elaphe speed you back to us in the hour of our need.

Yours in Christ,

Frater Gregorius

One

February 24, 1866

The pillywiggin's remains shivered into the air until they were little more than shimmering mist. Standing on the front steps of Fearnan manor where she'd just witnessed the pillywiggin's horrible death, Corrine couldn't pay attention to anything Father Joe was trying to say. She ran down the steps and around the main house into the misty labyrinth, heedless of the shouts behind her. When she crested the little hill and entered the gazebo, she clutched her sides, gasping against the restraint of her corset. Her lungs were afire and aching, as if she had the swamp fever again. She held her face against the damp marble, unable to hear anything but her own labored breathing.

Corrine had once sworn a vow that no one, human or otherwise, would ever see her cry again. She had broken that vow by the end of her time at Falston, and many times over at Fearnan. But now Corrine longed to renew it. Crying seemed too much like admitting defeat. She yearned for someone she could trust, some-one who would never betray her. The marble chilled her hands. She slipped her fingers into the scarf draped around her throat. Euan had given it to her after the shipwreck of the *Great Eastern*, and later, a charm to use it to call him whenever she needed him. Back then, she'd trusted him, almost to the point of love.

But that was before she had known the truth, before she had discovered that Euan and the Prince were one and the same. Before she had discovered the depths of his guile and betrayal.

As if listening to her thoughts, the fog breathed in a shadowed corner of the gazebo, forming into a man's shape. He stepped toward her. Euan. The Prince.

Set me as a seal upon thine heart, as a seal upon thine arm; for love is strong as death; jealousy is cruel as the grave: the coals thereof are coals of fire, which hath a most vehement flame.

His mouth didn't move, but she heard him.

Is that not what your Song of Solomon says?

She didn't reply. She glanced toward the gazebo entrance, wondering if he could follow her, wondering if this meant he could now find her anywhere.

"You're not here," she whispered.

The pillywiggin's death summoned me. Corrine, why do you flee from me?

"You took my friends. You killed—" She choked. It occurred to her suddenly that perhaps neither of her parents' deaths had been accidental. Had he killed them as he'd killed the girls in the alley, as he had probably killed Kenneth?

Death is in my nature. This he said with a sorrow as heavy as the shadows in which he stood. *As is love.*

"Love?" Corrine asked. The thought that he loved her, that this murdering creature was now professing love to her, after all he had done—it was too much.

4

Why else do I plead with you now?

"Plead with me? What can you possibly expect me to do?"

You are so young. You cannot know . . . His image wavered as he sighed.

"I know that too many have died because of you; I know that every day more are at risk because of *you*. I think that's all I need to know."

I love you, Corrine. Why is that so difficult to believe?

"Because—" she whispered hopelessly. "You killed all those people. You're not *human*."

I will not stop, Corrine. I let you escape before, but I will not do so again. You will be with me, here in my rath.

Corrine thought of the Prince's decaying city, its towers gleaming with witch-light. Long ago, before she knew what her dreams really were, it had seemed like such an enchanted place, but she knew now that any beauty it appeared to contain was a lie. She forced herself to stand straighter and move closer to him. "And what if I don't wish to?" The fog reached toward the gazebo with gray tentacles.

Then I will arrange it so you have no choice.

She rushed at him then, hoping to rip or tear or claw, hoping to *hurt* him.

Her hands passed through shadow and gripped something solid. She yanked it free.

"Corrine!" Miss Brown called from the entrance to the labyrinth.

The mist swirled and the Prince was gone.

Corrine closed her hand and put it behind her back. Whatever was in her palm was hard and curved, like a ring.

Miss Brown entered the gazebo, her flannel petticoats peeking from under her wide wool skirt. She wore a matching jacket with black piping and large black buttons. She looked ready to go riding, if the weather were not so foul. *And there were not Unhallowed afoot*, Corrine thought.

"Corrine, what are you doing out here alone? Was someone with you?" Miss Brown asked.

Corrine swallowed. "The Prince."

"The Prince? He was here?" Miss Brown came to her.

Corrine tried to breathe. "He appeared. He said—" She blushed, embarrassed by his declarations of love. "He said he would take me with him to his city, whether I wanted him to or no."

Miss Brown put a hand on her forearm. "We must tell the Council about this," Miss Brown said. "If he's able to enter here now, despite Mara's new wards—"

Corrine shook her head. "I don't think it was really him. I think it was some kind of message."

"A sending?"

Corrine nodded. Father Joe had mentioned the term offhandedly once in a magic lesson, though he hadn't explained it further.

"He shouldn't be able to do that," Miss Brown said.

Corrine was grateful that Miss Brown never implied that the Prince's new powers were her fault, despite all the mistakes she'd made. Miss Brown drew her out of the gazebo. "Come. Let's see what Father Joe and Sir James think."

As they entered the house, Miss Brown asked Mr. Turnbull to bring Sir James and Father Joe to the study. Mrs. Guthrie came at the ring of the bell, and nodded as

Miss Brown requested tea while they waited.

Corrine sat at the round table, remembering how Mara had leaped over it in the shape of a panther, how she had borne the cuideag imposter to the hearth and knocked him into the fire. Corrine wondered if the magic she was learning, the heritage she possessed, would someday turn her into a beast like that.

Sir James and Father Joe arrived with the tea. Mara came with Mrs. Guthrie, and took over her tasks as everyone seated themselves. Corrine bit her lip. It still bothered her at some level that Mara had to serve all of them in this way, even though she was the most valuable member of the Council. She tried to rationalize that Mara was not a slave, but a freed servant paid a wage and allowed to come or go as she pleased. But was she really?

"The Prince came to Corrine just now," Miss Brown said.

"What?" Sir James and Father Joe said almost simultaneously.

"Corrine," Miss Brown urged, nodding to her.

"He came to me while I was out in the gazebo. He stood in the shadows. I don't think he was really there. I think he was a . . ." She looked at Miss Brown.

"Sending," Miss Brown offered.

"Yes," Corrine sighed.

"And?" Father Joe said. It took five seconds for his glasses to come off this time.

Corrine blushed. *Set me as a seal upon thine heart* . . .

"He vowed to take her to his city," Miss Brown finished for her.

"The Iron Oath," Father Joe said. He examined his

glasses and polished them again. "He is appearing in his true form in daylight and despite Mara's wards."

"What shall we do?" Sir James asked.

"We have two choices. Stay and fight. Or leave and hope for better days," Father Joe said.

Sir James's brow furrowed.

"Or so the Unhallowed believe," Father Joe continued. "There's one choice they probably haven't considered. That we conquer them with their own tactics. I say we bring the battle to them. The pillywiggin told us they would next seek the Stone of Destiny. The Stone of Destiny was once also called the Stone of Scone, and for centuries, Scottish kings were crowned upon it."

Corrine suppressed a sigh. She sensed the beginning of another history lesson. "However," Father Joe said, "Edward the Confessor captured it in 1296 and brought it back to England as a sign of his victory over the Scottish. Some legends say that the monks of Scone hid the stone in the River Tay and that Edward was fooled. But others say that the Stone of Destiny rests under Edward the Confessor's throne in Westminster Abbey, and kings and queens of England have been crowned upon it ever since."

"Thieving English," Sir James muttered.

"Why not go to London and take it first?" Father Joe asked, ignoring Sir James. "The Unhallowed will try to use Corrine or Mara to get it for them. If we retrieve it first, if we can stay ahead of them, we'll keep them from taking both the girls and the stones. Perhaps we'll even weaken them enough to get the stone they possess back from them."

Corrine nodded, but her mind shrank from the

thought of the Prince's stone heart. *The Prince. Locked in his rath forever, the golden beetle scales raining down eternally in the dark . . .* She peeked down at the thing in her hand and saw a hint of silver.

"You should probably leave, regardless," Sir James said. "I must sadly admit that Fearnan isn't safe any longer."

"But will you be safe if we leave you here?" Miss Brown asked.

"Certainly, dear girl," Sir James said. "After all, it's the girls they want. I doubt they'll try using another cuideag, and they have no further use for me."

Except to get your rathstone, Corrine thought.

"We'll set as many wards as we can," Father Joe said. "You'll be as protected as we can make you."

Sir James half-smiled at him, but Corrine could see he wasn't entirely comforted.

"Why not try to close the rath?" Corrine asked.

Everyone looked at her.

"We know there's a gate right under the gazebo. Why not try to close it so they can't come through on the Fearnan grounds? They wouldn't expect that, would they?"

Father Joe laughed sharply, a sound startling in its cynicism. Hurt, Corrine looked to the others for support, but no one said anything.

"You have quite the imagination, Corrine," Father Joe said. "It would be wonderful if we could do what you suggest. But it's impossible to close a rath entirely without all the rathstones together. The Unhallowed raths are like rabbit warrens. Gates are everywhere. Close one and there are still many others available."

"But why not close this one and make it harder for them to trouble Sir James?" Corrine asked.

"It would take much magical energy that we can't spare now," Father Joe said. "No, let us focus on getting to London as quickly as possible. Agreed?"

Everyone nodded, except for Corrine. Mara caught her eye and shook her head a little. Corrine dropped her eyes.

Miss Brown sighed before she sipped her tea.

"Thea?" Father Joe said. "You have an objection?"

She shook her head with a small smile. "I was simply wondering how I would explain this move yet again to Ilona's and Christina's parents. They were suspicious after the events at Falston." Her cup chimed as she set it back on its saucer.

"Tell them it's an extended field trip," Father Joe said. "After all, London is one of the most famous cities in the British Isles. Certainly, our studies don't preclude forays into the field now and then."

He paused to drink his tea.

"And," he continued, "it will be good to get the girls away, I think. Perhaps Christina will escape thoughts of Rory. And Corrine . . ." He wouldn't speak of the Prince.

Corrine kept her eyes firmly on her teacup.

"Well," Miss Brown said. "I suppose we'd best begin packing then. Corrine, will you alert the girls and tell them to lay out their traveling things?"

Corrine eyed Mara where she stood at the edge of the table, loading the teacups and saucers onto the tray. There was obviously something the rest of the Council wanted to talk about without her. She stood from the table and made a small farewell bow before she left. With or without their help, she would find a way to close that rathgate.

She pulled the study door shut behind her, glad to be away. So much scheming and plotting made her long for the Euan she had known. She stopped on her way up the stairs and opened her hand.

Set me as a seal upon thine heart . . .

A silver signet ring glittered in her palm. Two tiny serpents—light and dark—circled its face, eating one another's tails, like the serpents on the cover of the Unhallowed book. The serpents were encrusted with something, dark wax or possibly . . . Corrine didn't want to think about it.

She had stolen the Prince's signet ring and he had sworn to steal her.

Love is as strong as death.

And though it seemed a strange and perhaps foolish thing to do, she unhooked the gold clasp of her locket and slid the signet ring down the chain. She slid the ring so it hung next to the golden book. She sensed power in this ring, and perhaps she could find some way to turn it against the Prince. So often, he had used her own power, her curiosity and trust, against her. The ring impressed a cold circle on her breastbone as she walked back up the ancient staircase to her room. She would prove to herself that his memory had no power to hold her.

Weak morning light filtered through the window. She crossed to the fire where it burned sullen and low on the hearth. The heat barely penetrated the woolen layers of skirts and petticoats. Corrine unwound the scarf at her throat and held it for a long moment, her fingers wound in its incredible softness. She pushed away the memories of Euan—saving her as the *Great Eastern* sank, talking with her quietly as Ilona and Kenneth fenced, and baring the wound in his chest to her, inviting her to kill him if his death pleased her best. Instead, she thought of poor Kenneth ripped to pieces, the nameless little girl who had died in her arms, the pillywiggin's shining blood, seizing the ring from him just now. She tossed the scarf into the flames.

The fabric burned a dark hole into the fire. Blue sparks trailed around it; whispered Unhallowed words unwove the fabric. Legs and eyes crumpled in a creaking heap. The fireplace exhaled a terrible stench, like the rotting caterpillar Miss Brown had once thrown onto the fire at Falston.

Daoi.

Corrine's stomach clenched. A daoi had been disguised as a scarf? A daoi had been the thing she carried with her against the cold, that she had held to her face in comfort? She stepped back, nauseated. She went to the window and tried feebly to open it, but when it wouldn't open, she ran out into the hall and shut her door.

She needed to be with someone, anyone. Someone human and warm and ordinary. She left her room, and knocked at Christina's door. She entered to find her two friends engaged in a game of baccarat.

"Corrine," Ilona said, looking over her shoulder, "we hoped you would come up after the Council meeting. Come play! Perhaps you'll feel better."

That was the closest either of them would come, Corrine knew, to mentioning the death of the pillywiggin.

As Corrine approached them, Christina held her cards over her mouth in horror. "Whatever happened to your dress?"

"It was scorched," Corrine said. She took the chair near them that Ilona indicated.

"Well, yes, of course," Christina said. "But why? And what is that smell?" She fanned her cards in front of her nose before laying a card on the table. Ilona snorted in disgust.

Corrine swallowed. The Prince's words stuck in her throat. "I stood too close to the fire."

"Fire does tend to scorch things, you ninny," Christina said, half-laughing. She must have seen Corrine's dejected expression, for she waved her cards at her and said, "I'm sure something can be done, *mon ami*. Perhaps we can embroider little flowers over the burn marks. Wouldn't that be lovely?"

The falseness in her voice clanged against Corrine's ears. This wasn't helping. Why wouldn't they acknowledge what was really going on? She stood. "I suppose," she said.

The two of them looked over their cards at her.

"Are you well?" Ilona asked. "You haven't seemed well since you returned from the rath."

Corrine fluttered her hand in what she hoped was a convincing dismissive gesture. She wanted to talk about the pillywiggin, the Prince, but their false cheer forbade her. "Perhaps I'll lie down for a while," Corrine said. "Maybe I should rest."

Ilona nodded, and Christina flashed her familiar smile. Next to her, Corrine felt tawdry and somehow gray. The girls resumed their game as easily as if she had never been there; she heard a short burst of laughter as she passed into the hallway.

She returned to her room, and dug in her nightstand

drawer for the Unhallowed book. The horrible smell lingered near the fireplace, so she went to the window, and, as she had often done these many days, curled on its cold, cramped sill.

The serpents on the book cover slivered restlessly beneath her fingers. She opened it.

"Closing a rath," she whispered.

Words boiled up in sticky gouts from the book's depths. The covers trembled and the serpents hissed. The book seemed *angry*.

To punish those who would deny their Rightful Lords

The great raths cannot be closed but by conjunction of the thirteen rathstones. Thus has the Great Deceiver assured that certain raths are sealed for perpetuity while others remain open to incursion. He has stolen Hallowmere from its true rulers forever. Still, one rathstone may seal certain gates into the great raths, though the smaller raths, enclaves of those who dare to call themselves the Hallowed, may be sealed entirely. Slow starvation will ensue for all inhabitants of a closed rath—a fitting end to those who would defy the Lords of Hallowmere.

To close a gate requires mortal blood and hateful iron, in addition to the rathstone. Cut the flesh with the iron and let it be stained with blood. Plunge it then into the earth, and holding the rathstone, say: "As room with no door and door with no key, seal this gate. With blood and iron, so mote it be."

As Corrine read the final words, the page shuddered and went completely black. She closed it and the snakes on its cover coiled under her hand. She knew what she had to do.

~Two~

March 17, 1866

CORRINE WAITED NEARLY THREE WEEKS UNTIL SHE COULD put her plan in motion. It took that long before a morning arrived when matters of the estate kept Sir James from his usual routine of retiring to his study for his second cup of tea.

After breakfast, Corrine slipped into the study. Sir James had placed the rathstone she'd given him on the mantel in an iron box. No Unhallowed would dare to touch the box, and as the windows were blocked by heavy draperies, no daoi could see it. She was surprised to find a little iron lock on the box, a lock for which no key was evident.

Corrine listened for a moment, then began her search. Where in all the vastness of Fearnan would he keep the key? Surely not here. That would be too obvious. Or would it? She rifled through his desk drawers, most of which were unlocked. She agonized over the ones that were locked, wondering if a tiny iron key was imprisoned inside, and how she'd ever find it. She tried to remind herself that there were always finding charms.

She looked at the box again. It seemed strange that Sir

James hadn't taken it directly to the Council chamber in Fearnan's cellar. Everything else of import to the Council was locked up there. She shuddered a little at the memory of the place and the scorpion-tailed cuideag that had haunted it. And then the thought came. *Perhaps the key is locked there, too.*

She couldn't stay here alone much longer. Father Joe was expecting her in the turret study for a final lesson before the packing for London began in earnest. And who knew when Sir James would come, since he seemed to spend the bulk of his time here.

Father Joe had mentioned at breakfast that he'd received a letter from Madame DuBois in London. She had made arrangements for them to stay on Primrose Hill at a Council sympathizer's house, a merchant who was away in India on business. All the preparations were in place. If Corrine was going to close the gate, she'd need to do it soon.

Father Joe was waiting for her in the turret room, gazing out of the window that looked onto the labyrinth. He held something at his side that looked oddly like a hand mirror. There was a strange expression on his face, a look not unlike those Melanie had given Corrine back at Falston when Rory was around. She followed his gaze to the labyrinth, where Miss Brown talked with a gardener over a bird's nest that had fallen from the hedge.

The priest gestured toward the table. "Well. Shall we?"

Corrine nodded and seated herself.

"Am I correct in guessing that you've been unable to concentrate on your studies since your return from the Prince's rath?" He settled himself opposite her.

"Yes, Father."

"Since you've finished copying Angus's letters, have you started with Brighde's? Perhaps that would keep your mind and hands occupied."

The perfect opportunity.

"They're still in the chamber," Corrine said. "Sir James said not to remove them. I need the key to the chamber before I can copy them."

Father Joe removed his spectacles and rubbed at his eyes. He seemed suddenly old and tired. "Yes, well. I'll give you the key when we're finished here. You can go to the chamber this afternoon."

Corrine nodded. That had been far too easy.

"Today," Father Joe said, "I want to work first with glamoury. We've had to use glamours several times to protect you, but it would be wisest for you to learn this skill for yourself." He opened a book and pushed it toward her. She wrinkled her nose at the mold speckling its pages.

"Glamoury is a magical art form the Unhallowed have practiced to perfection. It takes great skill to maintain a glamour; I do not know how the Prince managed it on our voyage across the ocean. It must have drained him terribly."

Corrine wondered how many of the people on board the ship had died to feed the Prince's power. She stared hard at the thin ink on the grimoire's pages, trying to ignore her guilt.

"So," Father Joe said. He slid the hand mirror across the table. "Pick up the mirror."

She took its tarnished silver handle and looked into it. Her eyes haunted her.

"Now, start with the breaths. I want you to think of

someone about whom you have strong feelings. Preferably someone of your own gender; it's easier on the first try. The first person who enters your mind. Think about the features of her face, try to see through her eyes, try to feel what she feels. Slip into her as though you're wearing a mask."

Corrine inhaled sharply as her face shifted in the mirror. Her eyes tilted and darkened; her hair brightened and coiled into golden curls. Rage and sorrow clogged her throat against speech.

Melanie.

She dropped the mirror and it shattered on the table as the glamour receded.

"Corrine!" Father Joe said.

She drew a long breath, put her hands over her face to make sure she was who she had always been.

"You did well," Father Joe said. "It was fairly convincing. Keep practicing. Perhaps with an upright mirror." He smiled.

Corrine didn't return it. "Why *her?*" she asked.

"Who knows? Revulsion and fear are strong emotions. Don't be alarmed by it—until you learn to control the magic, it will often choose what is uppermost on your mind. It was a good likeness and may be useful at some point."

Corrine's fingers trembled over the grimoire's pages. The broken mirror mocked her.

"Learning how to make a glamour should also help you to recognize when someone is using one. Keep practicing and don't let whatever comes frighten you," Father Joe said.

"I'll try." Corrine repressed the urge to bite her

cuticles, a habit her mother had forced her to banish long ago.

Father Joe stood. "Let's leave that and work in the astral domains. We'll attempt the domain of water this time. I'm sure it won't be easy, but it's necessary for you to progress."

Memories of the horrid mermaid who had worn Melanie's face, the ghosts dancing across the sinking *Great Eastern* made Corrine clutch the table. So many people had died for her onboard that ship. Much as she'd tried to forget, their faces haunted her.

"You'll not go unprotected," Father Joe said. "We found a charm in one of the chamber books." He removed a small jar of ointment from his pocket and uncapped the lid. Camphor laced with bergamot and myrrh drowned out the smell of moldy books. Father Joe dipped his finger in the balm and leaned to paint a dark cross on Corrine's forehead. The red binding on his aura flared, a binding she'd only seen in the shadows of the *Great Eastern.* He whispered words she couldn't quite catch; her forehead tingled with power.

"This will hide you in the domain of magic. It will not keep the Unhallowed from coming into your dreams or from finding you here. But in the domains, let us pray that it will keep you hidden long enough to learn."

Corrine nodded.

Father Joe lit a single white candle and placed it between them on the table. Then he rose and pulled all the draperies closed, shutting out the day. He came to stand behind her. "Close your eyes," he said. He took her through the five-count breathing exercise, then across the towers of the east and into the garden of the sun. As she watched the green fire of life moving through the garden, he said, "What do you see?"

"Bees, hummingbirds, June bugs . . ." Corrine said. Their drowsy hum made her crave sleep.

"Nothing else? No sign of rot, burning, or decay? No sign of intrusion?"

There was nothing. The garden was quiet. Busy with life, but quiet.

"Now, I want you to leave the bower," he said. "Walk in whichever direction seems most pleasant to you. What do you see?"

She heard the swish of his cassock as though from a great distance as he moved to her left side. "Grape vines," she said. "Sunflowers. My grandmother's hollyhocks."

"What else?"

"Wait. The vines are growing over something."

"Can you clear them away?"

In the garden of the sun, she reached to push the grape vine away from the structure. It was strong and resisted her somewhat, but at last she pushed it away. "A well," she said.

"Look in," Father Joe said. "Tell me what you see."

"It's made of stone. It seems . . . scorched, blackened around the rim. The rope for the bucket is cut."

Father Joe sighed. "Are you certain?"

"Yes. The rope is cut."

"Corrine, I want you to jump into the well."

She stared into the dark, mossy depths. Though she said nothing, though she dropped no stones, strange echoes came back to her that sounded like the sea. A face swam up from the darkness, a face with many rows of shark-teeth and eyes blacker than the deepest abyss.

The mermaid reached her long skinny arms to Corrine, trailing her scarves of decaying flesh.

Corrine gasped. She opened her eyes to the single candle flame and stuffy, camphor-scented room.

Father Joe's disappointment was plain.

"I can't go down there," she said. "*She* was down there. Waiting."

"Leanan?" he asked.

"No." She shook her head. "The mermaid."

Father Joe sighed. He crossed to the curtains and opened them. Corrine noticed he lingered a bit too long at the window where he'd been watching Miss Brown.

"The well knows you and your fears. Perhaps the glamour work triggered this, but you must work harder to conquer them. You are protected. The Unhallowed have no desire to harm you. You're far too precious to them."

That was little consolation. "You saw what happened to me, to my face! I can't jump into that well, Father," Corrine said. "She's waiting down there. She wants me. What if she uses me just as she used Melanie?"

"The well only shows you what's in your own mind, Corrine. The mermaid has what she wanted. She is not truly in the well. Nothing in the domains can harm you."

"But what about those other times—when Leanan and the Captain were waiting for me?" Corrine asked. She hugged herself against the room's chill.

Father Joe frowned. "That should not have happened. Air and fire are external elements. The Unhallowed were obviously trying to taint them for you. But water and earth—these are internal elements. They only mirror your own fears and anxieties. These elements are meant to help you overcome your self-doubt, so that you can move on to the final element, the domain of spirit."

Corrine nodded. She wasn't sure she completely understood. The mermaid's face swam up at her from the dark. She shut her eyes. Though the cuideag she had faced below the manor had been terrifying, something about the mermaid seemed even more so. Perhaps it was because she'd always believed that mermaids were friendly, beautiful creatures. Perhaps it was because of all the ghosts the mermaid ruled, waiting to exact vengeance at the bottom of the sea.

"Corrine?"

She met his concerned gaze. "I can't," she said. She looked down at the scarred table. "I just can't."

Father Joe sighed. "One day, you'll have to. You must progress, and you must trust that the charm will protect you. Otherwise, the visions may consume you." He placed a key on the table beside her.

"The key to the chamber?" she said.

He laid his handkerchief beside it and gestured at her forehead.

She wiped at her skin. The tarry ointment required much rubbing to remove.

"Shall I escort you?" he asked.

She thought of the ancient dungeons beneath the manor and the monster that had once haunted it, hanging from the ceiling. As she closed her fingers over the key, she recalled the cuideag's chirping screams. *The key! The key? The KEY!*

She would have appreciated his company, but then felt like a coward for her failure to accomplish the goals of the day's lesson. She sighed. "No," she said at last. "I'll do this on my own." She ventured a smile at him.

"Well enough then. Take the candle along with you and return the key to me when you're done."

"Yes, Father," she said, lifting the candle from the table. The candlestick was cool despite wax pooling at its base.

He hesitated, as though he had made up his mind to leave but still had things to say.

"I won't deny that the domain of water can be terrifying," Father Joe said. "But I believe that you will conquer it," he said. "I have faith in you."

Corrine looked at him sharply. A faint blush spread across his ageless cheeks. He had never spoken this way before. No one had said any such thing to her in a long time.

"Thank you," she said. Her voice was too small to disturb the candle flame.

He nodded and departed swiftly. He seemed embarrassed that he had revealed any sort of sentiment. Why?

Corrine nursed her candle slowly down the back stairs, across the hall, and through the little door that led to the cellar. She had considered asking someone for help, but her failure at the well shamed her. And what would her friends do here in the chamber anyway? There was no danger any longer. She couldn't face Melanie or the mermaid, but this was something she could do on her own. She pushed away a sudden fierce longing for Euan, who had so many times protected her against the Unhallowed. Except that he *was* Unhallowed. *Their Prince*, she reminded herself again.

She meandered through the expanse of broken chairs and rusting armor while the shadows leaped from the flickering light of the candle. Something scraped behind those shadows and echoed around her, making her heart skitter with fear. For a moment, she wondered if thoughts of the Prince had somehow called him to her again. Then she realized it was simply a rat scurrying away from the weak light.

She reached the chamber without incident and as she drew the key from her pocket, the door and its lock shimmered into being. She was careful not to look at the ceiling as she turned the key in the lock and went inside.

Honeyed light flooded the chamber room, light from some spell that the Council had placed on it. Corrine nearly doused her candle before she remembered she would need it to return through the dark. The octagonal room seemed small and intimate, yet its shelves were endless, filled from floor to ceiling with books, magical objects, chests, scrolls. Corrine simply couldn't comprehend it all. Faded banners hung on one wall above a waist-high door. Where it might lead, Corrine truly didn't want to know.

She quailed at the thought of trying to find the key to the iron box in all this magical wilderness. It would be small. She trailed her fingers along the shelves, looked in some chests that held mildewed, odd-shaped things she didn't want to explore further. She opened a case full of old brooches, touched a book that stung like nettles. Perhaps she had been wrong. Perhaps . . .

A ruby winked at her like a little red eye by the door. She went closer and saw that the ruby was woven into a filigreed iron key hanging from a chain on an iron hook. It certainly looked small enough to unlock the iron chest that held the rathstone. She used her handkerchief to take the key and place it in her pocket. The iron burned through the thin linen.

Dutifully, she went to the chest on the table and lifted out Brighde's letters. She supposed if she didn't let on to Sir James, that no one else would mind if she took them up to the turret room to copy. Interesting as this place was, she didn't want to stay here alone for very long.

She glanced around the chamber one last time before she departed, hoping the key would not be missed in the time it took her to use it.

She scrambled back across the echoing darkness, the candlelight swallowed in shadow.

Back in the turret room, Corrine unfolded the first of Brighde's letters. She readied her pen nib and set a blank sheet of paper before herself.

[March 1356]

From Sister Brighde of the Isle of Female Saints to Brother Angus of the Kirk of St. Fillan, greetings.

My dearest Brother in Christ:

The Abbess has given dispensation for me to write to thank you for your kindness at the market fair this Wednesday last.

Often has that man troubled me and I have only fended off his advances through my own resourcefulness, which I admit is paltry compared to that of one such as yourself. He has watched me since childhood, and only the Isle has kept him from me. Imagine my despair every year when I must submit myself to the possible horror of an encounter! I had begged not to be forced to it, but the sister who should have gone in my place was ill with the fever. There was no help for it. Praise be to our Lord that you were there.

You said that you thought the man was not so much a threat as perhaps a messenger. I pray you to explain how this might be so. You have knowledge that I lack, and I am eager to change my fortunes. There are so few in the sisterhood at present; that one of us should be spared any task is a burden on all. God willing, I could return again to shepherding or the fields beyond Taymouth. I am useless else.

Again, my sincerest thanks and hope that you may train me better in the ways of the world.

Your Sister in Christ,
Brighde

Corrine dipped her pen back in the inkwell. The letter unsettled her. She wondered if the Captain had in fact stalked Brighde since childhood. Had Angus truly intimated that the Captain might be a messenger so early on? And did that mean that he himself had preyed upon Brighde from the very first? If so, the abiding love Corrine had ascribed to Angus was false, little more than premeditated manipulation. But to what purpose?

She had met Brighde's sad shade on the Isle of Female Saints. Though Brighde had called her a fool, Corrine could not help but feel protective toward her and sorry that Brighde was denied eternal rest for some unknown purpose of the Unhallowed. Whatever the reason, Corrine hoped future letters would reveal it, along with a way that Brighde might rest in peace at last.

THREE

March 21, 1866

WHEN THE FULL MOON PRECLUDED THE NEED FOR A lantern, Corrine crept again into the study. She carried the key knotted in her handkerchief. An iron short sword that she'd wrestled from an old suit of armor was bundled in the folds of the heavy riding cloak she wore over her nightgown. She took the box from the mantel, pain arcing through her fingers. She wadded the handkerchief around the key's ornate bow and slid it into the lock.

Her fingertips smarted as she opened the box and drew the rathstone from its velvet-lined hiding place. The stone came into her palm like a bird finding its nest. Guilt didn't stab her quite as painfully as the touch of iron. This was different than the last two times she had stolen a rathstone, though she doubted any of the other Council members would agree if they caught her at it.

She replaced the box on the mantel and edged out of the study.

She didn't try the front doors, sure they'd be locked. Instead, she went into the empty ballroom to the glass doors that opened out on the veranda overlooking the garden. Corrine was both pleased and unnerved when one of them swung open and she slipped out into the moonbound fog.

The night air resounded with chittering voices, as though the Unhallowed were all around her. She frowned as she entered the labyrinth and wound her way through the knotted hedge. Why were they about? Could they see her? Last time she had come to the mound, she'd worn the glamour of a nix. They hadn't known her. Certainly now they would, and she considered that a glamour might have been a wise idea. But the thought of Melanie's face subsuming her own again sickened her. She hoped she'd have time to creep up to the rath entrance before they alerted the Prince. Perhaps the iron she bore would be enough to keep them at their distance.

She wondered what she would do if the Captain came. Corrine no longer knew whether to fear or pity him. He had allowed her to escape from the Unhallowed city the last time. Since then, the thorns of the rose anklet no longer tore into her, and her dreams were unremarkable. Corrine couldn't imagine the punishment the Captain had suffered for her freedom. Why had he let her go? And would he allow her to escape again?

She paused in the shadows of the hedge before going to the mound. The Unhallowed flitted like bats around her in the moonlight—chortling, pulling one another's twiggy hair, and sometimes coupling on the wing. Corrine's face grew hot under her hood, but she kept it pulled over her head. She cupped the old iron sword and let it bite into her hand. When the blood flowed, she wiped it carefully along the hilt; the pain of the iron was much greater than the wound itself.

She stepped out onto the gravel. Moonlight ringed the mound, but she could see a faint trail of witch-light, the entrance to the Prince's rath. Smaller Unhallowed beings flitted around it like a cloud of insects; they grabbed her cloak and tried sneaking under her hood, but she waved them away with the sword. For a long moment, she peered down into the mound. It was so similar to looking into the magical well of the astral domains that Corrine hesitated. However, the face that swam up to her was not the mermaid's, but Euan's. Her necklace slipped from the collar of her nightgown, the ring straining toward the gate. She knew the spell she was about to perform would not seal the Prince into his rath forever, but it would close *this* gate. She was certain he would know who had done it and why. It seemed a shame that she must do this to him when he had only ever been kind to her. Then she reminded herself that the Prince was not the kind gillie, the agile fencing master, the trustworthy if mysterious friend she had believed him to be. He and his people had killed or stolen more young girls than she could count. He had set a daoi to spy on her and most likely had sent the cuideag to muddle the Council's business. Who knew what other horrible crimes he had committed?

Jealousy is cruel as the grave . . . the ring whispered.

"No," she said. She held the rathstone tightly in one hand and shifted her grip on the sword. "As room with no door and door with no key, seal this gate. With blood and iron, so mote it be!" The Unhallowed tumbling about the mound shrieked and chittered, trying to grab her fingers, trying to pull her backward by her cape or strangle her with her own necklace. Corrine heard hooves on gravel behind her. She turned, fearful a satyr guard would drag her down to the Prince's throne room.

At first, four points of witch-light danced before her in the darkness. Then there were two. Then four again.

The moon shredded the clouds. A tall, black horse gazed at her, and the four points of witch-light were his eyes and the breath steaming in his nostrils. Three veiled women stood beside him, two on the left, one on the right. They lifted their hands to their veils. The memory of a dream flashed into Corrine's mind—a dream of a horrible face peeking out from behind the Prince's throne, cautioning her to be silent.

She turned and plunged the sword into the mound, shouting the spell again: "As room with no door and door with no key, seal this gate. With blood and iron, so mote it be!" The ring sighed against her.

The horse surged toward her, even as the mound crumpled in the moonlight. She heard the leap as all four hooves cleared the ground before the pain seized her. The marble gazebo trembled and toppled as if it was made of glass. An inky darkness issued from her chest in pursuit of the closing rathgate. It dripped and stretched from the ring, pulling her down toward the vanishing hole as though she was a puppet. The little Unhallowed creatures who had tried to torment her vanished into the vortex. Corrine gasped and choked, fighting against the sudden gravity. She clutched the sword while the darkness screamed toward the nearly-closed fissure.

Her vision flashed into elsewhere. *Gray walls. Crumbling plaster huddled in chalky piles on the warped floor. Rotted velvet curtains the color of old blood trailed the floor. The stench of mud and feces was overpowering despite the chill. Footsteps thudded outside. Buckled shoes scudded across the floor in vain fear . . .*

The strength of all the sensations almost made her faint, but the solid pain of the iron kept her from it. The damp spring air filled her lungs. Her left shoulder burned with frost. The rathstone shone milky-pale near the sword and she picked it up with numb fingers.

"Corrine!" Father Joe, Miss Brown, and Sir James surrounded her, followed by Mr. Turnbull, the butler, who swung his lantern stiffly through the air.

A few cracked columns leaned against one another, but the shattered remains of the gazebo were spread all around the gravel circle. The marble roof rested in three neat pieces opposite Corrine.

"What's happened here?" Father Joe asked, coming closer. He took her by the arms. "Corrine," he said, "why are you outside alone? What are you doing with the rathstone and that sword?"

Corrine was still too stunned to reply. Not even the visions of Jeanette's abduction at Falston had been so visceral. And then there was the dripping, choking darkness . . . Father Joe had to shake her a little before she managed to say, "What should have already been done."

Father Joe gripped her arm in a manner characteristic of Corrine's old anatomy teacher, Miss de Mornay. "I think you must explain this to us. At this moment," Father Joe said, making her stand none too gently.

Miss Brown and Sir James were looking at her with resignation and bewilderment. Miss Brown held her dressing gown shut over her nightgown. Father Joe marched Corrine past them, saying only, "This way."

"But—my gazebo," Sir James said, trailing behind them. Mr. Turnbull murmured something to him.

Guiding Corrine by the arm, Father Joe led them all

into the manor and down the hall to Sir James's study.

Before they could open their mouths, Father Joe shoved the pale rathstone under their noses.

"She had it," Father Joe said, handing the rathstone over to Sir James. "Please hide this somewhere *safe* later."

Corrine frowned. She knew what that meant. Somewhere where she couldn't find it. *The buckled shoes gleamed in the dim light.*

"What did you do?" Miss Brown said.

Corrine shook her head to clear away the vision. She stood as straight as she could. "What needed doing," Corrine said. Her shoulder burned. The hem of her cloak muddied the antique carpet. "I used the stone to seal the rathgate."

"How?" Miss Brown asked.

"A charm in the book," Corrine said. "It talked about punishing those who defied the Unhallowed by closing the gate to the rath."

"Repeat the charm," Father Joe said. His voice was dangerously calm now.

Corrine did so slowly, without the cadence the real spell had required.

"And what happened?" Father Joe said.

She shook her head. In all the time since this had begun, she had never said anything about the three ladies veiled in gloom. Truth be told, she was more afraid of them than the Prince and the witch Leanan put together. Corrine had not missed that one of three ravens had injured her eye when she first came to Fearnan. Nor that often in her dreams the veiled ones carried or cajoled her father in some way. One of the veiled ladies had cautioned silence, but Corrine was unsure why. And now they had brought something else to her. Something dark and deadly that had leaped within her, and given her a vision that still set her teeth on edge. Corrine hugged herself against the bitter cold in her shoulder.

"What?" Father Joe prompted.

"Something—a tall, black horse—came while I was trying to do the spell. But I closed the gate and now they won't bother us until we can get away to London." *Now the Prince cannot tempt me.* She still was unsure why thoughts of him spawned such sadness and yearning. She hoped her expression appeared more certain than she actually felt.

Miss Brown said, "Hush. Who knows what you've awakened with your foolishness on this night of all nights."

Corrine stared at her.

"It's the equinox," Father Joe said, pacing in front of the fireplace. "One of the nights when the Unhallowed are at their most powerful. You may have closed the gate, but I would wager you've angered the Unhallowed greatly and drawn further attention to yourself, if that was possible."

Corrine ached to reach and touch her icy shoulder, but drew her cloak closer about her instead. Sir James was looking elsewhere, obviously discomfited by seeing women in their nightgowns. "But . . . but . . . surely I did some good?" Corrine asked.

"I deeply doubt it. The Prince and Leanan will be even more angered than they are at present." Father Joe came to stand near her, and his eyes were hard with anger. "I told you not to waste your energies on this foolish endeavor."

Corrine hardly knew what she was doing as she turned and walked toward the door.

"Corrine!" Father Joe said.

"Joseph," Miss Brown murmured. Miss Brown reached out to restrain Father Joe as Corinne stepped out into the hall. She slammed the door hard behind her.

Corrine ran upstairs, lifting the muddy cloak and gown to keep from tripping over them. By the time she reached her door, she was gasping for breath. She shut it, wishing she could bolt it closed. She tore off her cloak and untied the strings to her nightgown. At the standing mirror by the wardrobe, she pushed her gown past her shoulder. Ice-white lines faded into the image of the Unhallowed horse that the three veiled ladies had led between them. She touched it lightly with her fingertips. Its edges were raised and puckered like a brand. What this meant, she had no idea.

She sighed and bound up the nightgown again. The icy pain thawed to an irritation. She supposed she would have to tell the Council what had happened, but not tonight.

Corrine was about to throw herself onto the bed when she noticed a bundle of parchment the color of yellowed bone lying on the coverlet. A scrap of mossy paper was secured to the bundle with withered vines. The scrap was blank, but when she touched it, Unhallowed words swam up from the aging parchment. *"If you would know your true enemy, read within."*

Had this come at any other time, Corrine would certainly have thrown it onto the fire. But now, angry and disconcerted as she was, she didn't care about the potential harm in it.

35

She opened the packet, saw that these letters were like those of Angus and Brighde, originals in unreadable archaic script with translations provided.

[December 1274]

My dearest lady—

You have left me again and I do not know by what strange chance it is that I must write to you even though it is but an hour since your departure. I cannot stop these thoughts of you. You cannot return soon enough.

I have found the sort of mortal you seek here at the abbey. In a fortnight's time, he will be yours, so long as I have the reward I am promised. You have said that the day is coming soon when I will be your consort for true. Sweet Leanan, golden lady, believe me, it cannot come quickly enough. Each day that keeps me from your side is another day in hell that could have been spent in paradise. I beg you to make your preparations with all speed, even as I hasten to complete the tasks you set before me.

I remain yours in body and soul,

Josephus

The door opened. Corrine slid the letters under the coverlet almost too late. She was so shocked she barely

saw Miss Brown step into the room and round the
bed.

Leanan? Josephus? *Father Joe?*

~Four~

March 21, 1866

ON THE SHORES OF LOCH TAY, LEANAN HAD CALLED Father Joe "beloved." Corrine knew that there had been something between them; she had long had visions of a golden-haired woman with a much younger Father Joe. But she had always assumed that he had been the witch's victim, somehow enspelled by her. She had never reckoned that he might have done her bidding at his own free will, even sought to be her consort.

So absorbed was she in these thoughts that Corrine barely acknowledged Miss Brown until she spoke.

"Corrine, I'm not sure what that display of temper was about, but I think we should discuss it," Miss Brown said. She had replaced her cloak with a shawl and pulled it tighter about her, as if arming herself for a fight.

Corrine tried to drive away thoughts of Father Joe and Leanan and the sound of footsteps on warped floorboards.

"Can you explain yourself?" Miss Brown said. "Why are you so belligerent toward those who would help you? Why do you persist in going against the Council's wishes?"

"No one said I shouldn't do what I did," Corrine said.

Miss Brown came to stand close to Corrine's side of the bed. Wisps of hair escaped from her nightcap and stirred in the near-constant draft.

"It was implied, Corrine. Do you not understand the difference between implication and direct admonition?"

Corrine knew her argument was futile, but she held to it. "No one said I shouldn't. And none of you were doing anything! You were all resting on your laurels, waiting for the next strike."

Miss Brown looked as though she might be angry, but then she smiled tightly. "I won't satisfy your accusations. The Council has decided what we must do. We will go to London and retrieve the Stone of Destiny." Then something occurred to her, and she said, "You didn't happen to let that slip during your escapade, did you?"

Corrine looked at her teacher in shock. "No! How could I? *Why* would I?"

"Good," Miss Brown said, though she was assessing Corrine with that piercing scrutiny that made Corrine wonder if the teacher thought she was lying.

"I know there is much you don't understand," Miss Brown continued. "I know that sometimes makes it difficult for you to do as we request. But, please trust us. Don't do any other foolish things like this on your own. We don't want to draw any more attention to ourselves than we must."

"But,"—the anger swelled until Corrine thought it would burst through her chest—"you've all lied to me.

You've all hidden things from me when you promised not to."

"What, Corrine? What have we kept from you?"

"That I was Half-Born, that . . ." Corrine trailed off. It was the Half-Born part that still upset her the most. It made her special and therefore in greater danger; it gave her power that she didn't know how to use, but that somehow could be used against whomever the Council or the Unhallowed wanted. And there were the other, older hurts—the loss of her father, her mother, all she'd ever known. What was her future?

Miss Brown fidgeted a little with the crocheted edges of her shawl as she spoke. "Corrine, it's true that we tried to hide that from you. Perhaps it was wrong of us. At first, we weren't certain. You bore many of the signs of Half-Born, but there were as many you didn't bear. We feared what would happen if we were wrong. We were wrong so many times at Falston. But we also feared that if we were correct, you might not understand your power and use it for ill. If we could shield you from the knowledge of what you were and train you to accept it gradually, we hoped that perhaps we could save you."

Corrine nodded. The knowledge didn't excuse them, nor did it alleviate all that so many had suffered because of their silence. Besides, Miss Brown might still be lying.

A brief flash of pain crossed Miss Brown's face. In that moment Corrine saw a young boy dressed in Confederate gray about to enter a forest, his gun held loosely at his side. A man wearing a dark coat and hat held out his scarlet-stained hand to the boy.

Corrine remembered where she'd seen the boy's face

before. On Miss Brown's desk back at Falston. *Her brother.*

But why would the Captain take a boy when he had only ever taken girls before?

In that way she had of catching thoughts, Miss Brown whispered, "Stop." She half-turned away.

"I'm sorry," Corrine said lamely.

"Just see you don't do it again," Miss Brown said. She didn't look at Corrine as she exited, and Corrine wondered whether Miss Brown was admonishing her for seeing into her past or behaving badly toward the other Council members. As Corrine pulled the chilly covers around her, she suspected a bit of both.

March 23, 1866

In two days, everyone was packed and ready to depart. The adult Council members hadn't said much to Corrine since the incident at the mound, and though the strong vision still haunted her, she hadn't yet experienced another. Father Joe hadn't called for another magic lesson, and Corrine guessed that she was meant to study on her own or not at all until he wished to deal with her again. Corrine avoided her friends and the servants, particularly Siobhan, as she was sure the girl would somehow sense the strange Unhallowed brand on Corrine's shoulder.

She spent the last afternoon in the Fearnan turret room, looking for information about the brand on her shoulder. More to the point, she was searching for a way to be rid of it. She wondered if the ring she had stolen might have some special power, something she could use to help free her. She flipped through *A Compendium of Unhallowed Fey,* which listed all the known Unhallowed with illustrations and cross-references to their other names. At last, she came to *Water-horse. See Kelpie.*

She turned moldy pages until the stallion's ghostly eyes stared at her again. She read:

Kelpie. Often appearing as a beautiful horse, this fairy haunts lochs and streams. Upon seeing the kelpie, most are taken with the irresistible desire to ride him, to which he graciously acquiesces. He will immediately plunge into a loch or nearby stream, taking his victim with him into the watery realm of death. The only way to tame a kelpie is to find his bridle.

Kelpies have often proven excellent studs. Several clans claim kelpie bloodlines as the origin of their fine, swift herds.

Corrine frowned as she shut the book. There was no mention of why a kelpie would brand a person, what it meant, or how that brand could be removed. The Unhallowed had once marked her with an anklet of roses, a device they'd also used to try to keep her in their rath. The Captain—oddly enough—had freed her from that manacle, and now she found herself shackled with yet another. Sometimes she wondered if there was any sense in fighting the inevitable.

Sighing, she turned to Brighde's letters, which she now kept in a letterbox for copying. She thought about the other bundle of letters that the Unhallowed had somehow sent her. She very much wanted to read them, but dared not bring them out of her room where someone else might see. Father Joe, she knew, would be mortified and possibly furious if he knew she had them. And Ilona and Christina would be upset if she didn't share with them. But Corrine remembered grudgingly how

42

Christina had kept the secret of her trysts with Rory, and how Ilona hadn't said a word either. *No. I'll keep my secret just a little longer,* Corrine thought.

She readied her ink pen and smoothed out a fresh sheet of paper.

[Trans note: April 1356]

To Brother Angus of the Kirk of St. Fillan from Sister Brighde of the Isle of Female Saints, greeting.

My dearest Brother:

I must commend you for your noble instruction during your visit of last week. Your discourses on those you call the Fey are fascinating. Of course, in my childhood, I had heard such stories, but your passionate belief is deeply affecting, your reason admirable. As you say, much has been said in Scripture of creatures we have yet to see with our mortal eyes; much has been written, and even more seen, that is still a dark mystery to us.

But I must humbly question the inherent goodness of these Fey you so insistently defend. How can the tales of travelers led astray, of wrecked cottages, and spoiled milk, of children exchanged with wizened corpses all be evidence of a just people? Perhaps you will point me to the punishment of Job or the sacrifice of Abraham. Good can be done in the guise of evil.

Is this not why there are brethren who mortify their flesh to lessen our burden of sin? You say that we have destroyed their homes, stolen their lands and treasures. Perhaps that is reason enough. But I would like to hope—and humbly again, I do beg pardon—that perhaps a people as wise as you say might find other ways to console themselves. Well and truly do I know how foolish a hope this must seem, for all our lives on this earth seem bound up in war and strife and sin until we are released into eternity and at last know ourselves free.

Our superiors willing, I pray that you may come again and teach your wisdom and that I may be even more able to receive it. It has been long since anyone spoke so intelligently to me of the domains beyond our reach. And most gladly would I desist in my fears of that which has haunted me all my childhood and driven me here to this island where I find my only solace and rest.

Your humble Sister in Christ,

Brighde

Corrine rested her pen in the inkwell. Brighde's words chilled her. The nun had been plagued all her life by the Fey, followed by the Captain. She had escaped and Angus had found her again, working deviously as a spider to trap her in the Unhallowed web.

Corrine remembered how young and sad Brighde's ghost had looked when Corrine had spoken to her on the Isle of Female Saints. Corrine wished she could have said so much more than she had. She thought of Brighde's reaction to the daoi scarf and recoiled. Why had Brighde not *told* her what she actually held? She wished she could speak to Brighde again, to understand what had truly happened. She also wondered if Brighde knew of the three veiled ladies who kept appearing in her dreams—who they were and what they might want. And were these new visions sent by Brighde? For what purpose? So many questions and no way to find the answers.

Perhaps she was seeking answers in the wrong place. Might one of Father Joe's letters mention the veiled ladies? She had hidden the odd packet of letters behind one of the panels in her writing case. Corrine was about to pull them out when Miss Brown entered.

"The carriages are here," she said. "Are your things ready?"

Corrine nodded. She blew gently on the freshly-copied letter and repacked all of her other things while it continued to dry. At last, she tucked in the letter, her gaze lingering over Brighde's long-dead words. If only the ghost could tell her what she needed to know.

Sir James and Father Joe had decided that it would be best to leave as soon as possible, hence Sir James had hired a midnight coach that would take them to Edinburgh to catch the early morning train to London. Everyone—even Mara, who was usually the most skeptical—seemed sure that since Corrine had closed the rathgate, no harm would befall them on the road. But Corrine hesitated as she climbed inside the coach with Ilona and Christina.

"Corrine," Christina said, as Miss Brown spread the rug around their knees, "are you quite sure you're all right?"

Corrine nodded. She didn't want to say anything that would make her friends afraid.

"You seem—" Ilona began, but Corrine cast a glance toward Miss Brown as she settled herself in the carriage and shook her head.

Later, she mouthed.

Ilona nodded, but the look of concern didn't leave her face.

They started out just as the sun fell from the sky. Corrine tightened her fingers in the rug and hoped that if the kelpie brand was going to bring trouble, it wouldn't be tonight. It occurred to her that the Prince's ring might cause trouble, as well, but she reasoned that he couldn't have possibly expected her to steal it, thus couldn't have cursed it. But then Corrine remembered Father Joe explaining how curses could be done at a distance and huddled closer to Ilona. She thought about throwing the ring out the carriage window, but couldn't bring herself to. Keeping something of the Prince's made her feel powerful, the way she had felt when she'd retrieved her locket from the Unhallowed treasury.

In the depths of the night, the carriage jolted Corrine awake. It tilted to the left so sharply that Corrine put her arms out to prevent Christina being thrown off the bench. Then the carriage slammed back down, and Corrine gritted her teeth, fearing that one of the wheels would break with so much force.

"What the Devil?" Father Joe said. He poked his head out from under the leather curtain flap, but clearly couldn't see anything because Corrine then saw him climb back over Siobhan and Mara's bench toward the window beneath the driver's seat.

"The driver is frozen," Father Joe said over his shoulder. "I'm going to climb up and get the horses under control."

After a moment, he disappeared through the window. The coach slowed and then stopped.

Miss Brown climbed over the benches and put her head near the driver's seat.

"Joseph?" she said.

Father Joe's voice drifted down through the window. "The driver's dead. We should—"

Cold light seared the inside of the coach. Corrine raised her arm to shield her eyes. The flash revealed a face peering into the carriage—an all-too-familiar face Corrine had hoped never to see again. The Captain's hood was back; in the flaring light, his black tongue hung from his mouth as his dog-eyes searched her out.

In the dying glow, the interior of the coach was a still life of terror. Miss Brown perched on the bench, twisted to see the Captain, her face hard as if she'd sighted a copperhead. Mara's arm stuck in the bag at her feet as she dug for a root. Siobhan was caught in mid-moan, turning her face away. Christina shrieked and hid her face against Corrine's side. Corrine wasn't surprised when Christina's body relaxed completely. Christina's faints were notorious; she had barely lasted through anatomy class.

The Captain grunted a harsh word, like a frog coughing. Outside, a slow Southern voice sang, "Come out, come out wherever you are!"

Ilona's fingers dug into Corrine's arm.

"Melanie," Mara hissed.

"Go!" Miss Brown yelled up to Father Joe, as another light flared.

The Captain gripped the side of the carriage, trying to haul himself in.

Corrine heard a thump next to the carriage. Father Joe called to the horses and snapped the reins. The carriage stuttered forward, but the Captain held fast. Mara pulled a black felt doll and a silver pin from her bag before the carriage went dark again. The Captain squealed in pain and lost his grip as Father Joe urged the horses into a gallop.

Melanie shouted again behind them. Ilona lifted the corner of the window-flap. Faint white shapes trailed the carriage, reminding Corrine of John Pelham at Kelly's Ford and Isambard Brunel and all the ghosts who now danced at the bottom of the sea on the *Great Eastern's* rotting decks. To distract herself, Corrine shook Christina and whispered her name, but Christina didn't respond. Mara's buckled shoes disappeared up through the driver's window.

Horses came up alongside them, Melanie flanked by a troop of masked riders. "Give me the Half-Born!" she shouted.

Corrine didn't hear Mara's reply, but a streak of green light arced back toward their pursuers. The light slowed them, revealing them for what they truly were. The riders were little more than an assemblage of bones and leaves; the horses were tired old nags. Melanie's face was pinched and hollow, and her calves were barely covered by the ragged skirts she wore.

48

Mara called down through the window, "Corrine, I need your power. Can you come up?"

Corrine glanced at her friends and Miss Brown. Their faces were white in the eerie witch-light.

"Yes, I'm coming." She clambered across the benches, and Mara's rough hands pulled her through the window.

Corrine struggled for balance on the narrow driver's box above the galloping horses. Father Joe leaned into the icy wind, urging the horses while trying to keep his eyes on the dark road ahead. Mara perched on the box beside him, looking back along the road for Melanie and her Unhallowed accomplices.

"Where's the driver?" Corrine asked.

"I said a prayer for his soul and pushed him off," Father Joe said, not looking at her. "We couldn't do anything more for him," he said before Corrine could protest.

Such callousness reminded Corrine of Father Joe's letter to Leanan. *I have found the sort of mortal you seek here at the abbey. In a fortnight's time, he will be yours, so long as I have the reward I am promised.*

"Now help Mara," Father Joe said.

Corrine swallowed and climbed up on the wooden bench next to Mara.

"I'm blown from all the warding," Mara said above the thunder of the carriage horses. "Can you feed me some power?"

Corrine looked back toward the light fading across Melanie and the Unhallowed. "How?" Corrine asked.

"Just breathe and let me take it," Mara said.

Corrine nodded and took five deep breaths, counting

up and down. She tried to visualize herself as a raven skimming across the sea, but then something went horribly wrong. Her wings wouldn't work. She plummeted toward the ocean and its waves opened like an angry, black maw. She swayed and slumped on the box.

"Corrine!" Father Joe said.

Mara's hand cracked across Corrine's face. The girl gripped Corrine's shoulder with one hand, her other drawn back for another slap. She searched Corrine's eyes in the darkness, and Corrine could smell her clean, sharp scent—like coal and lye.

"They bound your powers, didn't they?" Mara asked.

Corrine realized it was true. No matter how she tried to access the domains, to build the alchemy of mind required to do the magic, she couldn't do it. It was like touching a dead nerve.

Father Joe held the reins stiffly and said nothing. The carriage continued on its clattering way, racing to the train station ahead of the pursuing Unhallowed mob.

Corrine looked behind them. The carriage was pulling ahead; Melanie and her crew seemed chastened by Mara's pyrotechnics.

"Get back inside," Mara said. Her tone didn't invite argument.

Corrine pushed herself through the opening and back in the carriage.

"Is everything all right?" Miss Brown said. Her breath was metallic with fear.

"Yes," Corrine said. "I think they're giving up."

Christina sighed and straightened, then stiffened again when she remembered what had caused her to faint.

"Where is that horrible man?" she said.

"Mara got rid of him," Corrine said, just as Mara climbed back into the carriage.

"Mara?" Christina asked.

"That root won't work again," Mara said over the clattering wheels.

"Why not?" asked Miss Brown.

"Burned up," Mara said. "He's gettin' stronger than I can hold. 'Specially when I'm tearin' along the road in the middle of the night in a carriage."

Miss Brown sighed.

Corrine sensed Mara's eyes on her in the darkness. "And we have other problems," the maid said.

"What do you mean?" Miss Brown said.

"Her magic is bound," Mara said.

"What?" Miss Brown turned toward her. "What's happened, Corrine?"

"That's what comes of dealing with *them*," Siobhan moaned.

But before Corrine could answer the carriage was slowing and turning off the road toward a coach house in Doune. They were to change carriages here before proceeding to Edinburgh.

Corrine heard Father Joe explaining the driver's death to the gateman. "We were pursued by bandits," he said. "Unfortunately, we had to abandon the body along the road." There was more murmuring, but finally they were out of the carriage. Stable hands transferred their bags to the next coach.

Father Joe hurried them into the roadhouse where a few other people waited for their next coaches. Miss Brown stared at Corrine, but Corrine knew she wouldn't dare ask questions in public. Mara brought them each a mug of hot cider and a bit of warm bread from the inn-keeper, and then went outside with a nod from Father Joe, ostensibly to find their new driver. They all sat in silence, drinking the cider to warm themselves, but taking little pleasure in it. Father Joe avoided Corrine's gaze.

At last, Mara returned and they followed her to their new carriage.

Father Joe settled them all into the coach, his grim expression half-illuminated by the driver's lantern. "They are trying to find us." A chill fog crept up around him. "You laid the root?" he asked Mara.

She nodded. "I laid it. But whatever they got's strong."

"Then," Miss Brown said, pulling the heavy blanket over herself and Siobhan, "let us hope the root holds until we board the train. Once we're protected by iron, we should be harder to track."

Corrine didn't remind her of what had happened the last time they'd boarded an ironclad vessel, assured they'd be safe from the Unhallowed. Not only was it just a bad idea for her to speak right now, with everyone still angry over the discovery of her bound powers, but she had no idea what alternative they had than to hope that the train would protect them.

Father Joe shut the door of the carriage and climbed up to sit with the driver.

As they rolled away through the fog, Ilona snored softly beside Corrine. Christina was quiet, numbed by the journey and the escape from the Captain. Miss Brown hunched over herself like an old crow, whether sleeping or brooding, Corrine wasn't sure. It would have taken too much effort in any case to try to shout over the rattling carriage wheels. Corrine slumped against the coach, her back aching, her mind reeling at the thought that her magic, which she had only just come to accept as part of her, was gone.

~Five~

March 23, 1866

THEY TOOK THE BRILLIANT BLUE CALEDONIAN EXPRESSWAY train from Edinburgh to the border, then changed trains into a sleeper that stopped at Rugby, Leicester, Sheffield, and York before it reached its final destination at Euston Station in London. Corrine watched the greening countryside flash by, restlessly fingering the Prince's seal ring. *Set me as a seal upon thine heart . . .* For a moment, she regretted closing the gate, regretted leaving Fearnan. Despite all, Fearnan had come rather to seem like home, in a way Falston or her Uncle William's house could not. Nothing, of course, could replace the old farm on the Elk River in Maryland. She thought of it with a pang, her father driving the cattle to a new pasture on Magellan, his dark Morgan horse, her mother kneading bread with Nora in the kitchen. But the truth, she knew, was that Fearnan had offered her the slim chance of seeing the Prince again. Much as she hated him, the fact that he had come to her in the gazebo gave her a secret thrill.

The rocking motion of the train soon lulled Corrine into sleep.

Gray walls closed in. Someone's arms held her, and she leaned into them for comfort. Fading perfume hid under the ripeness of clothes worn far too long without laundering. Footsteps threatened on the stairs. She was squeezed so tightly she couldn't breathe. Then, the door opened.

Corrine jerked awake. A young woman in mourning passed their berth, and for a moment Corrine thought that she was one of the three veiled ladies. She shrank against her seat, still terrified by the door opening in that unknown room in her vision. She relaxed a little when she saw that the young woman led a little boy, just into trousers by the look of him. When he turned a blank stare on her, though, she shivered and stared back out the window.

The nearer they drew to London, the more excited Christina became. Ilona looked downcast, staring out of the window like a caged lion. Christina chattered on happily about all the wonders she had seen when she came here as a child—the social events, the wonderful clothes, the dolls. "But nothing can compare to Paris," she would say every now and then, as if to maintain loyalty to her home city.

Miss Brown smiled and nodded without sincerity, the lines at the corners of her eyes crinkling with weariness. Father Joe held a newspaper over his face, occasionally snapping the pages to and fro. One of the headlines caught Corrine's eye: *Heiress and companions in boating accident. Two survive, two drown.* Corrine looked away, tired of hearing about death.

She wondered if Father Joe was really reading or just using the paper to shield her from his anger until they could speak privately. He hadn't said a word to her in days, and Mara's discovery of Corrine's bound magic seemed to rouse his ire more than ever. Corrine didn't have much to say to him anyway. Though she'd not had time to read another of his letters to Leanan, she was firmly suspended between shock at his willing dalliance with the witch and suspicion that the letters were merely an Unhallowed device to sow distrust. Whatever the case, Father Joe's words were uppermost in her thoughts, yet she dared not speak of them to him.

In London, they disembarked at Euston Station without further incident. Corrine gazed in awe at the new station's Doric columns soaring overhead. Its grand skylights put her very much in mind of the *Great Eastern's* Grand Salon. While they waited with their baggage on the platform, Father Joe went to hire another coach to take them to the merchant's house at Primrose Hill. Coal dust and smoke made Corrine's eyes water, so she turned her gaze onto the crowd. She was relieved that she didn't recognize anyone, that Melanie wasn't lurking somewhere in the crowd. By the same token, she wondered what she might be missing without her magic.

The vision gripped her so hard she reached out to the nearby column for support. *Curtains bleeding onto the floor. Hiding. A terrible stench, like rotten, moldering skin. Two metal bowls slammed down, gray liquid slopping over their sides.*

"Corrine?" Miss Brown said.

Corrine gasped and tried to push the vision away.

"Are you ill?" Miss Brown asked.

Corrine was grateful she saw the headmistress's face and not whatever lurked in that terrifying room.

She swallowed and steadied herself. "Maybe just a little hungry," she said. She didn't want to discuss the visions in public. People stared at her curiously as they passed.

Miss Brown nodded, but her gaze was still concerned. "We'll be at the townhouse soon enough."

Father Joe returned then with the driver. Between them, the two men hauled the trunks and bags to the carriage while the women climbed aboard. Corrine coughed and held her sleeve over her nose and mouth against the London stench. In addition to the sulfurous fumes of burning coal, the odor of raw sewage was nearly unbearable. The smell reminded her very much of her first vision of the gray room. She gripped the bench so as not to slide into the vision again.

These visions were so strange, like a constantly-flowing river that Corrine was occasionally dunked into, catching a glimpse before she managed to haul herself out of the vision again. She sensed that these weren't images of the past, that these things were occurring in the present, perhaps even here in London. But there was too little to work with to be sure. And why were they coming to her now, when she had no magic to locate their source? She leaned her head back against the carriage wall for a moment in frustration.

Wedged between Ilona and Christina, she watched the yellow fog rising as the gas lanterns were lit. Costermongers went up and down the streets crying their wares. Men in top hats escorted ladies for short distances along the streets, taking care to keep the women out of the muddiest places. As Christina pointed out buildings and streets she recognized, Corrine watched a little boy in a worn derby hat run down the street, shouting and gesticulating, crashing into patrons who unwittingly lost their handkerchiefs, pocket watches, or wallets in the process. A door coughed out a stumbling young man escorted by two, black-robed Chinamen. A woman with vacant blue eyes and a tattered basket on her arm stood on the street corner.

Siobhan leaned against the carriage with her eyes closed, as though she could wish everything away if she only tried hard enough. Corrine sympathized with the notion, even if she knew it to be foolhardy.

At last, the bustle of the main streets subsided and the carriage halted before a narrow townhouse with a lilac-colored door. The driver assisted them out of the carriage and went to help Father Joe haul the baggage up the stairs. Corrine followed Miss Brown, who removed a key from her pocket and opened the door. A gust of moldy air, as if the house had been holding its breath for years, rushed out into the street. Miss Brown sneezed as she entered and said, "It wants a bit of work, but it'll do."

Siobhan and Mara immediately disappeared into the dim foyer. Corrine peeped into a nearby morning room. The ghosts of furniture huddled together under dusty white sheets.

"How long has it been since the merchant lived here?" Christina asked.

"A year or so at least," Miss Brown said. "I suppose that's why he stopped having it kept up by servants."

Christina nodded and went to the newel post, craning her neck to look up the curving stairs.

"Now," Miss Brown said, "as I understand it, the servant quarters are in the basement, and there are three bedrooms at the very top. As Father Joe will obviously need a room of his own"—here she blushed and busied herself with her trunk—"one of you will have to sleep in a room with me. Shall we draw lots or—" Before she could finish, Ilona and Christina raced up the stairs with Corrine in hot pursuit. Miss Brown's shout of disapproval was drowned out by their clattering boots.

With her longer legs, Ilona took two stairs at a time, leaping ahead like a gazelle in skirts. By the time Corrine huffed onto the final landing, Ilona and Christina stood smugly in one of the doorways, arms folded across their chests. Corrine rolled her eyes while the two of them hugged one another and went giggling into their room. As she walked alone into the other room, she found it difficult not to mope at the loss of all the midnight story-telling she'd miss.

Ever since returning from the Prince's rath, she had felt adrift, no longer part of their little circle. The magic and her association with the Council had branded her different. Now, her magic had been taken from her. She was left with nothing but these strange visions and their terror.

The room to be shared with Miss Brown was dim and small. She couldn't get much of an impression except for the olive green wallpaper and dusty still life above the sheet-covered double bed. The window opened onto Primrose Hill with its swath of green and dark trees disappearing into the sulfurous fog.

Corrine looked out onto the park, rolling the ring between her fingers, wondering again if she could use it to get rid of the kelpie brand on her shoulder. It occurred to her that perhaps she didn't want to. That maybe she was almost ordinary again—Corrine as she had been before the War when she had still had her family and life on the farm. Maybe this was a good thing. Perhaps she could forget about the Council, the rathstones, and go home to live with Uncle William to be his clerk and even find someone to marry.

But then memories of Euan tried to surface and she pushed them firmly away. Maybe she should take the ring off. Maybe it was reminding her of things she'd rather forget.

Boots rang down the hall and lantern shadow danced over the windowpanes. Corrine slipped the ring and her locket beneath her blouse.

"Siobhan's getting supper," Mara said. "Best you and the others come down while it's still light enough to see. They's a fire going in the hearth now."

Corrine still had trouble reconciling the ordinary-looking maid with the girl who had battled the cuideag in panther-shape and used a voodoo doll to scare away the Captain.

"I suppose you thought closing that rathgate was pretty clever," Mara said.

Corrine shook her head.

"When you ever gonna learn?" Mara asked. "You can't just go traipsing around, doing magic like you're God's own gift!"

"That wasn't what I was doing!" Corrine said. "No one else was doing anything. I was trying to protect us." Her shoulder stung. She rubbed it through her blouse.

Mara stepped closer, holding the lantern higher so that the light made her cheekbones sharp as knives. "No, ma'am. I don't think so. You were trying to protect *you*. The Prince scared you bad and you wanted to get back at him is what. Nothing else."

"That isn't true!" Corrine's voice rose.

Mara ignored her goad. "Let me see it."

Corrine stepped back. "No!"

"Let me see what they done."

"No!" Corrine turned sharply just as Mara gripped her blouse. The sound of ripping fabric tore through the room.

"Papa Legba! You don't do it halfway, do you?" Mara stared at the kelpie brand as Corrine tried to pull the tatters of her blouse back up.

But Mara held her still, bringing the lantern so close Corrine flinched.

"They want you bad. Worse than they ever wanted me." Mara released her and stepped back. "But that's no surprise. When the Prince wants something bad enough, he'll do whatever he can to take it."

"I don't think this was the Prince," Corrine said, before she could stop herself.

Mara eye's narrowed. "What?"

Corrine told her of how the kelpie had come, how the three veiled women had been with him, how the kelpie had leaped *through* her just as she'd closed the gate. Haltingly, she told about the visions, about how they'd confused her and made her wonder about their source. Perhaps the ladies were sending them? She had never tried to discover who the three veiled women were or what they wanted. She had just assumed that they were minions of the Prince, perhaps much like the Captain had once served Leanan. But now, having spoken it aloud, she wasn't quite so certain. They had always appeared independently of him, even had told her not to tell of their presence when they had been in the same dream as the Prince.

"Three veiled women?" Mara said. "And now you're having even stronger visions than before?" Her gaze grew distant, as though she was on the verge of remembering something. Finally, she shook her head. She pinned Corrine with the glare Corrine had learned to fear at Falston. "I'll have to think more on it. But in the meantime, stop being such a damned fool! This isn't like recess in the play yard. You could be killed. And so could all of us, if you're not careful. Think about that next time before you go sneaking out at night, trying to act all tough when you're nothing but running scared."

Just go away, Corrine thought at Mara. She felt more miserable than ever.

"I'll mend your dress later. Wrap your shawl about you to hide that tear and come downstairs now," Mara said. "It's too dark up here."

It wasn't quite an apology, but it would have to do. Corrine did as Mara said and followed her downstairs. As they passed the door to the room Ilona and Christina had commandeered, Corrine noticed that they'd already gone down without her.

Everyone had settled in the morning room, where a fire burned cheerily in the grate. Siobhan was setting out tea and toast and sundry other things she'd been able to beg at a moment's notice from a passing delivery boy. Dust and the smell of vacancy were still heavy in the air, but the white sheets had been removed from the furniture. Gold-gilt frames and porcelain plates reflected the fire's light. Corrine sat in the chair offered her, careful not to look at anyone.

Mara was about to depart, but Father Joe motioned her to sit.

"While we are all here together," he said, "I wish to speak to all of you about our purpose here." He looked at Christina and Ilona, and tried to catch Siobhan's eye, but failed. "Miss Brown, Corrine, and Mara are privy to the dealings of the Council here, but the rest of you are not." He shot a glance at Corrine as if he suspected that perhaps she had not kept the Council's secrets. "If we are to succeed, here and in the future, we need each and every one of you to promise your aid."

Ilona nodded sagely, while Christina gave him a calculating look. Siobhan's hands shook on the tea things and she stared at Father Joe wide-eyed.

"With the blessings of the others here, I should like to make you—Ilona, Christina, and Siobhan—informal members of the Council, if you will have it so." There were nods all around, though Siobhan's was hesitant. "There are ceremonies for this sort of thing," Father Joe said, "but we shall have to make do with my word for now and your sworn pledges of fealty to the Council."

He waited while each of them said softly, "I swear loyalty to the Council." Siobhan at her turn managed the words through stiff lips.

"Good," Father Joe said when they had finished. "We thank you for your willingness to trust us, despite everything you must have seen and encountered. God knows the Council needs your help now more than ever." He clasped his hands in his lap as though he would like to say more in that vein, but was restraining himself to the facts alone.

"We have come here with one purpose—to take the

Stone of Destiny from its place in Westminster Abbey back to Fearnan where it can be guarded with the other stones already in our possession. I assume that all of you understand the importance of these stones to the Council's work. The Stone of Destiny is a powerful rathstone in that it bestows prophetic powers upon the bearer; it may turn the tide in this battle and reveal whether we shall triumph for Elaphe and the Hallowed or forever be relegated to Unhallowed rule.

"Such theft would never have been easy in any case, but with Corrine's magic bound"—Corrine dropped her eyes to the gold patterns in the carpet by her feet—"it will be even more difficult. Only Mara and I and Miss Brown perhaps need be involved with this larceny; I would never ask it even of them if I could avoid it. The rest of you are needed for other purposes. We need information. Madame DuBois informs us that there may be another Half-Born carrying a rathstone here in London. It's a rumor, but we can't risk ignoring it. We also need to know how much the Unhallowed know, where they are stationed in London, and what their response might be to Corrine's . . . misfortune."

"We'll do whatever we can, Father," Ilona said.

The priest smiled sadly. "I know you will. But even this gathering of information is not without danger, Ilona. What we ask of you is more than any young woman, or man for that matter, should have to bear. But we hope that because you are with us still, despite all the dangers, that perhaps you are willing."

Ilona nodded, and Corrine knew somehow that she was thinking of all the girls lost—Jeanette, Penelope, and how many more before them? And Kenneth, so horribly murdered at Fearnan. There was much to avenge.

"So," Father Joe continued, "it seems to me that we require information on many levels. Siobhan, if you would befriend other servants and discover any untoward news in any households—disappearances, murders, possessions, anything of that sort would be a great help." Siobhan nodded tremulously, and Corrine wondered that she didn't throw her apron over her head and run out of the room. Though Siobhan seemed to have recovered bodily from the horrors on board the *Great Eastern* months ago, her mind was still fragile.

"Christina," Father Joe said, "your family is well-connected here. We hope that you will use your natural grace and charm to discover information within your social circle. Anything mysterious, any rumors of Half-Born and rathstones, any disappearances. We need any knowledge those of your station might possess. Be cautious and discreet. We cannot afford to be exposed."

"Yes, Father," Christina said. Her dark eyes gleamed with the thought of all the soirées and engagements she'd been missing.

Father Joe turned to Ilona. Save for the dark swath that she pushed back from her forehead, her hair was long enough now that most of it could be pulled back into a bun.

"Your work will be the most dangerous," Father Joe said to her. "And I deeply regret asking it of you. But you have proven yourself to be strong and courageous, and if you are willing, I see no reason why you should not help." His eyes darted to Miss Brown as he spoke, and she focused intently on the fraying ends of her shawl. This had evidently been another contest of wills between them.

Father Joe looked back at Ilona. "You must go among the people of the streets—the beggars and thieves and those of that ilk. It would be best if you cut off your hair again and disguised yourself as a boy; otherwise, I believe the danger would be far too great."

Ilona grinned. She had cut off her hair in mourning for Jeanette, but she had come to enjoy it short and had fretted about having to let it grow long again.

"Good," Father Joe said. "Then it appears we are all agreed. Tomorrow, we meet with Madame DuBois, who will instruct us on what she has learned thus far. Hopefully her report will set us on course for what we are to do next."

Everyone nodded, and Christina and Ilona pushed their tray tables away as if to leave. Corrine sat puzzled, wondering what her place might be. Father Joe hadn't even addressed her in his assignment-giving. Miss Brown cleared her throat, though, and stilled them with her commanding gaze. She said, "All of this does not mean that you are released from your studies. There will still be work to do and you will be expected to keep up and be examined in your subjects accordingly. Do you understand?"

"Yes, Miss Brown," Christina and Ilona said, almost in unison.

"You are dismissed, then," Miss Brown said.

Christina and Ilona rose and headed toward the foyer. Ilona turned back, grinning. "Coming, Corrine?"

Corrine shook her head. "Later," she said.

Ilona winked at her. Her happiness at the thought of

disguising herself as a boy and roaming the streets of London was incandescent. Corrine had to admit the freedom of being a boy would be a welcome change. Ilona and Christina rummaged in their trunks in the foyer before they disappeared with their lantern up the stairs.

Mara and Siobhan began carrying away the tea things to the kitchen. Corrine sat uncertainly, willing Father Joe to look at her, but he had picked up an old Bible from where it rested on the table near him and was leafing through it. Miss Brown was also engaged in a book, the title covered by her hand on the spine.

Corrine cleared her throat. "Father?"

Father Joe looked at her. "Yes, Corrine?"

"What . . . what am I to do?" she asked.

His face hardened, and for a moment she thought he would say something unpleasant. He sighed, though, and said, "I don't know. We must find a way to unbind your powers. And soon. Do you know how it happened?"

Corrine started to speak, but he interrupted, "You didn't do this yourself, did you? Because if you did . . ."

"Joseph!" Miss Brown was no longer even pretending to read her book. "How can you accuse her in such a fashion?"

Lifting the last teacup, Mara said loudly enough to quell all argument, "She didn't do it to herself, unless you count her foolishness in closing the gate on her own. Show them," she said, leveling her gaze at Corrine.

Corrine hesitated, clutching her shawl more tightly about her. Though she hadn't explicitly said as much, she had hoped Mara would be more discreet. Corrine had hoped that either alone or in concert with Mara, she'd discover a way to rid herself of the brand without having to let Miss Brown or Father Joe know about it. She should have asked for what she wanted when she had the chance.

"Show them," Mara said again.

Corrine dropped the shawl she'd been holding tightly around her shoulders and pushed the tatters of her blouse away from her shoulder. She touched the puckered skin, and a chill coursed through her fingertips.

"I'm not sure this is appropriate," Miss Brown murmured as she rose, looking over at Father Joe. Neither of them asked how her blouse had gotten torn.

Mara snorted.

Father Joe put down the Bible and readjusted his spectacles. Corrine turned away from them, glad she couldn't see their faces.

Miss Brown gasped. "Corrine," she said, touching her gently on her uninjured shoulder, "why didn't you tell us about this? Does it hurt at all?"

"A little," Corrine whispered. She readjusted the shawl over her shoulders.

"Tell us," Father Joe said.

So she told, as much as she was able, including her suspicion that the three ladies were sending the new visions that plagued her.

"You had all these visitations and you never once told us?" Father Joe asked. His voice was tight with anger.

"They asked my silence," Corrine said.

"And you would give it to them? You would trust unknown beings above the Council?" Father Joe asked. He set the Bible down hard on the coffee table. A puff of dust fled toward the fire.

Corrine's temper, always so carefully suppressed,

flared. "And why should I not? Perhaps they'd eventually tell me the truth instead of hiding everything from me!"

"Corrine," Miss Brown warned.

"What?" Father Joe said. He stood and removed his spectacles. "You cannot truly trust these three veiled ladies, whoever they are, more than the Council. They sent their creatures against you and wounded you, for heaven's sake! The Council has sheltered, fed, taught, even clothed you. We have——"

"Joseph," Miss Brown said. "It does us no good to fight against each other."

Father Joe stopped speaking. He looked young and vulnerable then, more like a man in his twenties than a centuries-old priest. He took his seat again and stared glumly into the fire. Corrine wondered if such vulnerability was how Leanan had twisted him into her service.

Miss Brown held Corrine's eyes. "You said they asked you to keep silent," she said. "Were you to keep information even from the Prince?"

"Especially," Corrine said, remembering the dream where the woman held a corpse-white finger against her lips, warning her to silence. The ring felt heavy against her chest and she pulled a little at the chain under the remains of her collar. She avoided looking at Father Joe, wishing she could be dismissed to change into other clothes.

"Who are they?" Miss Brown said. "Three ladies veiled in gloom. I shall have to research this. It's a pity you didn't tell us when we might have looked in the Council chamber. And you think they are sending you new visions?"

Corrine nodded.

"What are these visions of?" Father Joe asked.

Corrine described the gray room, the footsteps, the terror, and her suspicion that these things were taking place in London right now. "They're stronger than any other vision I've ever had," she said.

"This could mean many things. If, as you say, these things are taking place here and now in London, the Unhallowed are probably working here ahead of us. But why these women want you to know this or who they are . . . We need more information," Father Joe said.

"What am I to do?" Corrine said. Without magic, she felt useless. Everyone else had been given a job. She wanted one too.

"All you can," Father Joe said. His voice was still tense, and Corrine was almost grateful she couldn't feel the full force behind it. "Right now, that means copying the letters, studying, and telling us when you have more of these visions. Madame DuBois wishes to see you, and perhaps she may know how we can unbind your power. She may also have some notion of how to remove the brand. I do not."

"But should the brand be removed?" Miss Brown asked. "Perhaps it was put there to protect Corrine. You did say the ladies seemed independent of the Prince, didn't you?"

Corrine nodded.

"Maybe they're trying to protect her in some way."

Father Joe sighed. "I suppose it's possible, though it's difficult to see how."

"Perhaps the brand is their way of marking her as their own?" Miss Brown said.

Father Joe picked up the Bible again. Corrine sensed he was still angry, but his face didn't betray it. "I've witnessed many an internecine conflict between the Unhallowed—one seeking precedence over the other," he said.

Corrine shivered. If she had been apprehensive at being marked as the Prince's prize, she was even more so at the thought of belonging to the ladies. Who or what were they? Witches like Leanan? Or something even more dreadful than the mermaid who lay in wait for her in the domain of water?

"But this seems very different," Father Joe continued. "Most Unhallowed want to use the Half-Born for their magic, for the things they can do that the Unhallowed cannot. It makes very little sense that they'd want to bind her powers or prevent her moving forward with gaining all her skills. Unless they're trying to hide her from the Prince."

He looked at Corrine and she was disconcerted again by the fact that she couldn't read him as she once had. No needles coursed up and down her spine. There was no recognition.

"I must think on it more fully," he said. "In the meantime, I hope this has taught you not to meddle without full knowledge of the consequences, Corrine."

She nearly retorted another answer, but Miss Brown's watchful gaze forced her to hold her tongue.

"I think the best thing, Corrine, is for you to start fresh tomorrow," Miss Brown said. "Focus on your studies and on finishing the letters. Perhaps Madame DuBois may have more insight. She's very gifted in these matters."

"Yes, Miss Brown," Corrine said.

"Now run along to bed," Miss Brown said. "I'll be up shortly."

Corrine rose. She thought, as she left the room, that Father Joe reached out and clasped Miss Brown's waiting hand. But when she stopped to look more closely, it all seemed a trick of the shadows.

She took up a lantern on the foyer table and proceeded up the narrow stairs into the darkness.

~Six~

March 25, 1866

CORRINE HURRIED INTO HER NIGHTCLOTHES AS QUICKLY
as she could, so that she could read one of the
Unhallowed letters before Miss Brown came to bed.
She found her writing case near the washstand, opened
it, and pulled the letters from behind the secret panel.
She unwound the vine that held the letters together, and
unfolded the next letter in the series. She fingered the
ring and the locket on their chain as she read.

[January 1275]

My beloved, my Queen—

*It cheers me to hear that you received your gift with pleasure,
though for me it means an even deeper confinement until the
mystery of his disappearance is deemed solved. Though you have
told me of the many wonders of this life, you have never told me
of the regret and guilt. But perhaps it is not in your nature to
feel these things; you are made of different stuff than we weak*

mortals. I sacrifice much, but it is my lot to sacrifice all if it will appease you. Surely, as you say, the blood of mortals is a small price to pay when compared with the immortal life you offer.

And now you say the time has come for me. And that another gift is required. When I am no longer cloistered, I will bring him, damned and cursed though I may be for it. See that the Turning is true, my lady. You have my heart and body. Soon you shall have my soul. Have a care for your treatment of it.

Some would doubt that the reward is worth the price of destroying all the kingdoms of men for the love of one woman. Even so did the ancients speak of Helen, when the ramparts of Troy fell before the onslaught of Menelaus. And I will say, as did he, that yes, it is indeed worth it.

I am, as always, yours,
Josephus

Footsteps came down the hall. For a moment, Corrine saw the gray walls of the strange room again before she shook herself out of it. She shoved the letters back into the writing case, slammed down the lid, and jumped towards the washstand. She splashed water over her face nervously and dabbed at her forehead as Miss Brown entered the room.

"Corrine," Miss Brown said. "I thought you'd be asleep already."

"I thought I'd study for a bit," Corrine said, as she climbed into the rickety bed.

Miss Brown didn't say anything about Corrine's outburst downstairs. Worry lines creased her brow.

Corrine pulled up the covers and shut her eyes to give Miss Brown privacy. She listened to the bustle of skirts being exchanged for nightgown and cap. Her ears buzzed with the stunted vision, with Father Joe's voice in the letter—dark and insistent, more so than Angus had ever been.

The lantern went out and the bed creaked as Miss Brown climbed in.

"Good night, Corrine," Miss Brown said. "Let us hope tomorrow will be a better day."

"Good night," Corrine replied. Stiff with unsaid words, she at last drifted into an uneasy sleep.

March 26, 1866

The long tolling of a clock from downstairs signified the dreaded hour. Corrine tried to swallow her fear as best she could. Her companion hid her face in the corner and would not move. But today Corrine had decided that instead of cowering, she would stand when he came in. She would face him bravely, though the only weapon she had was the wrong end of a serving spoon. So when the footsteps shuffled up the stairs, when the door opened, she was ready. She sprang at him, trying to drive the end of the spoon into the back of his hand. The metal bent on his puckered, wriggling flesh. He grabbed her with a red-stained hand. The spoon gleamed as it fell end over end to the floor.

Corrine gasped awake. Miss Brown had apparently already risen, as her side of the bed was empty. Corrine tumbled out of bed and rushed to the window, expecting a glimpse of the Captain under the streetlights or in the trees near the park. But there was no one. She heaved a great sigh and crossed her arms over her chest to keep from shuddering. So, the Captain *was* responsible for the captivity of the two girls in her visions. For a moment, she almost thought the prisoners might be Jeanette and Penelope, both of whom had never been found after being abducted from Falston. But she had seen everything through Jeanette's eyes back then, and thus had come to know a bit of Jeanette's personality. This girl didn't feel like Jeanette at all. But if she wasn't, who was she? And who was the girl who cowered and refused to look at the Captain?

Corrine prayed silently that they weren't about to be sacrificed or drained as she'd seen in Killin. She sensed that the Prince wouldn't want her to see these visions, just as he probably would rather that she had never seen what happened to Jeanette or Penelope. Surely the ladies meant for these girls to be saved, but Corrine wondered how. Even if they were being held in London, the Captain could make himself invisible if he wished. It would be easy for him to come and go undetected by those not gifted with sight, and Corrine wasn't sure if she'd be able to see him herself, given how her powers were now bound. She also wondered why the ladies had suddenly taken an interest in the Prince's affairs, to the point of commandeering her visions expressly for their own purposes.

She went to the washstand and dashed at her face with the chilly water. Her mouth tasted slimy. She longed to use the tooth powder, but wouldn't dare foul the water in the washstand until Mara was ready to change it. She dressed slowly, forgoing the corset so as not to have to call anyone for help.

Downstairs, she found Ilona chattering with excitement as Siobhan brought her a stack of folded boy's clothes. Mara took the scissors to Ilona's hair, and as the locks fell on the worn carpet, Ilona's happiness only seemed to grow. She fled up the stairs as soon as Mara was done, clutching her new trousers and shirt. Her whoop of joy at the sight of herself in the mirror tumbled all the way down the stairs into the morning room.

Miss Brown shook her head. "I just pray that her parents don't bring me before the magistrate for this."

Corrine sat down and shakily stirred sugar into her coffee.

"Are you all right, Corrine?" Miss Brown asked.

"The Captain," Corrine said. "He's here in London."

Father Joe folded down his ironed newspaper. "Another vision?"

Corrine nodded. "He's keeping two girls in a room somewhere. One of them tried to escape. I saw his red hand when he grabbed her."

"Was she hurt?" Miss Brown asked.

Images crowded Corrine's mind of the Captain and Miss Brown's brother while trees blazed with cannon fire.

She put down her spoon and rested her head in her hands. "I don't know," she said. Mara had said once that if she didn't learn the magic, the visions would make her mad. Corrine believed her.

Siobhan carried in a letter tray that bore several neat envelopes. One she brought to Miss Brown, but the rest were for Christina.

Miss Brown raised a brow. "Word travels quickly in London."

Corrine lifted her head as Mara set a poached egg on her plate.

"Perhaps my mama told her friends," Christina said, as she took the invitations and parted their seals. She smiled. "Yes. This one is from a dear friend of Mama's, Lady Rosenthal. She wishes me to come to tea at three o'clock. Is that acceptable?"

Miss Brown nodded. "I shall go with you as chaperone."

Christina held the invitation to her breast as the roses came into her cheeks. Corrine could almost hear her thoughts. *At last. Proper society. Teas and balls and all that has been denied.* But there must also be nervousness. Whatever Christina had done, whatever had caused Christina's father to banish her to Falston surely must be known to her social circle, mustn't it? Yet Christina gave no hint that anything might be wrong or that any trouble might lay in wait for her entrance into London society.

Christina's eyelids fluttered for a moment and she slumped forward as though she might faint.

A hazy image of a woman—presumably Brighde— thrashing in a birthing bed, surrounded by masked mid-wives, came to Corrine. She clenched her butter knife.

"Christina?" Miss Brown said. She had the smelling salts at the ready, but Christina straightened on her own.

"Are you well?" Father Joe asked.

"Perhaps the dust," Christina offered. But her hands shook.

There was no time to think about it further, though, for Ilona bounded into the room, her boy's boots well-scuffed, her freshly-cut hair hidden beneath her tweed newsboy cap. Corrine's jaw dropped. To all appearances, Ilona was a tall, gawky boy, her trousers just a bit too short, her shirt just a bit too baggy. The only thing one might miss was the stubble of a first beard, but she looked so young that the lack of it didn't ruin her disguise.

"Call me Thomas," she said, with a bow.

Christina smiled. "You're enjoying this far too much, my friend," she said.

Miss Brown raised a brow while Ilona tried and failed to look demure. "Lessons first, Ilona," she said.

Ilona nodded. Corrine watched Christina writing a reply to Lady Rosenthal's invitation. Her hand trembled, but she managed to sign her name and seal the envelope with the hot wax Siobhan proffered.

Miss Brown ushered them all into the morning room for their studies. For the rest of the morning, they were drilled mercilessly in geometry and grammar. Corrine wondered if an eternity would pass before the dinner bell rang and freed them from their scholarly prison.

The food was light, as Siobhan was still finding her way around the kitchen and markets and Christina would be off to tea soon. As soon as she downed the last spoonful of soup, Ilona asked, "May I leave now?"

Father Joe nodded. Miss Brown looked so anxious that Ilona smiled and reassured her. "No need to worry, Miss Brown."

"Come back before the fog rolls in," Father Joe said.

"Yes, Father." Ilona stood, said her good-byes, and was gone almost before Corrine could reply to her.

Miss Brown shook her head. "I hope we won't have cause to regret this."

Father Joe watched Ilona through the window as she

adjusted the cap on her head and hurried down the street. "All will be well. I believe she'll do us credit."

"But I worry," Miss Brown said. "How do we know that she'll be well? How do we know that the Unhallowed won't—"

Father Joe silenced her with a look. "Euan had many chances to harm her and he didn't. Ilona is not who they seek."

He glanced over at Corrine and she looked away as though she hadn't been eavesdropping. She questioned sending Ilona out alone, too, but she also knew that it gave Ilona great happiness to have a task that might avenge her lost friends.

Miss Brown nodded and turned toward the sofa. "Well, then, Christina, we'd best ready ourselves," Miss Brown said. "I believe Siobhan and Mara have managed to unpack our things from the trunks."

Christina shut her notebook and laid it on the coffee table as she rose. She winked, as Ilona was wont to do, at Corrine's look of concern.

Father Joe said, "We leave for Madame DuBois's shop at half past three. Until then, work on copying Brighde's letters." Then, he left the room with his newspaper under his arm, dismissing further conversation or argument.

Corrine went upstairs to retrieve her writing case, and Miss Brown and Christina followed.

In their room, Corrine hefted the case and was about to leave, when Miss Brown stopped her with a hand on her arm. "I know the visions are troubling you, Corrine. I can only imagine what you must have suffered at Falston! But we'll sort this out. I'm sure Madame DuBois will be able to help you."

Corrine thought of all the other disappearances and deaths she had witnessed. None of those had ever been sorted out. She was losing faith that the Council could indeed sort anything out at all. But acting on her own had also gotten her into even more trouble.

Miss Brown hesitated, then said, "Also, don't let Father Joe's reactions hurt your feelings, Corrine. All of this is difficult for him, perhaps more than you can guess."

"It's difficult for me too," Corrine murmured. She looked down at the dusty floorboards.

"I know," Miss Brown said. "Just know that he—and I, for that matter, we care for you a great deal and hope you don't feel resentment toward us for things we must do or say that feel unjust to you."

"No," Corrine said. "I don't." But even as she said it, she knew it was a lie. She did resent deeply and she still suspected much that hadn't been shared with her.

"We tell you what we can as soon as we can," Miss Brown said. "I promise you."

Yes, Corrine thought. *But does Father Joe?* "I know."

Miss Brown pulled a gray watered silk tea dress from the others in their shared wardrobe. "May I extract then the same promise from you?" she asked. "That you will tell us what you know as soon as you know it, that there will be no more secrets or lies? If we are to keep Hallowmere from the Unhallowed, this is how it must be. They work through deceit and manipulation, and while we sometimes must stoop to it to further our aims, it is not the Council's desire to use such methods among ourselves."

The sincerity in her gaze made Corrine's head hurt. *In the forest, the canopy of fire spread overhead. Dark figures bearing muskets slunk through the burning forest. The boy reached out to the Captain and took his hand. Sparks of witch-light crept up from the ground, whirling like a cloud of fireflies until the Captain and his prisoner disappeared.*

"Corrine?"

Corrine blinked, trying to remember what Miss Brown had said. Something about promises. "Yes," Corrine said. "I will try." Her head hurt with the frequency of so many different visions. The locket and ring chimed together as she moved toward the door, reminding her of the Prince and all his old promises. *Thank goodness he isn't sending me dreams too.*

"Good," Miss Brown said, smiling. "And don't feel left out. Each of us has important work to do, and yours is no less valuable than mine or Christina's or Father Joe's." She dusted her dress and glanced in the wavering mirror at her reflection.

"Oh, I'd much rather stay here and copy letters than have tea," Corrine said. And that was very deeply true. The thought of a high society tea, after all the embarrassments of the Fearnan ball, didn't excite her.

"Well, don't think you're that easily excused. I'm quite sure you'll have to accompany Christina at some point. Having Ilona escort her would be quite unseemly now!" Miss Brown said.

Corrine choked down a giggle at the thought of Ilona in a dress with her terribly cropped hair, or what people would think if Christina appeared at a ball attended only by an effeminate young gentleman.

"Scandalous!" Miss Brown said, as though catching Corrine's thought. Then, she glanced out the window at the carriages rolling by, and said, "Heavens, I must get ready! Would you send Mara to help me when you go down?"

Corrine nodded and, clasping the writing case to her chest, made a beeline for the morning room. She alerted Mara, who was dusting the mantel, of Miss Brown's need, and settled herself at the desk by the ornate window.

The window itself was a bit maddening—more decorative than functional. Comprised of many faceted panes of glass joined by lead soldering and topped by a stained glass crest of some long-forgotten family, it didn't afford much of a view of Primrose Hill. Corrine only saw a watery green blur through its panes. But she supposed she should be grateful. If she couldn't see out, it meant that no one could see in. She could write by sunlight, such as it was, in comfort without fear of strangers, Unhallowed or otherwise, peering in at her.

Faintly, she heard Father Joe's newspaper snapping from the dining room as he turned the pages. Corrine could almost trick herself into believing that she had landed in some London family, with the mother and eldest daughter on their way out to tea, while the father reclined at his ease, reading the business reports over his cooling tea. Funny that such a common thing was less plausible than the reality—a centuries-old priest waiting to escort her to a tarot shop where a French medium would ostensibly learn the secret to unlocking Corrine's lost magic and finding the root of all these visions.

Corrine shook her head and removed the serpent-bound book and Brighde's letters from the case. Against her better judgment, she'd placed the book in the case because it was cumbersome to carry in her pockets all the time. In just the past week, the book seemed to have added pages to itself, though Corrine couldn't say how or why or what they even contained.

She opened the book, heeding the restless serpents on its cover, and passed her hands across the rippling pages.

"Kelpie," she whispered.

The book boiled and shuddered and threw itself violently on the floor. When she reached for it, the serpents reared, their hoods flaring in warning.

She withdrew her hand. She tried again, but the serpents hissed.

Shaking her head, she turned back to her writing case. There was no help for the book, it seemed, so she untied the loose-leaf journal that bound her copies, readied her ink pen, and smoothed Brighde's next letter on the desk.

[Trans. note: Beginning and end missing. Believed to be mid-May 1356]

. . . It was a glad time. Surely of that there can be no argument.

But did you not see that the cups were filled with blood and the plates stacked high with strange bones? You say there was wine and bread a-plenty, heavenly as you have never before encountered. But I saw what you did not. That they feed upon the flesh of humans and other Fey, that their bewitching hair is of cobwebs and their glittering eyes of stone.

They are not as you believe them to be, dear Brother, and I fear they have led you where I cannot follow. Much as I delighted in their music and dancing, much as their Prince spoke well of you and of the friendship he would have again with our kind, I cannot help but feel a darkness in my heart. I beg you to cease your relations with them and turn back to the Holy Father who shelters us both in His house. There is but one way, light, and truth, and the Fey do not hold it . . .

Corrine rested her pen in the inkwell. Small images of Primrose Hill sifted through the glass—a woman pushing a perambulator, three children throwing a ball across the soggy grass for a dog, a barely-budded tree. And that was all. Nothing supernatural. Nothing untoward. And yet, Brighde's revelations about the Unhallowed feast chilled her.

"Corrine?" Father Joe came into the morning room, his folded newspaper under his arm. He looked very different, his features and clothes altered so that he appeared to be an aging Anglican priest.

Corrine stared.

"Mara put a glamour on me," he said, fidgeting with the newspaper.

"It's probably safer," Corrine owned. She still felt his tenseness, but there was something else now, too, a sadness.

"Are you ready to . . . Why is the Unhallowed book on the floor?" Father Joe asked.

"It won't let me pick it up," she said.

"Won't let you?" He crossed to it.

"I tried to read it and it just shuddered and threw itself on the floor. And when I tried to pick it up, the serpents acted like they wanted to strike me."

He bent and retrieved the book. He turned it over a few times, examining it. The serpents didn't move.

"Odd," he said, and placed it beside Corrine.

The book leaped off the desk and landed at his feet.

"I don't understand," he said. "It recognized you before."

She didn't know whether to feel sad or relieved.

"Perhaps I should keep it again," he said. "Until we know something."

She nodded. She was strangely sorry to see the book disappear into his pocket. "Can you read it at all?" she asked.

"The pages do not speak to me anymore," he said. "But long ago they did." His gaze grew distant, and Corrine guessed he was thinking of the time when he had been Leanan's willing slave. She looked away.

Footsteps came down the stairs, and Christina and Miss Brown appeared in a cloud of perfume and whispering silk. Christina wore the new ensemble that had been made for her in the tailor's shop at Killin—a periwinkle velvet mantelet trimmed in ivory lace over a matching skirt. Corrine sank back into her chair, feeling her plainness painfully.

"Father Joe?" Christina covered her mouth with gloved hands.

Miss Brown started as she looked at him, and then she smiled. "A good glamour."

Father Joe's toothy grin unnerved Corrine.

"Well, we are off to Lady Rosenthal's," Miss Brown announced.

"You look charming," Father Joe said as they affixed their bonnets in front of the foyer mirror. "I wish you well of it." Christina's curls bounced on her shoulders as she smiled.

The carriage soon arrived at the front door, and Christina and Miss Brown, pulling on gloves and seizing their reticules, rushed out to meet it.

"We'll leave for Madame DuBois's within the hour," Father Joe said, turning back to Corrine.

She nodded and packed up her writing case, trying not to feel discouraged about being rejected by a book.

SEVEN

March 26, 1866

THE FOG ROLLED IN AS THE CARRIAGE PUSHED THROUGH THE sodden London streets. Again, the din of costermongers crying their wares, screaming children, the raised voices of haggling at the markets assailed Corrine through the carriage windows. At last the driver brought them in front of a shop that was hung with heavy, black curtains sewn with glittering symbols. A single crystal ball sat before them. A sign next to it read "Open."

"Be quick," Father Joe murmured as Corrine stooped to disembark. "A priest entering a Tarot shop will be noticed, even an Anglican."

Corrine grinned and hurried to the door. Over it, she glimpsed a freshly-painted sign that read "Madame LaFortune—Medium" in bright red letters above a hand with an open eye gazing from the palm.

The interior of the shop was dim, hung all around with claret-colored velvet hangings, except for an alcove where a portrait of a doughty Frenchwoman, presumably Madame DuBois's mentor, hung. A table covered in a gold cloth surrounded by four chairs sat in the middle of the room. Another crystal ball sat atop it on a gold filigreed stand, and a deck of Tarot cards rested facedown next to it. A set of cabinets filled with ghastly objects and arcane books slumped against one curtained wall.

At the jingling of the bells, Madame DuBois entered from behind the curtains. Corrine hadn't been sure what to expect, but her former French teacher was still as she remembered her—blowsy hair, sagging features, somewhat slovenly—despite her neat shawl and lace cap. Corrine noticed immediately, however, that her eyes weren't as red-rimmed as they had been at Falston, and that the pungent vapors of alcohol didn't follow Madame as they once had.

Madame didn't smile when she saw them. Instead, she peered at Corrine and shook her head, tsk-tsking.

"Just in time," she said. "Or too late, depending on how you look at it. You didn't heed me at all, did you?" This was said to Corrine as Madame turned her shop sign to "Closed" and bolted the door. She barely spared a glance for the glamoured priest.

"I tried," Corrine said, in a small voice.

Madame came back to the table and indicated two chairs.

"And you," she said to Father Joe, "you must pay more attention."

Corrine swore if Madame had had a ruler that she would have rapped Father Joe's knuckles. "Old you may be, but you are certainly not wise. How could you let this girl go alone into the Prince's rath?"

To Corrine's great surprise, Father Joe reddened. "She accounted well for herself. She brought back William's rathstone and Sir James. I doubt we'd have been able to save him, else."

Madame leaned closer and looked into Corrine's eyes. "She brought back more than that. Didn't you?" Her breath smelled of licorice.

"I don't know," Corrine said.

Madame pointed her chin towards Corrine's left shoulder. "They gave you a nice surprise, didn't they?" Leaning back, she took up the cards and began cutting them. "Or not-so-nice, I'd imagine."

"The book doesn't recognize her any longer, Maud," Father Joe said. "And she has no magic. It's as if . . ."

"She's no longer Half-Born." Madame nodded. Corrine turned Madame's name around in her mind. Maud. It sounded like a name that belonged entirely to someone else.

"There is a binding on you," she said to Corrine. "Can you not see it?" she asked Father Joe.

"You know I see very little these days," Father Joe said.

"Hmmph." Madame laid the cards on the table.

"But Mara has felt it," Father Joe rushed to add. "It was she who discovered it, in fact. Is it a spirit?"

Madame peered at Corrine again. Such scrutiny drove Corrine to examine the gold tablecloth. Little dark flecks, like tiny bloodstains, dotted it near the edge.

"I do not know," Madame said finally. "But we could test it in a séance. If it was placed there by the Unhallowed, though, triggering it could be a trap. Still," she said, tapping her fingers atop the cards, "it makes little sense as to why they would want to protect or shield your powers. The Prince certainly would not want to shield you from himself."

"Corrine said there were three ladies present when she closed the rathgate. Three ladies veiled in gloom."

"Three, eh?"

Corrine nodded.

Madame fanned the cards and slid them toward Corrine. "Choose ten," Madame said. "A spread might help us determine our course of action."

Corrine reached for the cards slowly, remembering her previous encounters with them. The first time, Madame had been trying to warn her about Falston and perhaps explain her place there. The second had also been a warning against foolish actions, a warning Corrine hadn't heeded. Each time, though, Madame had given her the card. Corrine had never chosen any for herself.

Corrine slid her hands over the cards, but she felt nothing. One by one, Corrine pulled out the cards and handed them to Madame, who assembled them in a cross pattern.

When the spread was laid, Madame reached for the first card.

"This card," she said, as she turned it over, "represents you in the matter at hand."

Corrine peered at it. A man ran away from a carnival, balancing five swords in his arms, while two stood in the ground behind him.

"Seven of Swords," Madame said. "Not surprising. This merely shows that you are seeking counsel, perhaps making an attempt at something new. I would guess, too, that swords are drawn to you—they are drawn to the very intelligent, those of lighter coloring and little humor."

Corrine tried not to frown, but she wasn't sure she liked what Madame insinuated.

Madame wasn't paying attention, however, and had

flipped the card that crossed the first one. A moon dropped sparks of silver on howling wolves, as an ugly black lobster crept from the depths of the sea. Corrine grimaced. The lobster reminded her somehow of the mermaid in the well.

Madame tsked. "Hidden enemies, terror, danger, deception. These are the obstacles you must face. But you've known that now for some time."

The next card was the Six of Pentacles, reversed. Madame gave Corrine a knowing glance. "This is your ideal, what you wish for but cannot have at present. Love and the magic of desire."

Corrine blushed and refused to look in Father Joe's direction.

"Beware, though—the love of the Six of Pentacles is all illusion," Madame warned.

Next came the Four of Cups reversed, the Eight of Cups, and the Page of Pentacles.

At the turning of the Page, Madame said, "You really do want him, don't you?"

"Stop," Corrine whispered. Her dreams of normalcy were far too private to share.

"Well," Madame said, pushing a stray strand of hair from her face, "beware of him. He may not be what he seems." She tapped the Four and Eight of Cups with a thick finger in rapid succession. "Work with what you have—your new knowledge—and let go of your former concerns. Allow yourself to move on to something new."

She flipped the last four cards quickly. The Star, Ten of Wands reversed, The King of Pentacles, Five of Cups reversed.

"The Star here represents your attitude," Madame

said. "Right now, you feel lost, abandoned, deprived. But there is another side to the star—one of bright prospects and hope. It is up to you to choose how to see your fate, though you wander now in a world of intrigue and difficulty."

Madame took a long, slow breath. "You may long for the magic of this love"—she pointed again to the Page—"but there is another who also pursues you, a dark lord of magic and illusion. You know him, of course."

The Prince.

"This last . . ." Madame's hands shook just a little as she rearranged them on the table. "This last is what will come."

There was such a long silence that Corrine could hear carriages passing beyond the dark curtains. She stared at the card. A person—the gender was uncertain—stood in a black mourning cloak on a riverbank. A far-away city beckoned over a bridge. At the person's feet, three cups spilled their bloody contents across the ground. Two remained standing, and Corrine sensed that they must be protected and that the cloaked person had no idea how he or she would do it.

"This is a card of loss," Madame said finally.

Corrine looked up at her.

"Loss, but strangely also inheritance, return, and ancestry. And . . ." she sighed, "consanguinity."

"No!" Father Joe shouted. He dashed his hand across the cards so that they scattered and spilled onto the floor like frightened mice.

"Father Joseph," Madame said disapprovingly.

"No," he said. "That cannot be what you see for her. I will not allow it."

"The cards seldom lie," Madame said.

"What do they mean?" Corrine asked. "What are you talking about?"

A look shot between Madame and Father Joe, one of those looks that Corrine had come to despise.

Madame shook her head slightly.

Corrine looked to Father Joe. His thick-jowled glamour disturbed her; there was nothing in his face that she recognized. His lips tightened.

"You won't tell me, will you?" she said.

"I . . ." Father Joe began.

"Listen," Madame interrupted. "Corrine, choices lie before you. Important choices resulting from important questions. What would the answers mean if we revealed them before you can make these choices on your own?"

Corrine gritted her teeth as she looked at the spilled cards. The last one was tilted on its edge, and the cloaked figure mocked her with knowledge she still didn't possess.

"I don't care about answers or choices," she said. "I want to know what you saw. What does that word mean?" She turned to Father Joe. "Why did it frighten you?" She looked between the two of them. "And why are you both still frightened now?"

There was nothing but silence.

Corrine stood.

Father Joe put out a hand. "Corrine, don't—"

"I'm not going to run away, or go to the Unhallowed, or whatever you're thinking," she said. "But I'm not staying here. If you won't tell me what I need to know, then I'll find out on my own."

Madame looked at her sadly. "This knowledge will only cause you pain."

Words boiled up Corrine's throat, but she clicked her teeth shut against them. "Very well," she managed to say. She remained standing.

Father Joe sighed and rose also, while Madame bent to retrieve the cards.

Corrine looked at him. "I want to go back to Primrose Hill," she said.

Father Joe's wrong-colored eyes darkened. "We were meant to go to Westminster."

Corrine shook her head. "I want to go back to Primrose Hill," she repeated.

Father Joe glanced at Madame, who was still busy with the cards, and sighed. "All right then. I shall send you back in a carriage, and go on to Westminster alone. Do I have your word that you'll stay put?"

Corrine knew that he was trying to maneuver her into swearing an oath.

"Yes," she said. *This time.*

Madame straightened and laid the deck of cards on the table.

"It was good to see you again, Maud," Father Joe said. "You have been missed."

Madame inclined her head and said, "See you take good care of this girl. We will hold a séance at the dark of the moon to try to unbind her power. Tell Mara to be ready. We'll need her." Corrine broke Madame's piercing gaze by staring at the threadbare carpet.

"Let's be off, then," Father Joe said too lightly.

Corrine followed him without saying good-bye or thanking Madame. Father Joe flagged down an omnibus and helped her into it in silence. She heard Father Joe tell the driver where to let her off as he paid the fare. The other passengers made room for her grudgingly. Corrine searched their faces for a moment, wondering if any of them were allied with her enemies, wondering how she'd know without the magic, but none of them would meet her eyes. She reached for the ring and ran her thumb across its worn surface. In times like these, it imparted an odd comfort.

No one spoke, except a young gentleman whose dark curls and thick eyelashes certainly bespoke a heritage different from his fellow passengers. He was well-dressed, but not ostentatiously so. As Corrine stared out the window at the changing of the Horse Guards near Whitehall, he said, "That's the Queen's cavalry there. Fine, aren't they?"

Without taking her eyes from the tall, Irish draft horses, Corrine nodded.

"Legend says that the Household Cavalry line began with a kelpie stallion," the gentleman said.

Corrine looked at him, but his half-smile was guileless, his almost-black eyes watching the horses disappear from view.

"What?" Corrine said.

"If you believe in that sort of thing," the young man said. Then he leaned across one of the other passengers and called to the driver.

The carriage halted, and the young man tipped his hat to Corrine as he climbed out.

Corrine nodded, speechless. Why would a complete stranger happen to mention kelpies to her? Could anything ever be simply coincidental again? Corrine wasn't sure. Without her magic, she could sense nothing about him, and no vision came.

Madame's Tarot reading rolled around in her mind. *Page of Pentacles . . . Seven of Swords . . . loss . . . hope . . . consanguinity.*

Corrine might not know about strangers with surprising knowledge of the Fey, but she knew one thing: She definitely needed a dictionary.

April 15, 1866

The next couple of weeks brought a hectic schedule of studying, tea parties, and scouting in the slums of Whitechapel for everyone else, while Corrine spent long, quiet afternoons copying Brighde's letters and trying as best she could to avoid the visions that threatened to overwhelm her mind. She had attempted to find a dictionary, and had even asked after one, but none seemed present anywhere in the townhouse's small library. She didn't dare ask Miss Brown what the strange word meant for fear Father Joe had already told the headmistress of the disastrous Tarot reading. She snuck reading Father Joe's old letters when she could, but that wasn't very often, as she never seemed to be alone in the morning room for very long. Father Joe came and went, conferring with Miss Brown endlessly about how to wrest the Stone of Destiny from its place under the throne without drawing too much attention to himself. He seldom spoke to her, unwilling, she guessed, to risk another spat with her.

Today was the new moon, when Madame DuBois would perform the séance to try to commune with whatever power bound Corrine. Corrine still wasn't sure whether this was the best idea. Who knew what would be summoned or what it would demand? The kelpie himself might come, and Corrine had read how the water-horses liked to plunge into rivers and lochs, to the doom of their riders.

She turned back to the fragment of letter she'd been transcribing, more about Brighde's fears of the Unhallowed.

[Trans. note: June 1356]

To Brother Angus of the Kirk of St. Fillan from Sister Brighde of the Isle of Female Saints, greeting.

My dear friend:

I am touched by your sincere repentance, such that, if you desire it, I will ask dispensation of the Mother Superior to allow a visit. I dislike deceit, however, and perhaps there may be a more suitable way of arranging a meeting that would not force me to tell falsehoods to one who has always shown me kindness. I am uncertain what you wish to say to me that you cannot say in these letters, private as they are, but I will hear you out.

Tell me where you wish to meet and I will contrive to be there. I've been taking the sheep alone to the higher pastures; perhaps there by the standing stone we will find a better meeting place than the abbey. Do you send your Fey friends to watch over me? Yester-noon, I thought I saw a horned man with a flute perched among the high rocks, but when I came closer, it was only a tree growing in the cleft of stone.

Despite the harsh words of my last letter, you must believe that I bear you no ill will. It is simply that I do not understand your decision to leave the Church which has sheltered and protected you and your brethren who love and miss you most painfully. If I should ever leave, I would feel it as a wound, as if someone had cut me from my true mother and sisters and from the Father who is father to us all. You say your friends the Fey offer this sort of love, but I fail to see how they can.

Nevertheless, I am willing to reconcile with you, for you are my dear brother and true teacher of Scripture; none wiser in the scholarly arts has there been since Iamblicus disappeared from your very own monastery years ago.

Tell me how we shall meet. I await your instruction.

Yours in devotion,

Brighde

Just as Corrine finished, Christina returned from yet another tea with Miss Brown. She bounded into the morning room where Corrine sat by the windows. "Oh, Corrine!" she called, coming and putting her arms around Corrine's shoulders and kissing her cheek.

"You must come with us next time! I have met the most wonderful companions!"

Corrine managed to put her pen back into the inkwell and turned to face Christina, who looked as if she might begin waltzing around the room. Corrine wasn't sure she wanted to hear about yet another delightful tea party, but Christina's happiness was infectious. "Tell me," she said.

"So many of these teas are dreadfully dull," Christina said, taking out a lace fan. "But today, I met a young heiress to the Ballantine fortune—Phyllida. She has the most perfect manners of anyone I've met here, and yet"— Christina leaned forward and whispered confidentially behind her fan—"she also has the most wicked sense of humor, as well. We were able to get out from under the chaperones, and stroll about the grounds for a bit. Her friend, Elizabeth Saylor—her father's a shipping merchant for the East India Company—came along, as well. You must meet them!"

Corrine nodded, though they sounded exactly like the sort of people she didn't wish to meet at all.

"Phyllida has several eligible suitors; one would think she would choose one and have done, but she is determined to play them for all they're worth."

Definitely not someone I want to meet. "Charming," Corrine said, trying to muster up a smile.

"Oh, she is indeed, and has the most exquisite parure of diamonds and sapphires I've ever seen."

"Parure?" Corrine asked. Once again, she felt the lack of a dictionary.

"A jewelry set, *ma cherie,*" Christina said, tapping Corrine lightly with her fan. "All the pieces are fashioned like serpents, and the serpent in the necklace holds a giant black star sapphire between his golden jaws. It's lovely."

Corrine nodded. What Christina spoke of was so far outside her experience that she knew little enough of what to say. "Where did she get it?" she asked, trying and failing again to muster true enthusiasm.

If Christina noticed the dullness in Corrine's tone, she failed to acknowledge it. "She said it was on loan to her father from a French museum dealer for all the fine whiskey her father has supplied his parties over the years. She said if we are invited to any balls soon, she'll loan it to me to wear."

Corrine imagined Christina draped in jeweled serpents and tried not to shudder.

"Ladies," Miss Brown said, pulling off her bonnet as she came into the room, "supper will be ready in just a little while, so make yourselves ready. Have either of you seen Ilona?"

They shook their heads and Miss Brown peered through the glazed window, her expression worried.

"She took something out with her today," Corrine said. "A big, cloth-wrapped package."

Christina looked at her as if she'd just tattled some kind of terrible secret.

"I'm sure all is well, Miss Brown," she said lightly, narrowing her eyes a bit at Corrine.

"I hope so. In any case, put your things away and make yourselves ready. Madame DuBois is joining us tonight."

Christina smiled and took Corrine by the arm, obviously brightening at the thought of being able to speak her native language with their former French teacher.

As Miss Brown went down the narrow hall toward the kitchen, Christina led Corrine upstairs.

"Now," she said when they were out of earshot, "I must warn you to be very careful in what you say about Ilona."

They paused on the stairs a moment, and Christina hugged Corrine's arm even closer to her side, so that Corrine could feel the iron stays of her corset through the soft quilting of her mantle.

"Why?" Corrine asked, turning to look at Christina.

But Christina didn't reply. Her expression was subsumed by a look of terror that made Corrine try to steady her in the narrow stairwell.

"Ah," Christina said with a little gasp of surprise. She clasped Corrine's fingers in a deathgrip, and as her eyes rolled backward, Corrine prepared herself for the inevitable faint.

But suddenly the eyes rolled forward again, and Christina looked at Corrine with a piercing dark gaze that did not belong to her at all. Her face altered to resemble a face Corrine had beheld only once before on the Isle of Female Saints.

"Brighde," Corrine whispered.

"He is coming for me, Corrine," Christina said in Brighde's voice. "And I cannot resist him." Her throat worked and her body trembled, as though Christina were desperately trying to cast the ghost out.

Then Christina went limp in Corrine's arms.

"Brighde," Corrine said, shaking Christina. "Christina!"

She shook her harder, but there was no response. She tried to lift her but the awkwardness of both their skirts in the narrow stairway made it almost impossible.

Boots clumped up the stairs and Ilona nearly tripped right into them.

"Corrine, what's happened?"

Ilona's cap sat askew, her lip cut and swollen. A bruise spread on her left cheek. Ilona shifted the cloth-wrapped package she held into the crook of one arm.

Corrine shook her head. "I don't know. Can you help? I can't quite lift her."

"Take her shoulders," Ilona said. "I'll take her feet."

Thus awkwardly, they made the landing and carried Christina into the bedroom she shared with Ilona. Corrine removed Christina's mantelet and helped Ilona loosen the lacings of her dress and corset.

"Always too tight," Ilona murmured. Corrine grabbed the bottle of smelling salts and waved them under Christina's nose.

Christina inhaled deeply, then looked at them both, her gaze lingering on Ilona. "What happened to you?"

"I might ask the same of you," Ilona said.

Christina looked to Corrine.

"You fainted. But before that, I think Brighde was trying to speak to me through you. She warned me about the Prince."

Christina's mouth turned down. "I wish she would just leave me be. I have never had a normal life because of her. Why won't she leave me alone?"

Corrine shook her head. "I wish I knew. Maybe Madame can call her in the séance. Maybe she can explain. I don't think she means to hurt anyone . . ."

But Christina had turned her head away on the pillow. She hated this nonsense about ghosts and fairies. She wanted nothing more than a normal life. Whatever had happened in her past had denied her that. And these fits, Corrine knew, continued to remind Christina of how she was so unlike everyone else. She could imagine Christina's thoughts: *How will I ever marry respectably? Will I end up an old spinster like Miss Brown?*

Corrine patted Christina's arm clumsily and rose. "Rest," she said. "We'll see if Madame can help."

She looked at Ilona until the girl growled, "I got in a fight. He was faster than me. No need to worry."

So tough. So like a boy that it made Corrine's heart bleed. No one would ever marry Ilona. She would be alone, fighting for whatever scraps she could, for the rest of her life. Corrine turned toward the door, and disliked the sinking feeling that no one would want to marry her, either, with her strange eye and bound magic powers. Who could love such a misfit? Who could feel at ease with such a woman as the mother of his child, knowing fairies would haunt that child all of its days?

She went into her room and slid down on the floor by the bed, trying not to weep. How had everything come to this? She sat for a long while, running her fingers around the ring's tarnished circle, trying to trace the series of events to this one strange moment. Her thoughts raced in circles. Then, no closer to a real answer than when she started, she rose and splashed water over her face at the washstand and went to the wavering mirror that hung in the wardrobe. She straightened her clothes, thinking how they were nothing so fine as Christina's.

Plain muslin with a little ribbon trim at the wrists and hem, a Princess-line cut that accentuated her one good feature, her narrow waist. Her new dress had been ruined when she'd thrown the daoi scarf into the fire at Fearnan, and though there had been talk of embroidering it, there hadn't been time. Corrine pulled a little at the corset under her blouse. She still despised it as much as ever, but it was a necessary evil. Her hair she left as it was. She had taken to pulling it up in a plain chignon. She couldn't imagine fussing with curls the way Christina did; there seemed to be no point.

She pulled a shawl around her, ignoring the stiffness in her branded shoulder. It was no longer as cold, but the puckered skin was sensitive to even the lightest touch.

She shut the wardrobe. *I'm ready*, she thought. But for what, she wasn't certain.

Dinner was a quiet affair, little more than mutton boiled with such root vegetables as could be had—mealy turnips by the taste of them. But Mara compensated with an apple pandowdy, the smell of which set Corrine's mouth watering long before it arrived at the table.

Madame and Christina carried on a conversation in French that Corrine, despite all her studies, caught only bits of. Ilona ate carefully throughout most of the meal, but the pandowdy overcame her reserve and she winced several times as she slid the hot apples across her swollen lip. No one had said anything to her about the bruise on her cheek, though Miss Brown cast a concerned glance her way every now and again.

At last, they retired to the morning room, where Siobhan had laid a fire and set out tea for everyone.

Madame insisted that Father Joe move the card table from its place in the corner to the center of the room, and gathered them all around it. She lit a candle in the center of the table.

"During the séance," Madame said, "I want all of you to do several things. One is to hold hands throughout the visit, if any spirits choose to attend. Another is to keep breathing deeply and evenly. Suspend your thoughts. Do not think about your next beautiful dress"—she eyed Christina—"or the food you just ate." The last was directed at Ilona. "Think of nothing. Let your mind be empty so that the spirit can find room to enter.

"We are seeking a spirit guide for Corrine, some knowledge of how her powers came to be bound and how we might unbind them. Without her continued training, we are at a great loss. And if she wishes to continue the work she has begun, I am confident that the spirit will make the way known to us. If anyone does not wish to be involved, he or she should leave the circle now."

Corrine glanced around the circle. Siobhan shivered in her seat, but she didn't move. Her fear filled Corrine with foreboding.

"Now, join hands," Madame said.

Corrine took Christina's and Mara's hands. Father Joe sat across the table from her. Incredulity fluttered across his features, as if he wondered how a priest could find himself in such straits, practicing a forbidden occult ritual.

"Now, take the five-count breath. Ilona, Christina, and Siobhan, it just means you breathe in for five—*un*, *deux, trois, quatre, cinq*—like so, you see?"—she took a great snorting breath—"and then out—*un, deux, trois, quatre, cinq.* And you just keep doing it until your mind is empty."

Corrine fell automatically into the pattern. She willed her mind not to see the dark ocean and the tower waiting for her at the eastern horizon. She didn't want to feel herself plummeting sickeningly into the ocean as she had before.

Madame began a low hum that seemed to pass through her and around the waiting circle. Corrine felt it tingle a little as it moved over her hands, the ghost of the sensation she normally felt in Father Joe's or the Prince's presence. The hum became an insistent buzz; Mara's and Christina's hands tightened on hers.

Then Madame said, "We call you, oh spirit who haunts our friend, who locks away her greatest treasure and clouds the mirror of her sight. We beseech you to appear within this our circle."

The light flared. Corrine opened her eyes and saw the candle flame sparking upward almost to the ceiling. Beyond it a shadow stalked, and as it drew closer to the flame, her shoulder ached with recognition. Its eyes glowed with witch-light. Its long, black mane was braided with waterweeds and knucklebones. It approached Corrine, solidifying even as it came around the table. A white light flared up in front of Christina.

Siobhan screamed and let go Father Joe's and Ilona's hands to cover her eyes. The kelpie leaped through the gap in the circle, through the wall, and out into the street. Even as he drew farther away, Corrine heard his hooves pounding the cobble. Father Joe and Ilona scrabbled after Siobhan's hands, and the drifting white shape materialized before Corrine.

"I warned you," Brighde said.

"But what can I do?" Corrine whispered. "They took my power."

"No," Brighde said. "They hid it, so that you could hide from the Prince. He comes for both of us. And now that ignorant girl has unleashed the one thing that could have protected you. On his own, he is dangerous. He will try to betray you. You must tame him."

"How?"

"You must find the bridle."

"The bridle?"

"Bring it into the circle. The kelpie will return to you every dawn until Beltane. Put the bridle on him before then and he will serve you. After that, you are vulnerable."

The candle flame returned to its normal flicker, and Brighde faded, like starlight into morning.

"Who are they?" Corrine whispered. It was as though no one but the two of them occupied the room. "The three women?"

Brighde smiled sadly. "You know them. They are the Treas Ulaidh. You have read of them before in the Unhallowed book." A wind blew through the walls; the candle guttered. Brighde flitted about the circle frantically as a moth. "He comes," she said, before she vanished again.

No one dared breathe. The room, save for the ticking of the clock on a bookshelf, was silent.

Corrine looked over at Christina. Her face was white, her grip on Corrine's hand clammy. Corrine reminded herself that Christina had never seen Brighde, much less a ghost, before.

"That is who causes all my trouble?" Christina whispered.

Corrine nodded. "I'm afraid so."

"Why will she not leave me?" Christina asked.

"We don't know," Father Joe said, releasing Siobhan and Miss Brown. "But I knew her in life, and believe me, if she wishes to stay with you, she will."

Madame looked at Siobhan with undisguised contempt. "You are very foolish," she said. "If you did not want to be part of this, you should not have sat to the circle."

"Maud," Father Joe warned, too late.

Siobhan crawled out of her chair, weeping, and ran from the room.

Corrine half-rose, but Mara put a hand on her. "I'll go. She trusts me a little more than she does you, even though I do all those devilish things I do."

Corrine nodded, and Mara slipped out of the room after Siobhan.

"I want to go to bed," Christina said. Her eyes were sunken. She looked to Ilona for help. Ilona came around the table and helped her up, and Corrine couldn't tell whether Ilona's glance at her was reproachful or fearful. Ilona used the candle on the table to light one of the lanterns and then they were off, Christina's arm draped over Ilona's shoulder while Ilona held the lantern high before them.

"The kelpie is free now," Miss Brown said. "What does that mean?"

"He is not entirely free," Madame said. "He must still return to Corrine until Beltane. We have until then to subdue him."

"The bridle," Corrine said.

Miss Brown frowned. "Where can we find a kelpie bridle?"

Corrine remembered the conversation with the stranger in the carriage.

"I think I know," she said.

April 16, 1866

Corrine heard Father Joe and Miss Brown arguing about it when she came down for breakfast the next morning.

"But, Joseph, you cannot just steal a bridle from the Queen's own cavalry! You'll be hanged or your hand cut off or God knows what!"

"Thea, I hardly think this would merit the loss of a limb. Besides, this is good practice for us. We can judge our execution and timing as an appreciation of how we will deal with the Stone of Destiny."

"The only execution I think we may end up appreciating is your own! Whoever thought a priest would stoop to such petty thievery!"

Before Father Joe could retort, Corrine entered the room. Both their faces were flushed with anger; Miss Brown's eyes were molten blue.

Corrine didn't smile, though these infrequent quarrels occasionally amused her. She was fairly certain the sub-text was completely opposite from the words that were spoken.

"Corrine," Father Joe said, "we were just discussing the bridle. More to the point, the procuring of this bridle."

"Yes," Corrine said, taking her seat, and spooning marmalade onto burned toast. "I'll bet Ilona could steal it."

"Steal what?" Ilona said, as she came to the table.

"The kelpie bridle," Corrine said. "We could go together. I could divert the stablehands while——"

"No, Corrine," Miss Brown interrupted. "It's too dangerous for you."

Father Joe considered it as he sipped his tea. "I think it's a grand idea. Ilona probably has many friends now who could do the job if she couldn't, correct?"

Ilona nodded. Corrine wondered if Miss Brown's seeming lack of concern for Ilona hurt. But perhaps Ilona considered it a sign of her growing talents in the underworld, a world that Corrine understood as little as the world of Christina's high society teas.

"But I think I can do it," Ilona said.

"I want to go," Corrine said.

Miss Brown was about to say something, but Father Joe shushed her. "If Ilona needs you," he said to Corrine, "she'll take you along. Let her decide."

Corrine met Ilona's dark gaze. "Fair enough," she said.

"Today, it will not be necessary," Ilona said. "I will need to find out where the bridle is kept."

Corrine nodded.

"Besides," Ilona said, scratching at her hair under her cap, "I think Christina wants you to play croquet with her today. That friend of hers—Phyllida—wanted to meet you."

The thought of Phyllida and her serpentine parure made even burned toast seem more appealing. But Corrine heard herself saying, "Of course. I'd be delighted." What she'd wear to meet a society girl, though, she had no idea. She'd much rather dress as a boy and go with Ilona, but she decided not to press.

Ilona went to the morning room to study before leaving for her day's work. Miss Brown looked none too happy, but Corrine was glad that Ilona was being allowed to play a vital part. She was just rising to follow Ilona when Father Joe said, "Corrine, would you mind studying with me this morning? I'd like to see how the kelpie has affected your magic. Have you tried to go into the domains at all?"

She sighed and shook her head. It was definitely going to be a long day.

She followed Father Joe into a small parlor off the narrow hall that led back to the kitchens. A few magic books lay open on a coffee table, and Corrine wondered if Father Joe had been trying to find spells to lift the kelpie binding. Father Joe indicated an old armchair and she sank into it.

"Let's just try something simple," Father Joe said, seating himself on the nearby settee. "Start the five-count breath, and then move through the domains until you get to the well."

Corrine nodded and closed her eyes. She descended into her breath, hearing echoes of Madame's voice counting the breaths in French last night.

The ocean tossed beneath her; the tower spires in the east were tipped in flame by the setting sun. She glided gently beyond the castle into the eye of the sun until she sat again in the garden bower. As she left the bower, she looked carefully for traces of Unhallowed encroachment—any signs that something might not be quite right. She traced the path through the hollyhocks and sunflowers to the vine-covered well. It was open and free of entanglements; its mossy breath enveloped her as she looked into it. Something swam far below in the black water—teeth, a shred of bloated skin . . . She pulled back from the well and realized something was watching her.

"There's a presence," she said, her voice slow and distant.

"What do you see?" Father Joe asked.

But she didn't answer. The kelpie watched her from the edge of the ivy. His midnight coat repelled sunlight, creating a black hole in the garden's eternal summer. In the light, his eyes were milky-pale as marbles. His heavy mane was festooned with water weeds and finger-bones where, Corrine supposed, his victims had clutched at him even as he dragged them to their deaths. Compulsion radiated from him in waves.

What do you want? Corrine asked.

The moment hung between them. The compulsion ceased. The kelpie seemed to be considering, as if he'd never been asked that question before. Even the bees were still, hovering suspended in the honeyed air.

Then the kelpie smelled or sensed something. He snorted and tossed his mane and tore away from the vines. She watched him carve a swath through the sunflowers until he disappeared.

At last, I find you, the Prince said.

She turned. Euan watched her, lazily cupping a rose between forefinger and thumb. He smiled and crushed it between his fingers, and blood squeezed from the petals.

His face was much more beautiful than she had allowed herself to remember.

Corrine inhaled sharply and opened her eyes. The room was fuzzy at first, the walls warped into pale green and gold.

Father Joe watched her. "Did you go into the domain of water?"

Corrine shook her head. "No. *He* was there."

"The kelpie?"

"Yes," Corrine said. "And the Prince."

"Both?" Father Joe said. He stood and began pacing before the empty fireplace. "Do you think the kelpie is bait? Was he there to divert you so the Prince could find you?"

Corrine considered. Even as she recognized the danger of the kelpie, he seemed melancholy and almost winsome. This, she knew, could be part of the danger; the legends said he lured travelers onto his back to drown them. But she had felt in that moment when she had spied him watching her that he was guileless, uninterested in harming her, perhaps even wanting to protect her, as Brighde had said.

"Corrine?"

"No," she said, at last. "I think the Prince frightened him off. I don't think the kelpie expected him there."

"He shouldn't have been there," Father Joe said. The force behind his words was like a fist slamming down on the table. "The Prince shouldn't be able to breach your mind like this. The domains should be impenetrable. Unless—" He looked at her. "Do you have feelings for Euan, Corrine?"

Corrine reddened all the way past her collar. The ring

burned against her chest. Her hands twisted in her lap. "I hardly know what you mean," she began.

"Don't play coy with me!" Father Joe said. "You're no good at it, Corrine."

Her mouth curved downward. "I know," she said. "I am not Christina."

Father Joe snorted. "Well of course, you're not. That has nothing to do with it. But if you once had feelings for Euan and still harbor them, without magical protection, it will be easy for him to seek you out. So, it's time for truth. Do you or don't you?"

Corrine bowed her head. "I don't know," she said, almost to herself.

"What? I can't hear you."

"I don't know," she said. She pressed her hands over her eyes to keep the tears from leaking out. She had deflected this question within herself for so long that, confronted with it now, she hardly knew how to answer.

"Corrine." Father Joe came to her and knelt in front of her so that she couldn't look away from him. He took her hands away from her eyes. "This is very serious. If you love the Prince even the tiniest bit, if your heart is turned toward him at all, he will find ways into your thoughts and dreams. Your feelings are an open invitation; he will not stint to use it."

Corrine's tears flowed, and the words came. "I tried. I tried to take the rathstone from him, but I couldn't. He begged me to cut it from him. He said he could bear death easier than my disregard . . ." She choked.

Father Joe gripped her hands so tightly she thought he might crush them in his own. "Why didn't you tell us this sooner? So it was not at all that you had no opportunity to take the second stone from him. He manipulated you into powerlessness, didn't he?"

She nodded.

He shook her and his voice was hoarse when he spoke, "You must stop this lying, do you hear! And you must banish him from your heart. Such feelings will do you and the Council no good!"

It was the last bit that transformed her sorrow into anger. She thought of Father Joe's love letters to Leanan, how he had said that the life of one mortal mattered not one whit compared to her love. He had obviously given himself completely over to the witch, while Corrine struggled day and night against the only man she'd known who had shown her true care and kindness. The Prince's only lie had been in his hidden identity, and how could he truly have revealed that to her? She felt almost sick now, as though she'd betrayed him.

"And what of you?" she asked, fuming. "Were you doing the Council good when you were Leanan's lover?"

The slap propelled Corrine's cheek into the musty upholstery. Corrine sat still, her hair unwinding from her chignon and obscuring much of her vision. Her face throbbed. Before arriving at Falston, Corrine had never been struck by anyone, anywhere. Her Transcendentalist parents did not believe in corporeal punishment. At school, Miss de Mornay had rapped her knuckles several times and threatened her with the switch. Mara had cuffed her to keep her from fainting atop the carriage. But no adult had ever slapped her.

"Don't ever speak her name to me again," Father Joe breathed. "No one will ever understand the price I paid. You least of all."

Corrine pushed out of the chair.

She barreled into Miss Brown at the door.

"Corrine, my goodness!" She brushed Corrine's hair out of her face.

Corrine desperately wanted to sink into her embrace, but Father Joe's voice tightened her resolve.

"Let her go," he said.

Miss Brown stepped aside, and Corrine thundered up the stairs before they could call her back.

In the end, she pulled the quilt off the bed and wrapped herself in it on the floor. She cried herself to sleep, clutching the ring and her little golden locket between her hands. Her dreams were refrains of the old dreams she'd had at Falston. The Prince called to her, and she saw his face wavering before her as though she looked at his image far below in a well. She walked again in the throne room with its golden rain, and the nix's gown clung to her like dark webbing. She looked into his face, ashamed, but there was only admiration in his gaze—admiration and that touch of sorrow he always bore.

Knocking at the door woke her. She lay still, hoping whoever it was would go away. But Miss Brown came around the bed, followed by Christina. Christina knelt and took her in her arms. Corrine closed her eyes.

"Corrine," Miss Brown said, kneeling down awkwardly in her wide skirts. "I know what happened."

Corrine didn't say anything.

Miss Brown placed her hand on Corrine's quilt-wrapped ankle. "Father Joe is very sorry. He begs your forgiveness. Under the circumstances, I am not sure what to do. My instincts are to punish you for talking out of turn to an elder—especially a priest!—but I cannot in all good conscience punish you when you were merely stating the truth."

Christina caressed her face and hair. Corrine knew there was no bruise or swelling, not as Ilona had suffered, but the wound to her dignity was infinitely worse than any physical mark.

"Help me here, Corrine," Miss Brown continued. "Because I truly do not know what to do. We must all work together. We must be able to rely on one another. If we can't trust each other, then the Unhallowed have already won."

Many ugly retorts fought to leave Corrine's lips, but she swallowed them all. Corrine knew Miss Brown was trying to help.

"I just don't want to see him for a while," Corrine said. She opened her eyes and looked at Miss Brown. She was amazed to see the headmistress smiling.

"I'll tell you a secret," Miss Brown said. "I've felt that way sometimes. Well, just this once, you shall have your wish. There are two choices. You may stay here and lie much more comfortably on the bed, or you may come with us for a possibly soggy picnic and croquet in the park. Which do you prefer?"

"Do come with us, Corrine," Christina said. "Phyllida and Elizabeth have both asked after you."

Corrine thought for a moment. It would be comforting, she thought, to lie here for a while longer with Christina stroking her brow and Miss Brown saying encouraging things at her feet. But it couldn't last. Eventually she would have to leave her room.

"All right," she said. "I'll come with you."

Miss Brown pushed herself to her feet and settled her skirts. "Very good. We'll depart in an hour's time."

Corrine let Christina help her up to sit on the bed.

"Now," Christina said, smiling, "let us do something with your hair."

Eight

April 16, 1866

WHEN THEY HAD LEFT THE HOUSE, FATHER JOE WAS nowhere to be seen. Corrine guessed that he'd gone out of the house and was glad of it. She didn't know what she'd say to him when next she saw him. She didn't know how she would continue to study magic with him. No one had ever laid a hand on her, certainly not someone she had come to trust and respect almost as much as her own father. He would have never done that to her. The tears almost welled again, but Miss Brown glanced at her as they climbed into the carriage and Corrine reined them back. Miss Brown always seemed to know what she was thinking or feeling. And in this case, she guessed that more tears would only be self-indulgent. She settled into her seat and as the carriage started off, she was drawn into a vision she couldn't stop.

The fire blazed high and for just a moment, Corrine saw the face of Miss Brown's brother fully revealed. His features were delicate—though his skin was dirty, he had large dark blue eyes like Miss Brown's and a smattering of freckles across his cheeks. If anything he looked like . . . a girl.

Corrine shook herself out of the vision and looked

at Miss Brown as understanding slowly dawned. Could Miss Brown's brother actually have been a *sister?* Had the Captain taken her *sister* with him into the Prince's rath? Corrine's mind reeled.

Miss Brown met her gaze for a moment before pointing something out to Christina out of the carriage window.

Corrine adjusted the ties of her bonnet nervously, considering. Now that she had her magic back, she hoped there was some way to sort out all these visions. Before the Captain or the Prince came to get her too.

They arrived at Green Park half an hour later. Corrine's stomach fluttered as she stepped out of the carriage and saw a group of picnickers assembled in a pavilion not too far off. Young men hammered croquet wickets into the ground enthusiastically, and it was just at that moment that Corrine realized she had no idea how to play.

"Christina, I don't . . ." But before she could finish, Christina drew her steadily across the lawn, waving at two young women who Corrine guessed must be Phyllida and her friend Elizabeth.

Phyllida rushed up to Corrine and took her hands before Corrine could blink.

"Why, Corrine!" the young woman gushed. "It's so delightful to finally meet you! We've heard so much about you, and we have just begged dear Christina and Miss Brown to allow you to visit."

Corrine looked up under the recesses of Phyllida's feathered hat, which curved over most of her face and left it in shadow. Her blue eyes sparkled with her sugary smile. Her hands felt large and mannish, like Ilona's, but when Corrine looked down, she saw that they were almost daintier than her own. However, there was no doubt that Phyllida was tall, nearly a head taller than Corrine.

The gray walls crawled with energy. The Captain put his red hand on the first girl's wrist. She ground her teeth in pain until he released her. He stooped over the girl in the corner and she screamed as he touched her with the red hand . . .

Phyllida poised, waiting for Corrine to speak.

"I'm . . . glad I could come," Corrine said weakly. The strength and frequency of the visions nearly turned her stomach.

Elizabeth sidled up next to Phyllida. Her eyes held a predatory malice as she smiled at Corrine and reached forward to pull her from Phyllida's embrace.

"So lovely to meet you," Elizabeth murmured, and for a moment her voice was so familiar that Corrine stiffened and withdrew from her lavender-scented arms. Corrine peered at her, at the dark curls fringing her forehead and her pale green eyes. She was quite certain that she would have seen through a glamour if Elizabeth was wearing one. But she only saw a girl staring at her curiously.

"Likewise," Corrine said, trying to recover herself.

Phyllida took Christina's arm and led her to the pavilion. Elizabeth didn't take Corrine's arm but trailed very closely behind Phyllida and Christina. Corrine looked at Miss Brown and she shook her head a little, as if to suggest that Corrine was on her own for this one. An older woman, whom Corrine guessed to be Lady Rosenthal, welcomed Miss Brown and motioned her toward a foldout chair out of the sun. Miss Brown shooed Corrine off toward the other young people before taking her seat among Lady Rosenthal's set. Corrine sighed. Perhaps it would have been better to stay in her room.

The young men returned from setting the wickets and invited the girls to join them. Corrine squinted at one of them, trying to make out features that seemed strangely familiar. At the same moment that she wondered if she needed spectacles, she remembered him. The man from the omnibus!

Corrine stepped back into the shade of the tent.

"Aren't you coming, Corrine?" Elizabeth asked.

"I'm . . . ah . . . feeling a bit tired," Corrine said lamely, and tried to burrow her way back into the shadows, almost stumbling over a chair in the process.

Elizabeth shrugged and followed her friends out onto the lawn.

But the young man had evidently heard her voice, for he came up beside her.

"My companion in the omnibus!" he said.

Corrine looked anywhere but his eyes, though she couldn't help noticing they were dark and gentle. She pretended to watch Phyllida and Christina giggling helplessly as their balls smashed into the wickets. No one noticed when Elizabeth cheated by moving her ball; they were too busy fluttering after Phyllida and Christina.

The young man watched them for a second. "It's strange how people change, isn't it?"

Corrine looked at him, but he was watching the girls on the lawn.

"I've known Phyllida and Elizabeth since we were children," he said. "Phyllida was always so quiet and Elizabeth such a sincere, gentle soul. It's only since the boating accident that they've become so . . . shallow—so selfish and rather crude . . ."

He glanced at Corrine, seemingly embarrassed, as though he hadn't meant to speak aloud. "But I forget myself entirely. May I bring you some punch, Miss . . . ?" His dark curls framed an overly serious face. He waited expectantly for her name.

"Jameson," Corrine said.

"Miss Jameson," he said. "Pleased to make your acquaintance." He made a small bow, which she returned with a brief curtsy. What did he know and how much should she try to find out? His presence here couldn't be coincidence; the omnibus exchange could no longer be discounted as a passing oddity.

"Yes," she said, not bothering to ask his name in return. "Punch would be wonderful."

He looked a bit surprised at her bad manners, but recovered gracefully enough and went off to procure the punch. Corrine watched as one of the young men offered to exchange mallets with Christina, claiming that hers was "perhaps too heavy for such delicate hands."

Corrine's mind raced, trying to think of how to approach further interactions with this young man. If anything he was not what he seemed, she should have sensed it by now. Unless he wore an undetectable glamour. She caught herself thinking of the Prince, of the petals slowly being crushed between his strong fingers, of his brilliant, ever-changing eyes. She reached to touch the silver signet ring where it rested against her locket. What should she do? Who was this man and what did he want?

He returned with her punch and handed it to her. She admitted to feeling a slight shiver as their gloved hands touched, but whether that was magic or some other form of chemistry, she couldn't say. She blushed furiously.

"I am Dimitrios Adamou, if you wondered," he said. "Most of my friends here call me Dimitri, though."

Men had lied to her so often in the last several months that Corrine wasn't sure she even believed he'd given his real name. "Thank you for the punch, Mr. Adamou," she said. She looked out across the lawn as she sipped.

When she didn't volunteer anything further, he said, "And am I not to have the pleasure of your Christian name, Miss Jameson? Forgive me for speaking so freely earlier; it was truly not my place."

Corrine looked at his earnest expression. For as much as she had seen Christina ply the charming act, she had occasionally witnessed her icy demeanor toward those Christina believed beneath her. She didn't know this man and doubted she could trust him. Though it went against her nature, Corrine hardened her heart and said, "I would prefer it if we kept our exchanges formal, Mr. Adamou."

His eyes glinted, and for a moment she feared he'd rebuke her just as coldly. But he said only, "Very well then, Miss Jameson. I shall leave you to your punch alone." He bowed and stepped out from under the tent to join his friends.

That wasn't what I meant, Corrine wanted to say. But she tightened her lips and stood a little straighter. It was better this way. If he were allied with the Unhallowed, she wouldn't so easily fall prey to his tricks. And if he weren't, she knew he would never understand the dangers and darkness she faced daily. For so long, she had hated the magic, the strangeness, the secrecy. But compared to this world with its small, polite cucumber sandwiches and scones with clotted cream, the domains of magic seemed completely inexplicable. No matter how she might wish to, how could she ever share any of it with an ordinary man?

At last, the ordeal was over and Corrine, Miss Brown, and Christina wandered away from the pavilion toward the carriage, which one of Christina's admirers had called for them.

"Wasn't that exciting, Corrine?" Christina said. Her face was flushed, but her hand trembled as she clutched Corrine's arm.

Oh yes. About as exciting as sticking a fork in my hand. But Corrine nodded, trying to seem grateful when it clearly meant so much to Christina. "You play croquet very well," Corrine said.

"Phyllida has invited us to a ball tomorrow night," Christina said. "She invited you, as well, Corrine. Will you come? Of course it's very last minute, but she said she hopes we can manage. It will be at the palace! The Queen is holding a ball in honor of the Princess Royal's visit. And Phyllida said I may wear her parure—necklace, earrings, all of it! You can borrow one of my gowns . . ."

Corrine let Christina chatter on happily, nodding and agreeing at the appropriate times. The thought of attending a ball at the Queen's palace with the same sort of people as had been present at the picnic made her heart sink.

They were nearly to the carriage, when Christina wavered and said, "Corrine, I think—"

Corrine sensed the surge of power through her fingertips.

Miss Brown apparently felt it, too, for she said, "Hurry, let's get her into the carriage before someone sees."

They helped Christina in and got her settled just as her knees buckled. Corrine put her arms around Christina as Miss Brown shouted for the driver to move along. She closed her eyes and summoned the five-count breath, and then she saw Christina in sunlight, sitting on a rock by a stream. She was talking to someone, sliding her hand through the glittering water. Rory. He took her hand and kissed it, and when he spoke it was as though something deep within him spoke to the soul of Brighde lodged in Christina's body. *My beloved, for so many centuries have I longed to see your face . . .*

"Brighde," Corrine whispered. She didn't know if acknowledging the spirit that lived in Christina would calm her, but there was obviously something Brighde wanted Corrine to know. Rory and Christina had met secretly at Fearnan; Rory had been responsible for making Christina deathly ill. But the vision Brighde had just sent her couldn't possibly have happened at Fearnan. The stream was different; the season wrong. Was this a possible future? A future centuries from now? Why else would Rory say he'd yearned for her for so long, unless . . .

"Angus," Corrine breathed.

"What was that, Corrine?" Miss Brown asked.

"Angus must be influencing Rory, just as Brighde possesses Christina," Corrine said, raising her voice over the rattling carriage. "That's why he can't help himself. That's why he's bound to serve the Prince, whether he wishes to or not."

Miss Brown held her gaze. "And why he'll most certainly find her again," she said, with no hint of disbelief. "We must be careful."

Corrine nodded. Christina leaned against her, her bonnet uncomfortably crushed against Corrine's neck and shoulder.

Corrine thought about the connection between Rory and Angus. A year ago, all of this would have seemed wildly impossible. Now, she accepted it more easily than a cup of punch from a kind young man. Angus's possession of Rory made sense. Corrine remembered how his attraction to Christina had begun—almost unwillingly, gradually growing into a passion neither of them seemed able to control. It seemed quite reasonable that Angus was behind Rory's obsession, doomed to carry out some curse or binding laid down by the Prince. And if that was so, then Christina and the soul she carried were in great danger.

"Should we even go to the ball tomorrow night?" Corrine asked.

Christina lifted her head then and looked at her so miserably that Corrine wished she hadn't spoken.

As Christina straightened her bonnet, Miss Brown said, "I understand your fears; you're right to have them. The masquerade was a near-disaster. But this is no masquerade; there will be many people and because it's in the palace, it'll be heavily guarded. I think it more important for us to go and perhaps meet more people. We've talked with Lady Rosenthal and Phyllida and have learned almost nothing. If there is another Half-Born about, as Madame suspected when we first arrived here, we must find that person and discover his or her alliances."

Corrine nodded as the carriage came to a halt outside their townhouse. She thought briefly of Mr. Adamou—could he be the Half-Born Madame had mentioned? But she had felt nothing from him, nothing that seemed out of the ordinary, anyway. As Miss Brown paid the driver, Corrine helped Christina inside. They removed their bonnets and went into the morning room. Corrine forgot about Mr. Adamou, steeling herself for an encounter with Father Joe.

But only Ilona was there, pacing restlessly, her thumbs thrust under her suspenders. Father Joe hadn't returned home yet from wherever he had gone for the evening, it seemed.

"Ilona?" Corrine asked, as Christina settled herself into the chaise lounge near the fire.

"I have found the bridle," Ilona said.

"Good!" Corrine said. "Where?"

"Tell us," Miss Brown said as she entered the room.

Ilona sighed. "In the Queen's stables at Buckingham Palace. Guarded by hundreds of cavalry and household guards."

Corrine smiled. "Perfect. You can steal the bridle while we waltz."

Ilona throw a sofa cushion at her in disgust.

NINE

April 17, 1866

MORNING CAME AND FATHER JOE WAS STILL NOWHERE TO be found. Corrine had woken drenched in sweat after a night of wrestling with dark dreams. Purple smudges under Miss Brown's eyes belied the fact that she had forgone sleep waiting for news of Father Joe. After breakfast, she called a meeting in the morning room, asking Mara to leave off the washing.

"He left no message, nothing," Miss Brown said. "Do either of you sense his presence?" she asked Corrine or Mara.

Corrine shook her head. The partial freeing of the kelpie seemed to have provided limited access to her magic, but how far that went, she didn't know. And since she'd been trying so hard to ignore Father Joe, she doubted she would have noticed anything.

"No, Miss Brown," Mara said. "I don't feel nothing."

"Would you if . . . if something bad happened?" Miss Brown said.

Corrine hated the fear in her voice.

"I think I would know it," Mara said. "I think if *they*

took him and did something to him, I would sense it somehow. But you know how he is. I reckon he just run off for a bit." Mara looked over at Corrine and Corrine's gaze fell to her lap.

"Maybe," Miss Brown said. She pulled out her handkerchief and threaded her fingers through the lace in an uncharacteristically young gesture. "But he hasn't done that since . . ."

Mara nodded. "Since he found me."

"It was a different time then," Miss Brown said. Corrine was very curious about what had happened between her uncle, Father Joe, and Miss Brown. It had obviously been very sad. Corrine guessed that Miss Brown was without friends in whom she could comfortably confide.

With her uncanny wisdom, Mara said, "Times change. He will, too. Maybe."

"Yes," Miss Brown sighed, "that is true." She smiled sadly. "But we shouldn't talk of him so casually. Let us hope if he is on a wander that he returns soon. Meanwhile, Ilona," she said, "mind you listen on your rambles for anything of import. If Father Joe doesn't return by this evening, I'll alert Madame DuBois to search for him."

"What do we do in the meantime?" Mara said.

"We must hold to our plans. Have I not taught all of you to be resourceful? We will continue our work as best we can without him. Ilona, much as I dislike putting you into danger, much as I don't condone stealing, we must have that kelpie bridle. Restoring Corrine's full magic is of utmost importance to us now, especially with Father Joe gone." Her face hardened and Corrine could see the

131

strength in her that men both feared and loved. Miss Brown rose, straightening her cuffs and returning her handkerchief to her pocket.

"Will we still go to the ball, Miss Brown?" Christina asked softly. She was readying herself for refusal, her mouth already turning down into a charming pout.

"I have said we will, Christina. I know it's dangerous, but information is critical. And every day we lack it, we are in even deeper danger. We need to know what's happening with these girls that Corrine keeps seeing, if there is another Half-Born, and what the Unhallowed plans are. We may just meet someone at the ball who can provide that knowledge." She looked sympathetically at Christina.

"We came to London to do the work of the Council," Miss Brown said. "Now we must be about it."

There were nods all around.

"All right then. We'll have a light supper before Corrine, Christina, Mara, and I depart for the ball. Ilona, spend the afternoon doing some careful reconnoitering, see if you hear any news of Father Joe. Come back before dusk; you can ride with us to the palace and take the bridle during the ball."

Ilona nodded. Corrine envied her. She'd much rather go creeping about the stables, finding out all sorts of interesting things and seeing the Queen's horses, than standing around in a puffy gown trying to avoid attention.

Corrine spent the rest of the afternoon preparing for the ball. Christina talked her into a new evening gown her mother had sent to her not long after they'd arrived in London. The skirt was layers of pale yellow organza, drawn up on either side with pink silk roses and sparkling crystal beads. Roses and crystal beads encrusted the neckline. A set of combs, ornamented with matching silk roses and dangling curtains of beads, nestled in a velvet-lined box.

"Mama still thinks of me as her sweet little girl," Christina said, as she laid the gown out for Corrine with an inscrutable expression.

Christina chose a gown that made her look older and more sophisticated. It was a deep shimmering burgundy moiré with black- tasseled trim. Opera-length black gloves were tasseled at the elbow and wrists. Christina held it against herself in the mirror, and Corrine knew that her friend was imagining Phyllida's parure resting elegantly above the neckline of her burgundy gown. Christina's eyes sparkled as she laid it across her bed.

Having chosen their dresses, they each went to their respective baths. Corrine touched the puckered brand on her shoulder as she soaked in the rose-scented water. She wondered where the kelpie was now and if he would submit to her once she had the bridle. *And then what will I do with him?* she thought. She wished she could go again into the domain of fire and discover what he might have said to her before the Prince came. Before Father Joe had slapped her for her impertinence. She sighed. She couldn't believe he would have just left, but Mara and Miss Brown feared that he might have. He had always been the one to stress the importance of loyalty and duty, the gravity of their mission to keep Hallowmere from the Unhallowed. Corrine would never have guessed that he might falter.

When she finished with her bath and was waiting on

Siobhan to dress her hair, she crept over to her writing case in her stockings and dressing gown and dug for Father Joe's letters. There were only a few more, she guessed all that the Unhallowed had managed to save from the love affair between a priest and their witch. She considered and discarded again the notion that the letters might be forgeries. She had seen Father Joe's penmanship in the other letter translations; she doubted anyone could mimic it or his voice so precisely.

[May 1275]

My beloved Queen—

As you have bade, so has all been done. The farmer who spurned you is drained of life and I have taken that life into me and found it sweet. I have sent his wife and son to you as a token of my abiding affection and loyalty. I have returned, as you desired, to the monastery where the one called Iamblicus dwells. Long have I watched him, and it is as you say: He allies himself with the cause of the Golden Serpent, forsaking the trust laid down by his ancestors on this sacred ground. He has stolen your magic and put it to common use as men are wont to do. I see now why you eschew the company of mortals as a rule, and am in even greater disbelief that you would seek me out when so often my kind has made such cheap use of your gifts.

It would be easy enough for me to kill him now; as you have said, the desire for flesh, once woken, is great. And no greater is that desire than in the presence of your enemies. Only give me the order and I will deal with this locust as we have dealt with so many of late. I will feed him to the Ghillie-Dhu and make of him a pleasing sacrifice to you and to the Morrigan both.

There is but one thing I humbly ask. That I again be ushered into the light of your presence, that I spend eternity in your arms.

Yours,
Josephus

A knock at the door and the click of the doorknob sent Corrine scrambling to stuff the letters back into the writing case. She latched the case shut and turned to meet Siobhan's nervous gaze. The maid held the hot hair iron with a heavy towel in one hand and an iron trivet in the other.

"Miss Christina sent me to do your hair, miss," Siobhan said.

"Yes, right," Corrine said, sitting down at the vanity.

Siobhan placed the iron on the trivet and began combing out Corrine's mostly dry hair. Corrine's hair was nearly down to her waist, which made the job of detangling it a painful ordeal. Corrine gritted her teeth as Siobhan tried to pull as gently as she could.

The vanity mirror betrayed the worry in Siobhan's face.

"You're anxious about Father Joe, aren't you?" Corrine said.

"Yes, miss," Siobhan nodded. "This isn't like him. This is like something *they'd* do." She lowered her voice as if the Unhallowed might be listening.

"Let us hope not," Corrine said. Guilt settled uncomfortably in her stomach.

"I saw him when he went out," Siobhan said. "His face was so dark."

"He was angry with me," Corrine said, as Siobhan began pulling her hair back from her face. "Have you seen something, anything that may help us discover where he might have gone?"

Siobhan shook her head. "That I haven't. I avoid *them* much as I can, and when a vision comes I just pray real hard that it will go away." She picked up the hot iron and Corrine tried not to cringe.

"I just hope nothing's befallen him," Corrine said. The memory of his words in the letters chilled her. *I have taken that life into me and found it sweet . . .* Had he been a vampire like the Unhallowed? A second thought almost made her jerk her head from Siobhan's fingers. Was he a vampire still?

"I pray all will be well, miss," Siobhan was saying. "That I do."

At last, cinched, singed, wedged, and otherwise accoutered, Corrine met Christina, Miss Brown, and Mara downstairs. Mara wore her best uniform and an apron starched so white it gleamed. Miss Brown's somber dark gown was set off by a jet necklace and earrings, which gave the impression that she was in mourning. At Corrine's glance, Miss Brown said, "The better to ward off unwanted suitors."

Corrine nodded. She imagined that the sort of heiress-seeking dandy one might meet at a ball would fail to enchant Miss Brown. Other than the masquerade at Fearnan, Corrine realized that the only royal ball she'd ever witnessed had been in the Prince's rath. She resisted the urge to shake her head. How was it that she had experienced more with the Fey than humans?

Miss Brown checked her timepiece, her jet bracelet glittering. "It's far past dark now. Where has Ilona gotten to?"

And still no sign of Father Joe, Corrine thought. Would he truly leave for good? What if the Unhallowed had taken him? If so, how had they done it? And what if something even worse had happened?

"Siobhan," Miss Brown, "do be a dear and go call a carriage for us."

Siobhan nodded, but before she'd fully opened the door, Ilona barreled through it.

She held a penny dreadful up to her face, as though shielding herself from the rain, and hurried toward the stairs. In her other arm, she carried the bundle she'd lately been taking with her when she left in the afternoons.

Siobhan slipped outside.

"Ilona?" Miss Brown said. She grasped Ilona's arm, pulling the pamphlet away from her face in the process. Blood trickled down Ilona's temple and she wiped it away with her free hand. The sudden stop caused Ilona's bundle to fall and unwind across the floor. A rapier spun in glittering arcs across the parquet.

"Ilona, what have you—" Miss Brown said. "Have you been fighting?"

Ilona clenched her jaw and stared straight ahead.

"Of all the nonsense—" Miss Brown began. "Take that to your room this instant! And be quick about it. We'll soon be late!"

Ilona threw down the penny dreadful in disgust, scooped up the rapier and the old coat she'd wrapped it in, and fled up the stairs without another word.

Corrine found herself staring down at the pamphlet Ilona had dropped. On its cover, a tusked, caped monster billowed, his hollow chest arching over a young girl as she slept. The title: "Varney the Vampire, or The Feast of Blood." Nausea forced Corrine to look away, just as Siobhan re-entered the foyer.

"The carriage is waiting, Miss Brown," she said.

Miss Brown pulled on the black velvet cape Siobhan offered her. Mara helped Christina and Corrine on with theirs. Ilona clumped back down the stairs, her face and hands clean and damp.

Miss Brown glanced at her, frowning, before she said, "Well, let's be off. Soonest left is soonest returned."

Everyone climbed in while Miss Brown gave instructions to the driver for "the boy" to be let off several streets before the palace as he had errands to run nearby. Then she joined them, carefully pulling the hem of her skirts into the coach. With all of their voluminous skirts, in addition to Mara and Ilona, it was a tight fit.

"Ilona," Miss Brown said.

Ilona glared at her from under her cap.

"I don't know what to say to you," Miss Brown

continued. "What have you been doing? Why have you been fighting? Surely you know the danger we're in!"

Ilona sulked.

"Father Joe and I trusted you not to draw attention to yourself, to blend in. And here you are, doing the very opposite! Why?"

But Ilona crossed her arms across her chest as well as she was able in the confined space and wouldn't speak.

Miss Brown sighed. "If you won't speak about that, I at least need to know: Can you perform your duty tonight without further incident? If you can't, then I must send you back to Primrose Hill."

Ilona eyed her. Corrine gritted her teeth. She had never seen Ilona fight, except in practice with Euan and Kenneth, and she didn't want to imagine how Ilona would fight if she were angry.

"I can do it," Ilona said. Her voice was gritty.

"Without complications?" Miss Brown asked.

"Without complications," Ilona said.

Miss Brown sighed then and sat back in her seat next to Mara. Worry made heavy shadows on her face.

Corrine looked out the window. The gaslight tricked out a hooded man standing on the corner, and Corrine stiffened. But then she saw that he was giving out handbills to passersby. She had not seen the Captain physically since their flight from Fearnan, and it had been a few days since her last vision of him with the girls in the gray room. He seemed different than Leanan or the Prince—an unwilling puppet, a twisted fool. She only hoped that her thoughts wouldn't draw him to her tonight.

More importantly, she hoped the Prince wouldn't make an appearance. If anything, she wanted to find

Rory and interrogate him until she ran out of questions or he ran out of breath. She had never wanted to throttle anyone, but Rory might very well be the first.

The driver slowed and called that they were just a couple blocks from the palace.

Ilona rose and Corrine touched her arm as she passed. "Good luck," Corrine whispered.

"Come back safely," Miss Brown said.

Ilona nodded stiffly, leaped free of the carriage, and disappeared into the crowd.

The carriage resumed and soon they fell into a line waiting to enter the palace gates, many of them more magnificent by far than their hired cab. Guards stopped them and demanded their invitation, at which point Christina told them that one had been left for her at the gatehouse, as instructed by Phyllida. One guard went to search it out while another inspected their carriage, assuring himself that nothing would threaten the Queen or the Princess Royal.

They followed the line of carriages into the wide courtyard and circled behind them to the east entrance. Butlers and lines of ladies-in-waiting received them and pointed them toward the cloakroom and the Grand Staircase that led up to the Queen's ballroom.

As soon as Corrine entered, the singing drowned out everything else—a sound such as she'd only heard after her magic had been awoken, the siren lure of a rathstone. Corrine looked at Mara and saw that Mara heard it as well. It made sense that the royal family might have a rathstone in their possession, but now that she'd felt it, Corrine wondered if this meant that she'd be compelled to steal it, like the kelpie bridle.

Even more, she wondered how she would do it if she had to. She sighed.

Miss Brown sensed her mood, as Mara helped them all with their cloaks. "What is it, Corrine?" Miss Brown asked under the murmur of the crowd.

Corrine leaned in as close as she could. Miss Brown smelled of velvet and rosewater.

"A rathstone, Miss Brown."

The headmistress's eyes grew wide. "Here?" she said.

Corrine nodded.

"What are we to do?" Corrine asked. She looked at Christina who had already been approached by a young gentleman asking after a dance on her dance card, which she hadn't even picked up yet.

Mara took their cloaks to the cloakroom for them and retrieved their tags. "We're all of us meant to go upstairs," Mara said. "They's a serving room off the ballroom with ices and such, so they say. I'm to wait there until you need freshening up between sets. Dance cards are at a table upstairs, too."

Corrine heard the frustration in her voice. Mara knew the rathstone was here, and she wanted to search for it just as much as everyone else. It was an unlooked-for prize. If they could retrieve an additional stone along with the Stone of Destiny, Hallowmere would be that much more secure. Corrine was deeply curious as to which stone it was and how it had come into the Queen's possession. And more importantly, whether the Unhallowed knew the rathstone was here somewhere.

As they climbed the curving arm of the carpeted staircase, Corrine tried not to gawk in wonder. Huge oil portraits of kings and queens long gone stared down from the Wedgwood blue walls, and two giant statues of Athena held gas lanterns at either side of the mirrored doors. The corridor, Corrine saw, was ablaze with light reflected from the crystal chandeliers and in the mirrored doors along the hallway to the ballroom. At the end of the corridor, the orchestra was striking up the first waltz, but the deafening song of the rathstone subsumed almost all other sound.

Phyllida and Elizabeth hurried toward Christina through the crowd. Phyllida wore the fabled parure, the golden serpent of the pendant clasping a black star sapphire between its golden jaws. Serpents dripped from her ears and a heavy serpentine bracelet circled her gloved wrist. Mara moved on past Phyllida with the other servants as if she'd taken no notice, but Corrine stared, speechless. The singing emanated from the stone glimmering darkly on Phyllida's bosom. The rathstone was the setpiece of the heiress's parure.

"Christina, darling," Phyllida said. "We are so happy you and your friend could come! We were worried you mightn't, at such short notice." Phyllida spared a glance and a tight smile for Corrine.

"Come, let us find dance cards," Phyllida said, linking arms with Christina. "I know all the young men will want to dance with you."

Christina glanced longingly at the parure, and Corrine remembered Phyllida's promise—that Christina could wear the parure during the ball. Phyllida seemed to notice Christina's gaze, for she said, "I shall wear it just for this little bit, and after the first set, would you like to try it?"

Christina's smile returned. "Yes, I should like that very much."

"Well enough, then," Phyllida said, leading Christina forward. Elizabeth looked at Corrine dully, shrugged and followed. Corrine fell back to keep pace with Miss Brown.

"The rathstone is in the necklace," Corrine said in her ear.

Miss Brown turned from looking at the portraits along the gallery. "What?"

Corrine tilted her head in the direction of Christina and Phyllida.

"Phyllida?" Miss Brown said.

Corrine nodded slightly.

Just then, Lady Rosenthal saw Miss Brown and came to her, trailing a doughty-looking lady all done up in green taffeta.

"Why, Miss Brown!" Lady Rosenthal said. Corrine hadn't noticed how large her nose was before or how round her eyes. With all the feathers trimming her gown, she looked rather like a startled owl.

Before Miss Brown could say anything, Lady Rosenthal was telling her friend all about Miss Brown's school and the charity cases she was kind enough to take, sliding her eyes none too subtly in Corrine's direction.

Miss Brown rushed to correct her, but Lady Rosenthal insisted on praising Miss Brown's patience and sacrifice for taking on such a hopeless mission. Corrine tried not to roll her eyes.

Christina was about to disappear into the ballroom. Miss Brown tilted her head in that direction, while Lady Rosenthal continued her philosophizing about the problems inherent in modern charity.

Corrine fled after Christina.

She picked up her dance card and tried to keep her hands from shaking as she wrote her name at the top with the little pencil attached by a velvet cord. A rathstone was here, a rathstone that obviously was completely unrecognizable to its bearer except as a precious bit of jewelry. How Phyllida had come by it, who might have stolen it from the Fey, Corrine didn't know and almost didn't care. What she wondered was how she could possibly expect to get the rathstone away from Phyllida without her noticing. Corrine needed to get Christina alone. Maybe Christina could convince Phyllida to allow her to borrow the parure for a little while. But Corrine knew that if they took the pendant back with them to Scotland, Phyllida's father's people would surely come after them. Christina had said Mr. Ballantine brewed scotch almost exclusively for the nobility; he'd get wind of where they were and send someone after the necklace. Of that, Corrine was sure.

So intent was Corrine on talking to Christina that she barely noticed the vaulted, gold ceiling, the red and gold wallpaper, and *trompe l'oeil* columns, cleverly painted to look like malachite. The hall echoed with music, and couples whirled in a whisper of organza and rushed conversation. Corrine observed them, looking for a burgundy dress and black tassels, for Christina's glossy chestnut curls and creamy skin. She skirted the edge of the dance floor, passing before a row of damask-covered chairs that sat before ornately framed mirrors alternating with oil portraits of hunting scenes. She tried not to trip over the vast skirts of ladies who were already taking a breather with their gentlemen. A young man caught her eye and tried to stop her, but Corrine pushed past him without apology.

Christina was at the other end of the hall with Phyllida. Corrine couldn't see Elizabeth through the crowd; she guessed that the green-eyed girl had been pulled onto the dance floor. Corrine was nearly to the musicians' dais before she finally found a way to cross the tiled floor. The waltz ended, and dancers streamed from the floor. Corrine lost Christina and Phyllida in the crowd. Then she saw them again, moving toward the middle of the room, toward a mirror next to a painting of a woman coiled suggestively around a swan. It reminded her of some Greek myth she had read with her mother long ago--something about Zeus courting a woman in the form of a swan. She thought the woman's name was Leda, but she wasn't sure.

She picked up her skirts and toddled forward in the ridiculous heeled shoes she'd been forced to wear. She wished fiercely that she could kick them off and run.

She collided with the man before she saw him.

"Excuse me, Miss Jameson," he said. His voice was low and uncertain.

Corrine looked him full in the face. "Mr. Adamou!" Her cheeks burned.

He smiled hesitantly. His teeth were very white.

"I was not certain you would remember me," he said. "Or speak to me for that matter."

Corrine looked beyond him to where Phyllida threaded her arm through Christina's and led her to the mirror. Elizabeth slid out of the crowd like a shark.

"Miss Jameson?"

Corrine looked into Mr. Adamou's face. The way he looked at her, his eyes searching hers, made her regret yesterday's behavior. She tried to sense anything magical about him, to see the outline of power that she'd once seen with Father Joe. But she saw and felt nothing extraordinary.

"Mr. Adamou—" she began.

The next waltz was beginning. "Talking seems to be bothersome to you," he said. "Let us just dance instead. My English mother has taught me all about this sort of thing."

The mirror across the room flashed. Christina and Phyllida were gone.

"I wish I could," Corrine said. "Truly, I would love to, and I regret yesterday very much. But I cannot stay just now. Excuse me." And she pushed past him, picking up her skirts and hurrying as best she could to the mirror beside the swan painting.

People murmured as she passed, "That girl just turned down the Greek ambassador's son!" "The nerve of her!" and so on. She gasped and looked back and only now saw the braid decorating his uniform, attendants hovering around him like well-dressed flies. Mr. Adamou still watched her. Reddening to the roots of her hair, she ducked between the dancers.

Corrine came to the mirror door and found it locked. "Christina!" Corrine gasped. Elizabeth glided toward her, grinning, until two gentlemen stopped her. Elizabeth's face froze.

Corrine stood at the mirror door, her hand on its latch, terrified someone—Mr. Adamou perhaps—would come and inquire what in heavens she thought she was doing. She looked in the mirror. *Christina,* she mouthed, wondering if her friend could somehow see her from the other side. She glanced over at Elizabeth, who glared at her would-be suitors as if she would stab both of them with her gaze alone.

The dancers whirled in the mirror-world before her, the men's black trousers flanking the wide, bright bells of the women's skirts. A black vapor took shape in the mirror, forming into a familiar, dreadful shape. The kelpie looked out at her, his eyes glowing witch-light. He struck one hoof against the tiled floor and shook his shaggy mane. Waterweeds dripped from his back. Corrine sensed somehow that if she willed it, she could open the door.

She took a deep breath, struggling against the tightness of her corset.

"Open," she whispered.

A glimmer of witch-light and the latch turned. Corrine slid inside, locking the door behind her just as Elizabeth broke free.

She stood for several seconds, utterly mystified. She was in a beautifully ornate drawing room. Lanterns and candles illumined lacquered tables crowded with Chinese curios—vases, bowls, great bowing horses draped in silk.

Phyllida stood behind Christina and clasped the serpentine pendant around Christina's throat. As she did so, she bent and kissed Christina's nape lingeringly. Corrine didn't understand. Had she wandered into some bizarre rath? She stared, unable to form words.

Phyllida glanced up, and in that moment, the glamour fell away. Rory wrapped his arms possessively around Christina's waist.

His blue eyes sparked with certainty. It reminded Corrine of how he had looked at her that night so long ago in Falston's barn. "You can't take her from me, Corrine. She's mine now," he said. He stepped back, tugging Christina with him.

Corrine focused on Christina's face and her torn expression of love and guilt.

"Christina," she said, "you don't want this. He's lying to you. I promise—"

"Quiet!" Rory said. "We don't need any of your mealy-mouthed promises!" He released Christina's waist and took her hand. "Come, my darling. Our Prince awaits."

He touched the stone at her throat and said a word Corrine couldn't catch. In another mirror by one of the tables, a city slid into view. Its glistening towers and empty streets beckoned.

"No!" Corrine said, stepping forward.

Rory pulled Christina to the mirror. Corrine rushed toward them, and only as she reached for Christina did she realize her danger. Rory grinned and encircled her wrist as if his hand was an iron manacle.

The Prince looked out of the mirror at them. Christina's eyelids fluttered.

"Excellent work," the Prince said. "Come."

Rory pulled and the mirror slid over Corrine's shoulders like silver skin. She saw the Prince walking through the haze. The ring hanging next to her locket strained toward him.

And then a tall, equine shadow fell between them. Flat equine teeth closed around Rory's hand on her wrist.

Corrine put one hand in the kelpie's mane, crunching bones and weeds and hair indiscriminately. She reached with all her strength for Christina.

"TRAITOR!" Rory shouted. Corrine's eardrums ached with his screams as the kelpie pulled her and Christina back into the drawing room. The mirror shattered behind them. Rory and the Unhallowed city were gone.

Corrine bent over Christina, trying and failing to rouse her. She unclasped the rathstone from her neck. Breath stirred the short hairs on Corrine's nape and she looked up.

The kelpie was looking down at them both, fell light in his eyes. Foam quivered on his lips and dew sheened his midnight coat. Corrine had the distinct feeling that if she climbed on his back now, he would carry her as quickly as he could to a watery grave. Hunger was in every twitch of his muscles and flick of his tail.

"What do you want?" Corrine said. "You have done your part. There is nothing more for you here."

"Payment," the kelpie said. His voice was like bone scraped across gravel. The little fins at his fetlocks flexed. He eyed the rathstone.

"Seek payment from your mistresses. I have nothing to give," Corrine said.

"The bargain is already struck with them," the kelpie said. "I protect you. But there is nothing in the bargain about *her*." He arched his neck in Christina's direction.

"No," Corrine said, "there is not. But she is already mine, you see. And I cannot just give her up."

Corrine tightened her grip on the humming rathstone. The serpent's golden coils snagged in her glove.

"Something must be paid," the kelpie said. He pawed delicately near the edge of Christina's skirt.

"She is not payment," Corrine said. She stepped forward, trying to breathe deeply and draw power from the rathstone. She wasn't sure how or what she would do, only that somehow she had to keep the kelpie in check. "Obey me," she said.

The kelpie snorted. "Only the one who bridles me may command me."

Corrine swallowed.

A low rumbling began, and Corrine quailed at first to think that the sound might be the kelpie's empty stomach. But it came up through the floor, through the walls, shaking portraits and rattling the Chinese figurines, just as Corrine imagined an earthquake would.

The kelpie squealed and paced. Then, he said, "He comes," and leaped toward Corrine, sliding into streamers of black vapor that diffused into her. A horrible slimy sensation coated Corrine's tongue and she felt drenched, just as she had this morning when she'd woken. She went to Christina, shook her, and pinched at her cheeks until she revived.

"Corrine," she said, "where are we? Are you in Fairy-land with me? Where is Rory?"

Corrine shook her head. "There's no time. We must get out of here."

She helped Christina up and slipped with her out of the mirror door into the ballroom.

Elizabeth—*Melanie,* Corrine realized, under a glamour that Corrine knew she should have noticed had she been paying close enough attention—was nowhere to be seen. Everyone was still waltzing as though nothing had happened. *And, as far as they were concerned,* Corrine thought, *perhaps nothing had.*

She pulled Christina through the room, her only thought to find Miss Brown and Mara and get out. She would like very much to warn Ilona in the stables, but she had to hope that Ilona's task was already complete and that Ilona was even now returning to Primrose Hill. She tried to bundle the serpentine pendant more carefully in her free hand as she dragged Christina into the gallery and toward the Grand Staircase. The rathstone curved to fit in her palm, just as the others had.

A hand on her arm spun her about. Melanie. The glamour had fallen from her in tatters. Rage carved lean hollows in her cheeks.

"Give me that pendant!" Melanie said. "And what have you done to Rory?"

Christina was still too in shock to speak.

"Rory is gone," Corrine said. "And we must be going, as well."

"Not so fast, you crazy-eyed carpetbagger," Melanie said. "I want that rathstone. Now."

Corrine gripped Christina's wrist more tightly and ran past Melanie through the gallery.

Melanie's cries of "Thief! Thief!" echoed after her. Heads turned and indignant exclamations followed them. Corrine ducked into what appeared to be the refreshments room, where rows of servants stood stiffly against the walls, trying to look as though they weren't eyeing the ices melting on the tables.

Corrine hurried over to Mara. "We have to go. And we all need glamours, now."

Mara looked down where Corrine clutched the

rathstone and half-smiled. She nodded slightly. "On the third breath . . ."

Corrine closed her eyes, trying to drown out the sounds of soldiers and Melanie's echoing accusations. The horrid sensation of her flesh rearranging over her bones subsumed her other thoughts. She looked at Christina and saw a plain-looking girl in a rose-colored gown. Her own gown was dark blue now and very sparsely trimmed with black lace. Though Mara still wore a maid's uniform, she had altered her dark skin and hair so that she looked like a light-skinned, auburn-haired Creole. Corrine slipped the rathstone pendant into her reticule.

"Come on now," Mara said. "Let's find Miss Brown."

They walked calmly from the room and began hunting in the salons for Miss Brown. Corrine was just on the verge of worrying that the Unhallowed had somehow captured the headmistress, when they at last found her standing in a circle of men and women presided over by Lady Rosenthal. Miss Brown looked uncomfortable, as though she'd very much like to leave but couldn't find a way to do so politely. Mara fortunately gave her the opening she was looking for, bobbing a curtsy and telling her that one of her students required her attention. Miss Brown excused herself under Lady Rosenthal's baleful eye and breathless gab.

"Time to go, Miss Brown," Mara said as the guards entered the room and began inquiring as to the where-abouts of a certain thief. Miss Brown looked a little askance at the disguised girls, but knew better than to ask. They went carefully down the Grand Staircase and to the cloakroom. Mara retrieved their cloaks just as Melanie came down the stairs with two of the Queen's guard. Though they tried to hurry, Melanie spotted Miss Brown and shouted, "There's their chaperone!"

They ran out of the door before the guards could close it, pulling their hoods over their faces, and leaped into the first hired carriage they could find. Miss Brown urged the driver to make haste, but other carriages were also leaving. Mara took Corrine's hand and together they worked as best they could to disguise Miss Brown. Corrine's hands shook with the effort of keeping so much magic steady in so many different directions at once. She wrapped the edge of her cloak around them to keep them still.

"It won't hold long," Mara said. "Let's pray they get this over quickly."

The soldiers came and searched their carriage as they waited in a line to be released from the palace gates. Melanie came along with them, inspecting each carriage before reluctantly passing them onward. As the soldiers searched their carriage, Corrine gritted her teeth against Christina's ragged breathing. She refused to look at her, silently begging the glamour to hold. In the end, the glamours held, though Melanie skewered them all with her dark gaze.

Corrine didn't exhale until they were finally past the gate and out into the street. The glamoury dropped from all of them. She glanced back as the carriage turned, willing Melanie not to look beyond the iron fence.

The gray walls vibrated. Corrine felt the Captain's hand on her forehead, draining her of energy, of life, of her visage. A shadow hovered near the curtains as they bled onto the floor. The shadow moved closer and Corrine gasped as she saw the familiar ever-changing eyes. *His face was dark with anger; she had only seen it this way when she looked back after fleeing his rath.*

They have failed, *the Prince said.* These two are of no further use.

The girl in the corner whimpered.

He leaned close to the girl and Corrine felt a deep, startling pain in her throat.

NO! *she shouted through the girl's mouth.*

The Prince stepped back, his lips scarlet. Corrine?

"Corrine!" Miss Brown said. Corrine looked into her blue eyes. "What did you see?"

"Phyllida and Elizabeth—the real ones," Corrine said, drawing a deep breath. "The Captain was keeping them to help Rory and Melanie with their glamoury. I saw the Prince with them. He—" She had trouble saying it, even though she knew she'd seen his victims before. She had never actually *seen* him taking life. She had felt it once, in her dreams, but she'd not known then what was happening.

"Those poor girls," Miss Brown said. "How can we find them? There must be some way."

"I wish I knew," Corrine said.

She reached into her reticule and took out the serpentine pendant, spreading it across her knees. Corrine stared into its dark heart as if she could read how to find Elizabeth and Phyllida there. The rathstone's singing had dulled to a buzz, but she could still feel its power through her fingertips. Christina glanced at it and wept.

Miss Brown looked down and her face hardened. "Unexpected treasure brings unexpected problems. The Unhallowed know we're here now and will be even more irate that you wrested a rathstone from their possession. But I'm very glad you managed it, nonetheless."

Corrine tightened her fingers around the golden scales. She wondered how they would keep the rathstone safe until it could be locked deep in the Council chamber in Fearnan. And even then, was it truly safe? Once all the stones were gathered, how would they possibly keep them safe from the Unhallowed? What did the Council want with the stones? It was a new, uncomfortable thought. Corrine tried to think more about how to save the two girls. She had frightened the Prince away somehow, but she knew he wouldn't wait much longer.

"I just hope Ilona got away all right. Maybe she can help us find the other two girls," Corrine said.

Everyone nodded in agreement, except Christina, who stared out the window while tears made dark tracks down her cheeks.

No one else said anything the rest of the way home, but Corrine heard echoes of other hopes—especially that Father Joe would have returned safely when they arrived at the townhouse.

Corrine entered the townhouse cautiously, worried that the Unhallowed would seek revenge on Siobhan and Ilona as they waited alone. But the house was quiet, lanterns glowing in the foyer and along the stairs. Firelight reflected from the grate in the morning room. Ilona sat staring into the fire, a moldy, worn bridle with tarnished silver fittings draped across her knee. She turned when she heard them enter and rose, holding the bridle by her side.

Father Joe was still nowhere in evidence.

"Before anyone says anything," Miss Brown said, "I

move that we all change into our dressing gowns and meet back here. You and Siobhan included, Mara, so long as you don't mind bringing some tea for all of us."

Mara nodded and disappeared down the hall toward the kitchen. Wordlessly, Christina preceded Corrine and Miss Brown up the stairs, while Ilona returned to her armchair by the fire.

Corrine was relieved when the pale yellow layers fell away and she was at last left standing in her chemise and stockings. She shoved the reticule with its precious rathstone deep on the top wardrobe shelf, then hurried into her nightgown and pulled her dressing gown over it, while Miss Brown discreetly did the same behind the wardrobe door. Neither acknowledged the soft sobbing that filtered through the wall from Christina's room.

Corrine shoved the ring and her locket under the neckline of her dressing gown. She thought again, as she often had, that perhaps it wasn't safe, that maybe she should put the ring in the reticule alongside the rathstone. She remembered the way it had yearned toward the Prince, and she knew he had tricked her before with the daoi scarf. But, she reminded herself, she had taken the ring from him. He certainly hadn't given it to her. And no harm had come of wearing it thus far that she could see. Power stolen was power earned in this game it seemed, though what power she could glean from the ring she still hadn't figured out.

They returned downstairs. With each moment, Corrine was more convinced that Father Joe would not return to them. Christina came a few minutes after them, her face smudged where she had scrubbed away her tears. Even as Corrine settled on the sofa with a throw and gratefully accepted the tea Mara and Siobhan brought, she couldn't feel comfortable thinking about the two girls trapped somewhere in London, soon to become the Prince's next feast.

Corrine felt foolish for not having worn a glamour to the ball. But would it really have helped? Perhaps it would have been wiser, but they had only gone to seek what information they could and provide cover for Ilona's theft.

Rory and Melanie's glamoury had been so perfect as to be almost flawless. Corrine remembered her little suspicions of them at the croquet party, but she honestly would have suspected more of Mr. Adamou than the two vain young women. She certainly would never have suspected Rory of disguising himself as a woman to lure Christina. She would have been amused by it was she not still so horrified by the plight of the real Phyllida and Elizabeth in their captivity.

And now that her magic was unbound, the Prince could find her easily. She worried that any moment he and his satyr guards might burst through the door. Corrine shuddered so much that her saucer and teacup rattled before she recovered herself.

"Now," Miss Brown said when they'd all finished, "tell me exactly what happened. It seemed I was trying to disengage myself from Lady Rosenthal for hours. I was terrified that something was happening to you."

Christina stared straight into the fire, so Corrine related the tale. She told of Mr. Adamou with a little hitch of regret that she hoped no one noticed. She even included the part about the kelpie demanding payment for Christina, though she couldn't look at Christina as she related that detail. When she had finished, everyone was silent for a bit.

Miss Brown said, "Very good work on your part, Corrine. I'm proud of you and sorry that no one else was there to help you during your ordeal."

Corrine nodded. She had the strange feeling now that Mr. Adamou would have helped if only she had let him. But now she would never know.

"But Christina," Miss Brown continued, "I must say I am deeply disappointed in you. After all that happened at Fearnan and all that was done to save you, your behavior truly surprises me."

Christina's expression was so stricken that Corrine wished Miss Brown would take back her words. However Christina might play at bucking authority, she truly hated to disappoint people she admired.

"I could not help it, Miss Brown," Christina whispered, so low that her words could barely be heard above the crackling fire.

"But you knew the risks, the dangers!" Miss Brown said.

Christina bowed her head. Some of her curls escaped around the fringe of her nightcap.

"How long had you known about Rory's disguise?" Miss Brown asked.

Christina's fingers worked along the embroidered edge of her nightgown but she didn't answer.

"How long?" Miss Brown said, her voice strained.

"Just a week or so," Christina finally whispered. "Phyllida—He began acting strangely toward me and finally, when I protested, he revealed to me who he really was."

"Did you know about the plot to trap Corrine with the rathstone?"

Christina looked frantically at Corrine. "No," she said, shaking her head so that more curls escaped. "No, I didn't. I thought it was only me he was taking. I thought it would do no harm."

"Do no harm? Why would his kidnapping of you do no harm?" Miss Brown said.

"Because," Christina said, "I am not special like Corrine or . . . or Mara or Ilona. Who would really care if I am gone? I want to be with him. No one will ever want to marry me, after what I did. I know what he did to you"—this to Corrine pleadingly—"but I cannot help myself. Something compels me. *He* compels me."

Corrine thought of the Prince and sympathized. Knowing who and what he was had certainly confused and unsettled her. There were moments when she very nearly hated him. And much of that hate, though she couldn't admit it aloud, stemmed from a strange fascination that she knew was dangerously close to affection. Despite all he had done, despite all that he might do, Euan had reached her in ways Rory never had. The worst part about tonight, she thought, besides dealing with the kelpie, had been seeing the Prince, first in the mirror and then in the room with the real Phyllida and Elizabeth. She knew what Christina felt, even if she couldn't confess it. And if Rory truly was possessed by Angus, then Christina's protests that she couldn't help herself were somewhat valid.

"You are foolish," Ilona growled. "We would all care if you are gone! And how do you know what will happen if he takes you away? How do you know what it's like there? Corrine told us how horrible it was. Do you really want to be there forever?"

Christina held Corrine's eyes as she spoke. "Everything about the city is beautiful. The Prince and his court are very kind. He offered us a villa with a beautiful garden—"

Corrine shook her head. "That's only what he wants you to see, Christina. And he can make you see that because you want to believe it. Do you want to know what the Prince really is?" She told of the vision she'd had as they fled the palace, though it hurt her heart to say the words, how the prince would likely murder those helpless girls he'd kidnapped.

Christina looked away, her lips flattening in an angry line.

"Christina," Miss Brown said, trying to catch her eye, "Corrine is telling you the truth. The Prince does not care for you, except for what you can give him—whether that's your blood, greater leverage over Corrine, or something else. You are stronger than your inclinations. All is not yet lost in this world. Don't give up your future here before you've had a chance to live it."

Christina didn't reply, and Miss Brown sighed.

Corrine worried that no matter her inclinations, Christina wouldn't be able to resist the powerful bond between the souls of Angus and Brighde.

"Speaking of the future," Mara said, "what do we do about Father Joe and these girls Corrine keeps seeing? What about the Stone of Destiny?"

Corrine was a bit startled when she spoke; she'd almost forgotten Mara was still in the room.

"Well—" Miss Brown sighed, "I think we must

move forward with our original plans. Madame DuBois said we should alert her when the bridle was secured. Apparently, we need to tame that kelpie as quickly as possible. I doubt he will help us again without some sort of payment."

Corrine shuddered.

Miss Brown turned to Ilona. "As to Father Joe and these girls, have you heard anything at all from the people in any of your haunts?"

Ilona shook her head. "Tomorrow, I will go among the mudlarks—those that comb the banks of the Thames for whatever they can find—and ask."

Miss Brown's stricken expression told of her deep and inadmissible fear for Father Joe. But Corrine was certain that she would know if Father Joe had died. Somehow, she would have felt it. She looked to Mara for confirmation of her thoughts, but Mara's face was shielded in shadow.

"Go and seek what information you can," Miss Brown said. "But I must ask you not to engage in more fighting, Ilona. You put all of us at risk. What if something were to happen to you?"

Ilona scowled, but nodded. The rough spikes of her hair stood out in the firelight.

"Well, then. All of you know your assigned tasks. Christina, do I have your promise that you will not endanger yourself further with Rory? This is very serious. I do not want to have to contact your parents again."

"And what would you tell them?" Christina said, rising from her seat. "That I've gone to live with fairies? That I've fallen prey to some spell? Doing that would only expose your precious Council!"

"Christina!" Miss Brown said. She also stood, and it seemed that she might give Christina a good shaking, but her outstretched hand fell to her side.

Christina looked at all of them. "You can rest easy. I will do no such thing. I have my own reputation—what is left of it—to protect. And I will not seek Rory out. I doubt he can be found anyway." Her lips quivered as she said the last, as if she would weep again. But she turned instead and fled. Her door slammed shut upstairs a few moments later.

"I'd better go and speak with her," Miss Brown said, sighing.

"Talk some sense into her," Mara said.

"I hope so," Miss Brown said. Her dressing gown and nightcap made her look oddly vulnerable. A vision of Miss Brown's brother (sister?) walking over a hill with the Captain floated to Corrine from the fire. "Ilona, give us half an hour before you come up, will you?" Miss Brown asked.

Ilona nodded.

"Good night then," Miss Brown said.

Everyone stared at the fire for a while before Corrine finally uncurled from the sofa, hoping it was safe to go to bed.

"Good night," she said softly.

Ilona looked up at her. "I'm going to find him, Corrine. And those girls."

"I want to go with you," Corrine said.

Ilona nodded stiffly, and Corrine was relieved. She'd feared Ilona would deny her.

Mara just sighed and shook her head. "Pretty soon all

that'll be left will be me, Siobhan, and the rats."

Corrine tried to smile, but the fear on Siobhan's face went too close to the bone. She guessed what waited on the Thames's muddy shores.

~Ten~

April 20, 1866

CORRINE PERCHED ON THE DESOLATE CLAW OF A MOUNTAIN *peak. The Unhallowed city spread below her in all its chaotic ruin. She watched as the city filled with black water, as the landscape slowly morphed into the familiar hillside above Loch Tay. Below her, mists shrouded the loch. She turned and saw the mound open behind her and the dreaded glimmering within. This time, the gates were very clear—golden jaws that she feared would close around her if she attempted to step between them.*

You have been here before, *he said.*

The Prince was beside her, looking into the mound.

Yes, *she said.*

And you still do not know why you are here.

No, *she said.*

A pity. It would be much easier if you knew. *She felt he was discussing something trivial and yet of the utmost importance. His face was cold and hard, as she remembered it from the days aboard the Great Eastern, when they had both been ill from all the iron.*

If I knew what? *She tried to shift away from him, but found herself still standing quite close.*

How to find Hallowmere. How to open this gate. *He leaned against a nearby tree and stroked it. The bark stretched and sighed beneath his caress.*

Why? *she asked.*

Because I would not have to do this. *Father Joe was tied to the tree. It was as though he had always been there and she had simply not noticed. He had lost his spectacles and his face was bruised and bloodied.*

Corrine, *Father Joe said through broken teeth.*

But the Prince wouldn't allow him to speak any further. He signaled, and gauntleted satyr guards came forward with an iron spike and a hammer. They leveled the spike over Father Joe's chest.

This is what happens to Half-Born who betray me, *the Prince said.*

Then the hammer struck the spike.

Corrine woke screaming.

Miss Brown sat up and put her arms around her. "Corrine, what's the matter?"

Corrine's throat ached. A horrible, slimy taste coated the inside of her mouth. "I think the Prince has Father Joe, too." She couldn't bear to tell Miss Brown about his broken teeth, the iron spike. Miss Brown drooped against Corrine for a moment before she released her.

"Well," Miss Brown said, as she climbed from the bed, "let's give Ilona a chance to find out. Perhaps the Prince is just trying to trick you, knowing how that will make you feel."

"Maybe," Corrine said. *But I doubt it.* The Prince had never really lied to her. He had hidden his identity, but that was not difficult to understand. If she had known who Euan truly was, she certainly wouldn't have accepted him as readily. Corrine took off her nightcap and threw it on the bed in disgust. Still, after all this time, she found herself rationalizing the Prince's actions.

Miss Brown looked askance at her as she pulled a checked day-dress from their shared wardrobe.

Corrine just shook her head.

"Help me get dressed?" Miss Brown said. "I'll send a message to Madame DuBois. You will be ready to deal with the kelpie tonight?"

"Yes, Miss Brown," Corrine said. Even though she dreaded seeing those dead, milky eyes again, she knew she had little choice. The kelpie was with her, bound to her in some strange way. If she could control it, perhaps she would have some advantage against the Unhallowed. Rory had certainly been surprised and angered by it. Corrine smiled a little at the thought.

Corrine slid her feet onto the chilly floor and helped Miss Brown with her lacings and crinoline. Miss Brown helped her in turn. At last, they were both ready to descend. The headmistress knocked on Christina's and Ilona's door as they passed, calling, "Breakfast!" before continuing down the stairs with Corrine in tow.

Miss Brown dispatched Siobhan with a note to Madame DuBois while they waited on Ilona and Christina. Corrine watched the steam rising from her tea, thinking of the Prince and what he had said about the fact that she still didn't understand why she was here. She guessed that the glimmer within the cave mouth was Hallowmere, but the Prince's frustration and what the Treas Ulaidh wanted from her she still didn't know. She wondered now if the book could tell her more, if it would reject her as it had before. Corrine slid out of her seat to retrieve the writing case and then sat back down. Father Joe had taken the book back from her. Now that the Prince had him, had the Unhallowed gotten their hands on the book too?

"Corrine?" Miss Brown said.

Corrine shook her head and took her seat again.

Christina and Ilona finally joined them. It was a subdued breakfast; no one wanted to mention last night's events, even though it was very much on their minds. Miss Brown herded them into the morning room for their lessons afterwards, and Corrine tried to forget her worries over the Unhallowed book by studying Coleridge's work, especially "Christabel." But the poem filled her with dread.

The lovely lady Christabel,
Whom her father loves so well,
What makes her in the wood so late,
A furlong from the castle gate?
She had dreams all yesternight
Of her own betrothed knight;
And she in the midnight wood will pray
For the weal of her lover that's far away.

She couldn't help but think of Christina as she read the words.

After she had written an analysis of the poem, Corrine was released to copy more of Brighde's letters. Christina and Ilona struggled on with geometry, quietly fretting over the equations together. Corrine was glad to be excused from that chore, and went to the desk by the window to work on the copying.

The next letter was torn so that the last part was missing, which Corrine could plainly see on the original despite it not being remarked upon in the translator's usual note.

To Brother Angus, Kirk of St. Fillan, from Sister Brighde, Isle of Female Saints, greeting.

I write with great trepidation that my words will do more harm than good, though it is my sincere prayer that in the end, we will come to an understanding. Too long have your letters gone unanswered, you say. But there is a time for silence and for meditation upon whether our actions are pleasing in God's sight. Or have you forgotten? Since we last were together, my heart has been deeply troubled. I have been in seclusion to try to understand God's purpose for us. Greatly have we sinned. So much pleasure should not be taken in such sinning.

What befell us, whatever goodness your friends the Fey may have intended, must be forgotten. I will receive you as my brother in Christ, but nothing more . . .

Corrine sighed as she finished copying the last line. So Brighde had tried to break with Angus. All to no avail. Corrine wondered what that meant for Christina and Rory, if they were bound to a dark fate no matter what they did. Rory didn't seem to care, and Christina was rapidly following him. Corrine didn't know what she could do to convince her friend that following Rory into the Unhallowed rath was wrong. Why wouldn't it seem like paradise?

Ilona came and put a hand on her shoulder and bent

to her ear. "I'm going now," she whispered. "Go upstairs and change into some of my boy's clothes, then meet me at the end of the street."

Corrine nodded, looking at Christina. She was completely absorbed in a French novel and paid no attention whatsoever. Miss Brown was nowhere to be seen, though Corrine thought she could hear her from the direction of the kitchen. Ilona left.

Corrine waited a few minutes, then stood stretching and said, "I'm going for a nap, I think."

Christina nodded without looking at her.

Corrine hurried upstairs. Her heart hammered as she ducked into Ilona and Christina's room and rifled through the dresser. She found trousers, suspenders, a shirt, and cap. She took an old coat hanging in the wardrobe too. Her own old boots would have to do. She took them all into her room, threw off her clothes, and struggled out of her corset. The shirt and trousers were far too big for her, but the suspenders held them up. The coat luckily covered it all, so that she hoped she looked like any street urchin who had just taken whatever clothes he could find. She stuffed her hair under the cap and pulled it almost down over her eyes, trying not to think of the irony that Rory had tricked her into thinking he was a woman and now she would try to trick others into thinking she was a boy.

Rory's glamoury inspired her to try a little of her own. She looked into the wavering mirror and tried to see the boy she wanted to become. She forced herself to watch as the flesh rearranged itself over her bones. Soon, a boy her age peered out of the mirror at her, and nothing about him, not even his left eye, suggested a hint of Corrine.

Her heart catching in her throat, Corrine snuck out of her room and down the stairs, carrying her boots, praying that no one would see the strange boy in their midst. She listened at the corner of the stairs and leaned out to peep into the morning room. Christina was still reading. Corrine raced across the foyer, hoping the creaking floor wouldn't give her away before she could get out of the front door. She slid the bolt and slipped out. She stuffed her feet in her shoes and ran down the stairs and to the end of the street, where Ilona stood, hands in her pockets, looking out across the row houses of Primrose Hill. Ilona stared at Corrine before recognizing the clothes she had given her.

Ilona grinned. "You must do the same for me someday."

Corrine nodded. "When I'm better at it. Otherwise, who knows what you might end up looking like. You didn't see the glamoury last night!"

Ilona smiled. "Let's go, then. It's quite a walk," Ilona said. She turned and headed south toward where the Thames slunk through London, heavy with refuse and tidal debris.

When they finally arrived at the riverbank, Corrine was so tired she wondered how she'd ever get back to the townhouse. Her legs trembled as they climbed down the stairs toward the exposed mud where the mudlarks sought treasures left by the low tide. Most of them were thin children with heads too big for their bodies, so covered in grime that their skin color was indistinguishable from that of the river mud. Women with broken teeth and tattered skirts sifted through the muck, hoping for a penny or any bit of value they might be able to take to the rag-and-bones man.

"Act like you're looking for things," Ilona muttered, before moving off.

Corrine bent and pretended she was searching, her fingers skimming just above the mud. Out of the corner of her eye, she watched Ilona work along next to some people, then heard her speaking to them in her low, gruff voice.

"That ain't the way you find a body," someone said next to her.

Corrine started and looked around. No one was immediately near her; several children were combing the river's filthy foam but none had spoken to her.

"You're wasting time," the voice said from a battered bucket at her feet.

Corrine tried to lift it, but wizened brown arms pulled the bucket firmly back down to the mud.

"Don't touch my home; it's all I've got left!" Two bright green eyes peered at her from a hole where the bucket had rotted through.

"Sorry," Corrine whispered. "Are you—"

Before she could finish, a skinny arm thrust from the hole and she saw a tiny brand. A man holding two serpents. She tried to think where she'd seen that before.

"Hallowed. And a gainisg if you must know," the little creature said, as it drew its arm back into the bucket.

"Gainisg?" Corrine tried the unfamiliar word.

"I moan for deaths to come in rushes and so forth. Not very exciting," the gainisg said. "And no need to do it here. The people are already dead."

"Do you know why I'm here?" Corrine asked. She

looked around to make sure no one saw her talking to the bucket. But if they did, she guessed they'd assume she was insane as some of the rest of them.

"Of course I know. Anyone could see through that glamour you're wearing. If you're looking for the Stone of Destiny, you're wasting your time here. You get back to the River Tay and talk to my cousin up there. She's up at the Holy Well of St. Fillan. We used to go moaning together, when there was rushes and honest death a-plenty." He winked at her.

"How can you make light of people dying?" Corrine asked.

"People do it all the time," the gainisg said. "And so do we, for all that. Or at least, we used to. Now we just fade into nothing and get stuck living under buckets near dirty rivers."

Corrine covered her mouth to keep from laughing.

"Now, who's making light?" the gainisg asked, his eyes darkening.

"I'm not," Corrine said, trying to sober up. Her feet sunk a little in the mud.

"Best get a move on," the gainisg said. "The Prince is here. He's sworn and determined to have you as his bride. And when he gets that way, precious little can stop him."

"His bride?" Corrine choked.

The green eyes regarded her. "You're wearing his ring, aren't you? Why else would he give it to you?"

"He didn't—" Corrine began. But the gainisg's glare silenced her. Her feet had sunk so deeply in the mud, both literally and figuratively, she wondered if she'd ever work her way out.

Ilona came to her then, her boots squishing. "Let's go," she said. "No one's heard anything about a priest, but there's rumor of two girls being kept down in Whitechapel. Worst place in town but wouldn't surprise me if they took them there."

Corrine nodded, memories of the gray room flashing through her mind. The green eyes disappeared from the bucket hole and a faint disapproving cluck emanated from the bucket.

"Good-bye," Corrine whispered. She remembered something her mother had once said, about leaving favors or milk or some expression of gratitude for kind fairies—or even the more capricious ones like the kelpie. She dug in her pocket and came up with an old ribbon Ilona must have saved. She shoved it through the bucket hole.

The green eyes slid back into view. "Good manners." it said. "But still very foolish. You go see my cousin now. And tell her to remember old Sedge."

Corrine nodded, blushing. He reminded her far too much of her first encounter with Bridghe. She wondered if the Hallowed would ever find her anything other than disappointing.

Ilona helped Corrine slog back to the stairs and they cleaned their boots on the worn stones as best they could.

Ilona glanced at her sidelong. "Why were you speaking to a bucket?" she asked.

Corrine blushed and pulled her cap down over her brow to hide her eyes. "There was a Hallowed—a gainisg. He lives there apparently."

"And he knew you? What did he say?" Ilona gave her a hand up the steep stairs.

"That we should hurry back to the Kirk of St. Fillan. He has a cousin there."

"Who also lives in a bucket?" Ilona asked.

Corrine lightly slapped Ilona's shoulder. "No, ninny. She lives in the holy well there. Maybe she knows something about the Stone of Destiny that will help us." Corrine thought again of what the gainisg had said of the Prince, though she really didn't want to think more about the ring and what it might mean. The same horrible sensation as when the kelpie had leaped into her at the ball rose in her mouth.

"What?" Ilona asked.

Corrine shook her head. "Just something he said about the Prince—" She remembered Madame's Tarot reading, the terrified way Father Joe had reacted. *Ancestors, inheritance . . . consanguinity.* She shook her head.

They had been wandering down a street toward the Seven Dials. A crowd bulged out of an alley, amid shouts of encouragement and money changing hands.

Ilona barely glanced at Corrine before she had wormed her way through the crowd, drawing Corrine after her.

Corrine followed her through what looked like the back entrance to a warehouse. After the initial boxes and bales of goods, however, Corrine saw that the place had once been something quite different. The shell of a stage loomed, its gilded plaster flaking, its curtains dusty and moth-eaten. Stray beams of sunlight pierced the rotten roof and tricked out more ornate carvings in the gloom, but Corrine's gaze was drawn to two men who danced around one another on stage, their rapiers flashing in the dust-laden air.

Something seemed odd about one of the duelists. His

rapier shone gold in the stray beams of sun, but it was his presence that alerted Corrine. Dark magic danced around his outline—a fierce, rough glamour. Prickling heat raced down her spine. He was almost certainly Unhallowed.

Corrine burrowed after Ilona through the crowd of people, many of them stinking of the dog feces they collected to sell to tanners down the row.

Ilona's eyes gleamed as she watched the swordsmen put one another through their paces. The swords hissed back and forth like dueling serpents across the boards. The swordsmen kicked up dust as they crab-stepped around one another.

"Sword duels have been illegal in London for many years," Ilona whispered. "How are they getting away with it this openly?"

Corrine was about to reply, but then she saw two young women huddled near the curtains in the shadows. Though their faces were dirty and their dresses torn, she recognized the true Phyllida and Elizabeth cowering together.

"Look!" she said, trying to point discreetly in their direction.

Ilona looked at her, puzzled. "Who are they?"

"The girls in my vision, the ones Rory and Melanie used for their glamoury. Phyllida and Elizabeth."

"But what are they doing here?" Ilona whispered.

Before Corrine could answer, the Unhallowed swordsman disarmed his opponent. The human's rapier clanged on the stage, its owner's hand bloodied and trembling.

A ruddy-cheeked man in a bowler hat and worn tweed suit shambled onto the stage. "Who's next?" he called.

He dragged Phyllida and Elizabeth from their hiding place, forcing them to stand straight and hold up their chins. "Who wants to be these ladies' next champion?" He cackled suggestively.

Ilona lunged and Corrine just barely caught her.

"Il—" Corrine began, but Ilona shot her a look of warning. "Thomas," Corrine amended. "Shouldn't we be going now?" Corrine had never seen so many ruffians gathered in one spot. They were almost more alarming than the dancers at the Unhallowed ball about which she had dreamed so many times. "Maybe we can go find the police . . ." She fell silent when she saw a bobby leaning on his billy club near the stage, egging on the man in the bowler hat.

"No," Ilona said, straightening her jacket. "I'm going to figure out how to free those girls. You go ask around. See if you can find out anything about Father Joe."

"But—" She wanted to tell Ilona that she was fairly certain one of the swordsmen was Unhallowed. There was no way Ilona could win, if she was thinking of fighting him.

"Just go!" Ilona said before pushing forward to the foot of the stage.

Corrine turned. She pulled on a man's grimy shirt sleeve and nearly got slapped for her trouble.

" 'Ere now! No pickin' my pocket!" he said.

"I wasn't," Corrine said. "I just wanted to ask—"

But he shoved her away and turned back to the stage, where the man was calling for someone who was not a coward. Several people shoved their friends forward, but all of them turned back into the crowd. The Unhallowed swordsman looked over all of them, his face impassive.

Corrine turned away in disgust. An old woman sat in a corner under the rotting balcony. Corrine threaded through the crowd toward her.

"Come now, surely one of you is man enough to try?" the man in bowler hat yelled.

"I am!" a familiar voice called.

Filled with dread, Corrine spun back toward the stage.

Ilona climbed onto the rickety boards to a chorus of laughter and jeers. "He's naught but a scrawny pick-pocket!" "Where'd you learn the sword—from the cheap-jack you stole it from?" The man in the bowler hat took Phyllida and Elizabeth back into the shadows.

There was silence as the Unhallowed swordsman bowed.

"If I may borrow this rapier," Ilona said, bending care-fully to the forgotten sword where it lay on the warped floorboards.

The swordsman inclined his head.

They saluted and the glittering swords leaped toward one another in the gloom. Corrine could barely follow their movements. Ilona's expressions veered from terror to delight. The Unhallowed swordsman was expressionless, pushing Ilona through the movements with a cat-like ease that sometimes made Corrine want to look away. She gasped when Ilona pushed back, her sword inscribing a black arc across the swordsman's gloved hand.

"First blood!" the man in the bowler hat cried.

The swordsman's careful neutrality faded in that moment. Even as Ilona grinned, he redoubled his attacks with a fury that Corrine knew Ilona had never before experienced. His golden rapier slid across her cheek, drawing a red line and knocking off her cap.

The audience roared. Ilona could hide her girlishness under large clothes and a cap. But without the cap, her feminine features were pronounced enough to make her duplicity obvious.

"What impropriety is this?" the man in the bowler hat shouted. His voice echoed throughout the musty hall. "A girl thinking she can stand in the place of men!"

Ilona hesitated, and in that moment, the swordsman disarmed her with a flick of his sword. The crowd surged, shouting in anger at Ilona's affront. The swordsman seized her and drew her against him, laying the golden sword across her throat.

Ilona turned her head toward the two girls cowering just off-stage. "Run!" she shouted as loudly as she could. The swordsman choked off anything else she might have said.

"Ilona!" Corrine cried, forgetting all pretense. She saw the two girls scurry away as the crowd pushed forward, but she could only think about Ilona. She lunged toward the stage, but someone beside her held her back. The old woman's bony claw gripped her and pulled her into a dark embrace.

"If you want her to live," a familiar voice said, "stop."

The Prince. Corrine could hear the gainisg saying again how foolish she was. She looked down. The old woman's claw transformed into his sinewy, weathered fingers.

Before she could say anything, he said, "He will get her out. Come with me now."

She planted her feet and stared defiantly into his

hood. His eyes gleamed in the shadows.

He stood to his full height. The crowd bashed her against him in their attempts to wrest Ilona from the swordsman. Corrine heard the wild song of his heart beneath his cloak.

"Do not tax me further," the Prince said. "They will rip both of you to pieces if they can. It's their way. I am your only hope of rescue."

Corrine bowed her head.

"Now, dearie," said the Prince as he resumed the guise of the old woman holding her arm, "could you kindly escort me out of here?"

Corrine nodded. All the crowd saw, if any of them looked, was a young boy leading an old woman from the fray.

They emerged from the shouting and stampeding into the twilit alley. For a few paces, the Prince kept his glamour, but as they passed into shadow, he cast it off.

"Keep walking," he said, pulling Corrine close to him and forcing her almost into a run to keep up with him.

They wended through the alleys until Corrine was too hopelessly lost to find her way out alone. At a dead end, the Unhallowed swordsman waited for them, holding Ilona with a bronze dagger to her throat. She looked the worse for wear, her face deeply bruised in addition to the red weal across her cheek. Her eyes glittered at Corrine.

Corrine pulled toward her but the Prince held her.

"*Reveal,*" the Prince said. Corrine's glamour dropped from her as easily as scissors cutting through cloth. But she stared in horror at the swordsman as his glamour fell away also. His hood was drawn up over his terrifying face, but she saw the scarlet edges of his hand. The Captain held Ilona fast.

Corrine struggled. "Let her go! It's me you want."

The Prince turned Corrine and shoved her against the nearest soot-stained wall. He lowered his face so that it was only inches from hers. She stared as long as she dared at his flickering eyes—dancing and changing like witch-light—before she dropped her gaze.

"You've no idea what I want, more's the pity," the Prince said. His breath was faintly sweet and cloying—wild roses with hints of bergamot and blood underneath. "This charade would have been over long ago if you had only come to me as I asked. But now, all is altered. Your friends have chosen to involve themselves, and thus they too will know the consequences of toying with me and mine."

"Leave her be!" Ilona shouted. A string of Hungarian curses was silenced abruptly when the Captain clapped his hand across her mouth.

"Stop it," Corrine said to the Prince. "You've no need to hurt her or anyone else."

But the Prince ignored her as though she hadn't spoken. "Take her and put her with the others," he said to the Captain.

The Captain shifted his grip on Ilona, as if to carry her off. Ilona stiffened. Corrine knew she wouldn't go without another fight.

"Stop!" Corrine screamed.

The Captain's hooded head turned toward the Prince for confirmation, and the Prince held up his hand.

"Why do you do this? Why did you take those girls and do such horrible things to them?" Corrine said. She wanted to beat at him with her fists but shoved them deep in her coat pockets instead.

"The girls were a lure, nothing more. I knew you wouldn't come to me of your own free will. But I knew that she"—he gestured toward Ilona—"would be drawn here to fight, and you would come with her. I tire of playing these games, Corrine. Understand that if you or your friends betray or steal from me again, I will not stint to repay them in kind."

"I *don't* understand," Corrine said. "She's done nothing to you. Nothing."

"Has she not been seeking information for you all along? Has she not stolen and fought in the name of your Council?"

Corrine looked at him in confusion.

"Not to mention that you have stolen two rathstones from me now—"

"Three," Corrine said, unable to resist. "When I found Sir James in your rath, he was carrying the Fearnan stone in his pocket."

The Prince's eyes went malevolent and dark. For a moment, she thought she'd gone too far.

"I want them back, Corrine. All of them. I know that you've also come for the Stone of Destiny. I want that, as well."

"Well, take it then," Corrine said. Her knees trembled with the fear and anger racing through her.

"You know I cannot!" he spat. "The Stone is on Hallowed ground. Even though any fool could find it under the throne of the kings, no Unhallowed may pass through the abbey's gates."

Hallowed ground . . . She had always taken that word to

mean "sacred," but perhaps it meant something more, something to do with the Hallowed Fey.

Fury twisted his features, and she guessed that this was closer to his true appearance than the face he usually wore. Corrine stared.

"And if I bring you the Stone, will you return Father Joe to us?" she asked.

"You would bargain with me?" He half-drew his dagger, but the Captain grunted and the Prince seemed to think better of it.

She lifted her chin. "I want Father Joe. And you will stop hurting him."

"Very well," he said. He bent close to her. "You will give me the Stone for the priest. Though I assure you, I shall be the winner in that bargain."

She was about to speak, but he held up his hand.

"There is more." He leaned into her, the long, muscular lines of his body pressing through her loose trousers. He whispered in her ear, his breath tickling her skin like butterfly feet. "When you bring me the Stone of Destiny, you will come with me to my rath where in time you may become my consort."

Corrine struggled against the thought, but he pressed her shoulder hard against the wall. "And if you do not do this, all of your friends will die." He withdrew enough to look into her eyes.

Corrine dropped her gaze.

"I must have your word," he said. "You know I have never lied. I will kill them if I must. Your friends matter only to you; they are little more than chaff blowing on the wind to me."

She nodded once and gritted her teeth as he kissed

her throat just below her earlobe. Heat slipped down her neckline toward her heart, and the ring slid from under the collar of her shirt.

"And what's this?" the Prince said. He slid his hand under it and cupped the ring where it rested next to the little golden book of her locket. *"Set me as a seal upon thine heart . . .* So my little thief took this too. Do you know what it means to wear my ring around your throat, sweet child?"

Corrine shook her head, all her defiance gone.

"I didn't think so," he said, releasing it and stepping back. "Or else you wouldn't wear it so readily." His wolfish smile grew as his eyes held hers. "You have already bound yourself to me, without even knowing it."

Corrine's fingers trembled as she moved to undo the clasp.

"No, no," he said. "The bargain is made. Keep the ring as a symbol of my promise. And should you pine for me, you have but to speak the charm I taught you long ago."

"I won't call on you," she said, her voice shaking. "Ever, ever again."

The Prince chuckled. "Soon, you'll have no need."

He signaled to the Captain, who released Ilona.

"Give me a sword," Ilona said to the Captain. "And I'll do more than give you a flesh wound."

The Prince laughed. "I've no doubt you'd try. You might even succeed—did I not train you myself?"

The Captain held out his red hand in warning.

Ilona glared at the Prince, but he ignored her.

"Go now," he said to Corrine. "You have sworn to me. I will await you on Beltane. If you do not come, be forsworn and forever bind your spirit to my command, even as Brighde and Angus were bound."

Corrine nodded, trying not to look at Ilona as the girl came toward her.

"What have you done?" Ilona said.

Corrine heard echoes of her mother's ghost long ago. *Oh, what have you done?*

She shook her head, looking back at the Prince and his man. "Let's get back," she said.

And throughout the long walk to Primrose Hill, when Ilona asked the same question again, she only shook her head in response.

~Eleven~

April 20, 1866

"WHERE HAVE YOU BEEN?" MISS BROWN SAID WHEN AT last the two of them dragged through the door. Miss Brown's face was white, her mouth carving deep lines in her face. She looked like she'd aged ten years since the morning.

"We freed the girls, but the Unhallowed have taken Father Joe," Corrine said. "We didn't see the girls after they ran away, but I hope they went back to their families."

"And she has made some kind of bargain—" Ilona began. But Madame DuBois advanced swiftly out of the morning room where she had been waiting and signaled for their silence.

"Mara and I have protected this room," she said, as she led them into the morning room. "Whatever you say in here will be safe."

Miss Brown sent Siobhan for water and clean linen with which to bathe Ilona's face. Corrine told the story as well as she could, including her hope that Phyllida and Elizabeth had indeed escaped from the Prince. Siobhan returned and began dabbing at Ilona's face. The girl tried not to wince.

"I don't understand why he didn't just take you," Miss Brown said, shaking her head. "I'm grateful that he didn't, but . . ." Corrine could tell Miss Brown was frightened and perhaps could guess at the implications.

"He needs her to get the Stone of Destiny for him," Mara said. "He won't risk losing that opportunity while he has it."

Corrine remembered his body leaning into hers. She blushed.

"What else did he say?" Madame DuBois asked, her eyes narrowing.

"Mara's correct. He'll bring Father Joe back to us if I give him the Stone of Destiny on Beltane," she said.

Miss Brown looked down, shaking her head. "That is no choice at all," she whispered.

Everyone was silent. Ilona stared at Corrine, and Corrine prayed that her friend wouldn't press the matter further.

"Our only hope is to get the Stone of Destiny back later," Madame said at last. "Use it as leverage now against a time when we might recover it from him in the future. We will have to find the remaining rathstones, at any rate. This way we'll know the location of at least one." Her smile was thin and sharp, a hollow attempt at optimism.

Miss Brown nodded. "We must have Father Joe back," she said.

Corrine remembered with guilt their fight before Father Joe was taken. If she could do this one thing for him . . . Maybe there was still time to make amends.

Corrine watched Christina as she embroidered list-lessly. She seemed not to hear them or care what they spoke of at all. Corrine pitied her and hated her at once. How could she still choose Rory over helping her friends? How could she not care about the evil the Unhallowed had done? Corrine wondered if she'd wake up one morning and find Christina gone.

"That we must," Madame DuBois said. "And that will mean that we'll need your magic fully unbound. It's time to call the kelpie and bridle him." She gestured to Ilona, who rose and went to retrieve the bridle from her room. Siobhan stood as though she wasn't sure what to do, holding the compress she'd been pressing against Ilona's face.

"You may go if you like, Siobhan and Christina," Miss Brown said. "I think we'll only need Mara, Ilona, and Corrine for this."

Madame nodded, and Siobhan and Christina left, Siobhan casting nervous glances behind her.

Corrine felt again the strangeness of being without Father Joe. Something about his presence anchored the magic they did, even if he couldn't fully participate.

"Why has no one ever unbound Father Joe's powers?" Corrine asked.

There was a silence in which everyone refused to meet her eyes.

"No one can unbind them save the one who bound him," Madame said at last.

"Leanan?" Corrine asked. Miss Brown blushed. She wondered just how much Miss Brown knew.

"No," Mara said. "My father. The Marsh King." Old visions of a tree swaying through a deep swamp surfaced in Corrine's mind.

"Your father—" Corrine said. She knew that Mara

was Half-Born like her, but she had never been sure how it had come to pass. Corrine wasn't even sure how she herself had come to be Half-Born. Corrine didn't know who the Marsh King was, but if the images she had once had in Mara's presence were of him . . . She shuddered.

"We don't yet know how this happened," Madame said. "The Unhallowed have long been sterile, ever since Father Joe cursed them long ago. Mara's birth should have been impossible."

"It's just another sign that the battle is closing in on us," Miss Brown said, as Ilona returned with the bridle. "And we need all of our strength to fight it."

Madame nodded. "Gather round, then," she said, gesturing toward the table at the center of the room. A pentagram had been laid out with the crystal ball at its center and white candles at the tips. "Seat yourself at one of the candles," Madame said. Corrine took the southernmost point of the pentagram.

Madame and Mara alternated calling the directions, and when they came to water in the west, the room visibly darkened as if a black mist had crawled in through the chimney. Drops of sweat beaded on Corrine's skin; the horrible algal taste coated the inside of her mouth.

"The kelpie," she whispered. Before she could say more, before Mara could begin the intonation to north, black smoke boiled from Corrine's throat. Her shoulder burned as the kelpie materialized between her and Ilona.

"Ilona, now!" Madame shouted. There had been no plan, no training in what to do, but Ilona leaped up before the kelpie could back away or bite and slid the rotted leather over his nose with her right hand, pulling the tarnished bit against his closed lips. She grabbed his jaw with her left hand and stuck her thumb into the corner of his mouth behind his teeth, pressing his tongue so that, like any mortal horse, he was forced to open his mouth. For a moment the kelpie twisted into something else—an eldritch boy with wild hair and barrel-stave ribs perhaps—but the vision flickered so quickly that Corrine wasn't sure she'd seen it. The bit was in his mouth now, the headpiece firmly behind his ears. There was nothing he could do to rid himself of it, and the knowledge was in his glowing eyes.

"Bound only to be free," he said. "That was what they promised." His voice was slow and dark as an underground spring.

"The Treas Ulaidh bound you to me," Corrine said. "Why did they bind my powers?"

The kelpie snorted. His lips curled against the bit in his mouth.

"Your powers were not bound, foolish child. I was sent to help you, that you would not come into the domain of water unaided. You saw what waits for you there."

Corrine thought of the mermaid at the bottom of the well, her black eyes, her grin full of shark's teeth. She had been right about her fear after all.

"But you are Unhallowed—"

"And thus, I know the ways to defeat my own kind." The kelpie shook his knotted mane and the knuckle-bones chimed.

"But—" Corrine still didn't understand.

"The Three Treasures struck a bargain with me. They released me from my imprisonment if I would aid them.

And when I have done so, when I have brought you to them, then will they release me forever." Images moved through his darkening eye—of thrashing white limbs, blood swirling away on darker currents, the plunge and roll of the loch waves drowning out human cries.

Corrine swallowed. "You will not—"

"If the bridle is removed, you alone can withstand me. The brand you bear is proof of our bond. But if others were to cross my path, they would not fare so well as you. Up until now, I have only spared them because I could not free myself." His lips drew into a sneer, and for a moment, she saw the wild boy's face she had seen before.

She looked down.

"What are the Three Treasures? Why do they want Corrine?" Madame asked.

"I answer only to you," the kelpie said to Corrine.

"But you heard her question," Corrine said. "Who or what are they? What do they want of me?"

Witch-light returned to the kelpie's eyes. "They are the reason my former masters want Hallowmere. They are the three great weapons of the old gods. Once, they were gods themselves. Now they are but ghosts and shadows. They cannot speak but through images and yearnings, and are little more than nightmares to most." The kelpie pranced a little. "They want you to free them."

"What are the weapons?" Miss Brown said.

The kelpie did not answer her. Corrine saw the veiled ladies again, as she had the day Falston had been destroyed. She saw again the horrifying mask, its long ribbons trailing like shrouds under the veil. "The mask," she whispered.

The kelpie nodded. "And?"

"I don't know," she said.

"The Mask of Medusa, the Spear of Athena, the Shield of Neith," the kelpie said.

"And these . . . weapons . . . they want Corrine to free them?" Miss Brown asked.

The kelpie looked to Corrine for direction.

"Answer her," she said.

"Yes," the kelpie said. "They have tested you and found you . . . adequate."

"Tested?" Corrine thought of how the raven had nearly torn out her eye at Fearnan. "Blinding me was a test?"

"They needed to know that you could recover from adversity and that your magic ran deeper than sight alone," the kelpie replied. His voice was the sound of streams running underground, the blind cavefish, the fathomless abyss.

"And why should I help them?"

"Because if you do not, the Prince will use you to find them. And when he takes possession of them, he will take possession of all," the kelpie said.

Corrine ignored him and looked to Madame DuBois and Miss Brown instead. "And what will the Council do with them? If I free the Treasures, how will the Council use them?"

"We will destroy the Prince and free those who serve him to be cleansed in Hallowmere," Madame DuBois said without hesitation. "We will restore the balance between mortal and Fey, as it was before Leanan began all this mess."

The kelpie snorted.

"If the Unhallowed will not be restored, then they will be destroyed," Madame DuBois said.

The kelpie said nothing.

Corrine put her hand on his withers so that he looked at her. "And how can I know that they sent you to help me?"

"I know what waits at the bottom of that well in the garden," he said. "Do you wish to face it alone? Who better than I to fight alongside you?"

Corrine shuddered, whether at the thought of the mermaid's teeth or the clamminess of the kelpie's coat she couldn't say.

She remembered when she had questioned her father once about how he knew his crops would grow. He had smiled, as he chewed on a stalk of grass, and looked out over the newly-planted field. "Sometimes," he'd said at last, "you must just have faith, Corrine."

And it was faith or the lack of it that faced her now. She had often been unsure who to trust in this strange battle. It seemed the greatest unlikelihood that she would find herself trusting a kelpie, a servant of the Unhallowed, but she had no other choice. Something had gotten inside her on the voyage to Scotland, something that made her fear what waited for her. She didn't know how it had happened, but she couldn't face the mermaid in the well alone.

"Are you ready?" the kelpie asked.

"Now?" Corrine blanched. Everyone's eyes seemed to be on her.

"Now is always the best time for anything," the kelpie said, smiling.

A smile on a horse that is not a horse is a gruesome thing indeed,

Corrine thought. "Fine," was all she said.

"Take my reins, then," the kelpie said. "And do not let go."

Corrine gripped the rotten reins tightly, wondering as she did so if they might break. She closed her eyes and took the five breaths.

She flew. Over the dark sea, beyond the empty towers of the east and into the eye of the sun. Into the garden where the bees drowsed and the flowers hummed. Down the path to the well where she had first spoken to the kelpie and where the Prince had startled her out of her trance. The kelpie was there beside her, the only velvet patch of night in the garden.

They peered into the well together. Corrine saw the kelpie's lips curl; saw his yellowed, worn teeth. She imagined them grinding bones and flesh beneath the loch and shivered. He eyed her as though he knew quite well what she thought.

The well's mossy depths gave back no light, no reflection. Corrine couldn't even see the mermaid lurking there.

"Maybe she's gone?" she asked.

The kelpie sniffed the dank well-breath like a dog.

"No," he said. "She is in there, because she is in you."

Corrine looked away from his flaring gaze.

"Climb up," the kelpie said. "And we will go to the domain of water together." He turned toward the well's stone lip so that she could use it easily as a mounting block. She climbed up onto the stones and was about to board the kelpie when she stopped.

He had turned his head to watch her, and there was a

flickering gleam in his eye that spoke of blood and bone and the dark waves of the loch.

"The bridle keeps you safe," the kelpie said. "That and the bond forged between us by the Treas Ulaidh."

Faith, she thought again.

She hauled herself aboard the kelpie's broad back. He was solid as a draft horse, like the Friesians she'd seen drawing the wealthy in their hansoms at the Queen's ball.

Corrine had barely adjusted the reins before he leaped and they plunged down the well. The dank air swallowed her scream.

They were in the black ocean. Corrine couldn't see anything, and she choked on the inky darkness as her final breath escaped.

Put your face in my mane. She heard his whisper as though his velvety lips tickled her ear.

She put her face down. Between the knotted mane and his hide, she opened her mouth and inhaled his clammy darkness. Something changed in her lungs; the water rushed into them, but she could still breathe. She raised her head and realized she could also see.

Far below, a ship lolled on its side like a broken dancer, beyond the reach of wind and current, hidden from the sun. Despite the depth, there was light—a hectic witch-light that played across the ship as figures waltzed across the rotting decks. An eerie symphony that never seemed to finish one movement before careening to the next wailed up from the shattered salon.

Corrine knew the *Great Eastern* without having to see the name flickering along its side, just as she knew the figure who sang in the toppled mast, her wordless notes intertwining with the endless symphony.

The kelpie came to rest at one end of the tilted deck. Corrine watched the ghosts whirling through their paces, oblivious of all but the music, as the Unhallowed dancers had been in all her dreams. Guilt filled her, black as the ocean in her lungs. Because of her, these people had died. Because of her, they were eternally bound to the *Great Eastern*, endlessly tracing their tattered patterns across the deck until even the boards crumbled into sand. She sobbed.

This is why you are here, the kelpie said in her mind. *Guilt and fear have locked your full power from you.*

What must I do? she thought back at him. *How can I free them?*

The mermaid's form glowed softly in the rigging as she sang. Though there was no current, the long shrouds of her loose skin and her oily hair fluttered around the mast.

You must force her to release her hold on the ship.

How?

The kelpie looked over his shoulder at her. *Either make a bargain she cannot refuse, or kill her.*

Corrine shook her head. She'd had enough of bargains with the Unhallowed, but killing? She had seen so much death. She wasn't sure she could be responsible for more.

What would you do? Corrine asked the kelpie.

The kelpie grimaced, though she knew it was meant to be a smile. *What do you think?*

The mermaid's siren song ceased, but the symphony rattled on.

Decide quickly, the kelpie said. *She is aware of you.*

195

She remembered how almost without thought the green fire of life had raced across the forest floor toward the Captain after Kenneth's death. She thought of Mara killing the cuideag, of tossing the daoi scarf into the fire at Fearnan. How was the mermaid any different than those creatures?

The mermaid drifted toward them. Her face was as tattered as her arms and the closer she came, the greater the rents in her flesh. Corrine clutched at the kelpie's reins. At last, the mermaid shed her skin entirely. What rose on the deck before them was little more than a hulking, finned *thing* with milky, round eyes and rows of needle-teeth.

What say you now? the kelpie said in Corrine's thoughts.

Traitor, the mermaid-thing said to the kelpie. The accusation hissed and bubbled, distorted by the weight of water.

Corrine bowed her head. The mermaid-thing waddled toward them, tentacles spurting from its back, its hissing jaw open wide.

Will you be swallowed by your fear or fight it? the kelpie asked.

Corrine closed her eyes and breathed. In the deeper darkness behind her lids, the air flashed through her, chased by the green fire of life. And now, a third element joined them—a slender silver thread, like the sparkle of sun on water. She reached for it, bound it to the air and fire, and opened her eyes.

A silver fountain poured through the darkness, engulfing the mermaid-thing and dissolving it into inky fragments. After the mermaid was gone, the silver fountain flooded the ship with light. The music ceased as the silver stream moved through the bow; the dancers halted and for the first time seemed to be cognizant of their surroundings. They all stopped, their dead eyes fixing on Corrine.

The kelpie stumbled a bit, and it was then that Corrine realized the ship was moving, that the silver current was carrying it upward. Gradually, the abyss fell away, the water turning from black to deep blue to cerulean. Corrine felt no pressure or pain whatsoever in the rising, but when the ship emerged above the waves, she choked and vomited seawater as her body struggled to breathe air again.

It was a pure, fair day on seas blue enough to burn Corrine's eyes. Gulls and terns cried above them, and white sand shimmered in the distance. The ship still moved, drawn on by the silver tide. The kelpie walked to the rail, and Corrine felt silly for still being astride him. She looked over his side into the depths and saw schools of shining fish leaping alongside. All the ghosts were crowded at the rail, pointing out the sights, and turning their faces up to the sun.

Corrine watched them as the ship moved toward the sand bar. She hadn't realized such a deep guilt and fear had ridden her since the sinking of the *Great Eastern*. She had shut away the cries of those who had died, even as she knew she was directly responsible for their deaths by her mere presence on board. She had tried not to see any of those faces again, but the thought of the *Great Eastern* at the bottom of the sea, the souls of the dead forever damned to dance on its decks had haunted her.

The ship ran aground with a bone-grinding lurch that nearly threw Corrine from the kelpie's back. Far in the distance, a great mountain rose into cloud. The ghosts streamed off the ship onto the dunes, led by a familiar, bearded man sporting a top hat and striped trousers. He checked his pocket watch before climbing the first dune. Isambard Kingdom Brunel. He turned at the crest and raised his hand to Corrine.

She took the reins into her left hand and responded with a wave.

Then, Brunel disappeared over the dune, while the orchestra players, the boilermen, the ladies in their crinolines, and gentlemen in their smoking jackets fanned out behind him. Corrine sighed.

"Well done," the kelpie said. "You have mastered this element. Shall we return?"

"Yes," Corrine said. "But tell me one thing."

The kelpie stilled beneath her.

"Why did you not tell me what it means to wear the Prince's seal ring?"

The kelpie snorted, as though he'd expected her to ask something else. "I thought you knew. Do not you mortals play similar games with rings of engagement and gold bands and the like?"

"Yes, but . . ."

"Where do you think the tradition started, then?"

Corrine didn't know how to respond, and before she could say more, he leaped. She fell up until the hard chair in the drawing room was underneath her, and the reins were in her hand, the kelpie's cheek dragged close to hers.

She startled at having him so close, his blood-and-bone breath, his witch-light eye peering into hers with deep amusement.

Then he was gone, and the horrid, clammy taste was on her tongue.

~TWELVE~

*April 21, 1866*

SNOW FELL IN A FEATHERED CLOAK AROUND CORRINE AS SHE *trudged up the mountainside. She had been climbing this mountain for years, it seemed. Her hands and feet had gone white at first, but blackened now with frostbite. Her chemise clung to her skin, as frozen as the tears on her cheeks. She wasn't sure anymore if she was fleeing from or toward something.*

You cannot escape me, you know. *The Prince's voice echoed around her in the silence.* We made a bargain.

Corrine tried to run, but her numb feet wouldn't cooperate. She sprawled in the snow.

He lifted her up, and for a moment, the shadow of a gate loomed over her—golden, fanged jaws that threatened to swallow her. She looked for the glimmering light between them, but something else peered at her out of the gloom. A face of frost. A white finger placed against white lips. Black eyes that forbade her to speak. And then two more faces. One leathery and withered, the other hard and motionless as stone. All three made beckoning gestures.

She screamed. The Prince laughed. That will not help you, *he said, as he hauled her down the mountain.* You are mine.

Corrine sat up in bed. She was alone. Apparently, she had slept through Miss Brown rising and departing.

She ached all over, as if she'd been diving deep into the ocean all night long. Which, in a way, she had been. She threw back the coverlet and looked at her feet. They were rosy and pink, the skin cracked a little at the heels. Not blackened, not numb with frozen blood. Corrine sighed.

The sun beckoned her from bed. She looked through the grimy window where a couple boys chased hoops down the hill. A man on a liver chestnut took the bridle path at the edge of the hill up through the trees. Three ladies whispered to one another under their parasols as he passed.

She turned toward the wardrobe, thinking of the three women in her dream. The Treas Ulaidh asked again for her silence. The kelpie said they wanted her help. But what, she wondered, would they give in return? She had bartered with the Prince for the lives of her friends and Father Joe. If the Three Treasures wanted her badly enough, would they bargain with the Prince for her life? Somehow she doubted it.

She rummaged unsuccessfully through her wardrobe, wondering what one wore to a prisoner exchange. There were only a few days left, she knew, until she would have to make good her end of the bargain. Corrine wondered if the Prince would truly return Father Joe; she suspected he had some trick up his sleeve.

Corrine's eyes slid to her writing case on the floor by the washstand. She listened for a moment, and then went and dug one of Father Joe's letters from its hiding place.

My dearest beloved—

It is cruel punishment that you have sent me out into the world again with recourse only to your courier. The transient image of you in a tarnished mirror or still water haunts me. It would seem you delight in my torment. For long, I could only consent to it for the brief bliss of being in your arms. That is no longer enough. I have done as you bid. I have slain in your name. Yet you have cast me from your presence as easily as a child tosses away a toy. By your most pernicious art, you made me believe and crave your love. The Father help me, I crave it still.

Even so, I have seen how my folly has led me to mistake domination for love and evil for justice. Though you may discern the torn and scattered pieces of my heart across this page, I shall no longer battle with you over unconquerable vice and infrequent affections. I shall spend the rest of what life is given to me cleansing myself of the sin you have wrought in me and atoning for the harm I have done in my pride and wickedness. I have seen the dream of Elaphe and realized it to be good, and I have accepted Iamblicus as my mentor and protector on this new journey. I shall bear my affliction alone, for all the rest of my days. And every day I shall refuse the gifts you have given, for the price of blood paid for them is far too high.

If Fey and mortal cannot live side by side on this earth, then are we all doomed. If you are willing to give last gifts, then I beg this of you, as one you claimed to love. Desist in your witcheries and give over your will to dominate the earth. It cannot be done but by love and faith. That I have seen. And though you may call me traitor and apostate to your cause, know that your image will remain forever as a seal upon my heart.

Frater Josephus

Set me as a seal upon thine heart . . .

Echoes of the Prince's words made her drop the letter in her lap. *So, he renounced her.* She shuddered to imagine what Leanan must have done when she read of Father Joe's betrayal. And what must others have thought? From what Corrine could glean, Father Joe had been a priest of St. Fillan's Kirk. He had befriended Elaphe and Iamblicus, but then had betrayed them for love of the witch Leanan. He had killed for her, and he had begged her for even more power. And now this letter seemed to indicate that he turned on her, back to Elaphe and Iamblicus. How could anyone trust him?

Corrine scanned the letter again. *I shall bear my affliction alone, for all the rest of my days. And every day I shall refuse the gifts you have given, for the price of blood paid for them is far too high.* She did not know what this could possibly mean. Was he speaking of his Half-Born gift of magic? She wasn't sure, but she guessed that he had often used his magic before it had been bound. So what had he meant? And what had Leanan done to him as retribution? For she surely wouldn't have allowed him to escape that easily. In her brief encounters with the Unhallowed witch, Corrine had sensed an overweening pride and avarice, and a determined desire for Father Joe that they had barely escaped at the Isle of Female Saints. She couldn't imagine that the witch would allow Father Joe to escape her this time.

But was there a way to *make* the Prince keep his end of the bargain? So often, as this morning, he had appeared in dreams to terrify her or cajole her into doing what he wanted. Corrine wondered whether she could reciprocate. The thought of frightening the Prince made her smile and gave her a little shiver of horror all at once. How might he retaliate? But could it be done? And how?

Mastering the domain of water definitely made her feel stronger, but she wasn't sure she was strong enough to taunt the Prince. There were still two domains left: earth and spirit. The great mountain rose forbiddingly in her memory. *Will I manage to master them all?*

She shook her head. There was one letter left, but a knock came at the door and Mara pushed through with a tea tray laden with food.

There was no time to hide the letters. Corrine pushed them under the coverlet, hoping that Mara wouldn't see.

Mara looked at her with a raised brow as she rose. "Miss Brown sent me up with this to see if you was awake," she said.

Corrine nodded.

"Let me help you get dressed and then you eat your breakfast," Mara said, setting the tea tray down on the vanity.

Corrine shrugged off the nightgown and into her chemise and bloomers, trying not to think about the dream of wandering on the frozen mountainside. She stepped into the corset Mara held out for her, and grunted as the maid pulled the laces as tightly as she could. Neither of them said anything about the kelpie brand. Then came the hoops and the crinoline, the long, heavy skirt, the blouse, the jacket—all of which had replaced the gray dress she'd singed by the fire at Fearnan. For a moment, she longed for the loose trousers and coat she had worn just yesterday.

Mara usually left the hairdressing either to the girls themselves or to Siobhan if any was to be done. She was therefore on the verge of leaving Corrine to her breakfast when Corrine stopped her.

"Mara," she said, "I'm wondering . . ." She paused, unsure how to say what she was thinking.

Mara stared, her face too hard and worn for someone of her age.

"Is it possible for me to appear in dreams to the Prince the way he can appear to me?"

The maid considered. "May be possible. Though I don't think it's ever been tried. Why?"

"He's promised to bring Father Joe back to us at Beltane. I want to be sure he does."

Mara put her hands on her hips. "Girl, you're toying with forces you still don't fully understand yet." She tilted her head on one side. "Still . . . might be fun to send him a little message. Do you have anything of Euan's we could use?"

"I have this," she said, unclasping her pendant and holding out the signet ring on her palm.

A slow, wicked smile curved Mara's lips. "That'll do," she said.

"When?" Corrine asked.

"You come to the parlor tonight," Mara said. "We'll send him a message he won't soon forget."

Corrine smiled as Mara nodded and left the room. She turned to the breakfast tray, hugging herself so hard she almost couldn't breathe. She guessed that Father Joe wouldn't approve, but had he not said before they left Scotland that the Council needed to bring the offensive to the Unhallowed? The Prince had been doing everything in his power to show he wasn't playing. *I'm not either*, she thought as she sat to her toast and tea. *And now he'll know it.*

When Corrine finally went downstairs, she was greeted with the sight of her friends quietly studying in the morning room. Ilona fidgeted with her skirt on the divan, clearly longing for her boy's clothes. Her face was still bruised, but much less swollen than it had been yesterday. Corrine could imagine the guilt Miss Brown must feel about Ilona's fights, but if Ilona resented her scars, she gave no indication. Christina was listless and pale, her appearance far sloppier than usual. She wore the same dress as yesterday—something she seldom did—and had done nothing with her hair, which was usually elaborately coiffed no matter whether she was studying or going out for a tea party. Neither of them said anything when Corrine entered the room, carrying her writing case. Christina, in fact, didn't bother to acknowledge her presence.

If we don't do something, Corrine thought, *we'll lose her soon.*

She crossed to her desk and arranged her writing case in an attempt to distract herself from the near-constant chatter of her thoughts. But the thoughts just kept coming.

The first day of May—Beltane—was the earliest that anything could possibly be done. *Unless . . .* Corrine considered that they could attempt to steal the Stone of Destiny now and send it away to Scotland, and only give the Prince the parure rathstone. But surely he would not be foolish enough to believe that the Stone had been stolen from Westminster by someone else just before he was to receive it. It was hard to know what he would do in his wrath. He might kill Father Joe or anyone else who he felt deserved it. That wasn't something Corrine was willing to risk.

Corrine brooded as she opened the case and assembled her writing things. She hadn't realized how much she'd been forced to abide by the Prince's rules of combat. Truthfully, she hadn't wanted to admit that she was engaging in combat at all. But now, with all that had gone before, she knew she was fighting just as hard as Ilona did in her fencing matches, but on a very different plane.

She wished for a moment that she still had the Unhallowed book. Knowing more about them before she entered the rath might help her find a way to defeat the Prince once and for all. But Father Joe had taken it, and whether he had hidden it away in his room or the Unhallowed had reclaimed it, she was uncertain.

In the end, she knew, there was only one way to defeat the Prince. As Brighde had told her in the ring of standing stones, she would have to kill him. She would have to cut the rathstone from his chest. But now she began to wonder if the ghost was just using her as she used Christina. Why was she so terrified of the Prince? Had he done something even more terrible to her than keeping her soul from heaven?

She spread Brighde's last letter across the desk in hopes of finding out.

[Trans. note: Early December 1357. Middle page missing.]

To Brother Angus, Kirk of St. Fillan, from Sister Brighde of the Isle of Female Saints, greetings.

My dearest love—

It is my hope that these words will reach you wherever you might be in this world or out of it. The courier says he will deliver my letters to you, but I am ever uncertain, when for weeks I receive no response. Have you forgotten me? Are you even now lying in some Fey woman's arms? I am jealous of your attentions: I wish for them to be showered upon me alone. I am to be the mother of your child. Does that not merit your highest favor?

And yet, I am torn. Is not our love gravest sin? You say not. You say the Fey rejoice in our love. But who are they to absolve us?

[..]

My illness grows with the child, and I can no longer bear the disgrace of pretending. If you will not have me with you, then the loch shall be my final home. You once said the Prince would give us the highest honors of his court if we would accede to his will. What, I wonder, does he require in return? You have made it so that there are no choices left to me. It is either the loch or the rath. Tell me which you would have it be.

Yours forever fallen from grace,
Brighde

Corrine set the pen down with a sigh. That Brighde had threatened suicide was news to her, but her distress over the Prince's motives wasn't. *What did he want, indeed,* Corrine thought. She remembered the Prince speaking of her as his potential consort and cringed. This must have been his objective with Brighde too. Angus had been bait, a way to lure Brighde into trusting the Fey. But had the Prince hoped to gain her as his bride? And had Angus known all along? The romance that had once seemed like little more than forbidden love was rife with dark, scheming undercurrents. Corrine wished for a moment that she didn't know about any of it. If she had never seen the trunk, if she had never discovered the letters, if she had never listened to the Unhallowed in the hawthorn bush . . . Too many *ifs.*

She pondered on this all afternoon and throughout supper. Everyone was unusually silent. Miss Brown barely got through grace, her voice cracking as she recited the words Father Joe had always said. Corrine wondered again if the Prince would make good his promise to deliver Father Joe alive. She had been very specific about that in the bargain, but she wondered how many different interpretations of "alive" the Prince might use against her. Corrine sighed and pushed the mutton chop around with her fork. She missed a good ham steak about as much as anything.

The front bell rang and Siobhan rushed to answer it. Everyone looked at one another, except Christina who kept her head down, raking her fork over her boiled potatoes.

Christina's head came up, though, when a masculine voice was heard in the foyer.

Corrine froze. Could it really be . . . ?

Siobhan returned with a calling card and an invitation which she handed to Miss Brown. "A Mr. Adamou to see Corrine," Siobhan said, looking nervously in her direction.

Miss Brown held the card out and read. "Mr. Dimitrios Adamou, Esquire, Regent's Park." She looked up at Corrine. She glanced around the corner and lowered her voice. "Do you know this man, Corrine?"

Corrine swallowed. "I met him at the croquet party."

"Is he an ally?" Miss Brown asked.

"I don't know," Corrine whispered. "But he frightens me."

Siobhan waited, obviously unsure what to do.

"Tell him I'm ill," Corrine said.

Siobhan bobbed her head, though she looked unhappy about having to give the refusal. She went back into the foyer where Mr. Adamou still waited.

Everyone listened.

Siobhan murmured her apologies, obviously moving Mr. Adamou toward the door.

"But I wished to tell her—" He raised his voice in agitation. "Is there no way?"

Siobhan's voice was surprisingly firm. "She can't have visitors now, Mr. Adamou. I'll give her your card and she'll send along a response when she can."

"But I wanted to thank her for rescuing my—"

"Thank you for calling," Siobhan said. The door closed.

Corrine could almost feel him there, standing at the lilac door, trying to decide whether to knock again. Eventually, she heard a carriage going away down the street.

Miss Brown opened the invitation. "Mrs. Gillian Adamou requests the company of Miss Jameson, Miss Beaumont, and Miss Brown at high tea next Thursday at 3 p.m. The favor of a reply is requested."

Miss Brown looked up at Corrine. "He must be quite taken with you."

Corrine shook her head, "No, no. I really don't think so. He seems to know something about the kidnapped girls, but I'm not sure how much. He seems . . . strange." *What does it matter anyway?* Corrine thought. *In ten days, I'll be gone.*

Miss Brown nodded and refolded the invitation. "Well, if you have misgivings and in light of the present circumstances, perhaps we should decline the invitation," she said. She left to write her refusal in the parlor.

For the rest of the evening, there was little to do but play cards with Ilona—Christina continued reading her novel—and wait.

When bedtime came, Corrine was surprised to find that Miss Brown had decided, in the interest of comfort and better utilization of space, to sleep in Father Joe's old room until such time as he returned.

"We'll both sleep better," she said, smiling wearily at Corrine.

"Can you do something for me, then?" Corrine asked.

Miss Brown nodded, shadows jumping around her candle flame.

"Can you search for the Unhallowed book? Father Joe took it back from me before . . ." Corrine's voice trailed off.

"Yes," Miss Brown said. "Now, good night, Corrine."

"Good night," Corrine said, turning back to say good night to Ilona and Christina. Miss Brown's candle receded down the hall.

The dead expression on Christina's face made Corrine grasp her arm.

"Christina, tell me what's wrong," Corrine said. "Maybe I can help."

"You know damn well what's wrong." Christina pulled her arm away.

Corrine stared at her open-mouthed. Christina had never cursed and certainly not at her. Ilona looked at Corrine in sympathy but remained silent.

"But, Christina—"

"You ruined my one chance at happiness, Corrine. I was willing to accept my fate. Why can't you?"

Corrine felt the bright swathes of her illusions, illusions she hadn't known she'd held, shredding into ribbons. "When you were sick, you said you wanted help. Now you're saying that you don't? Brighde wouldn't . . ."

"Oh, Brighde!" Christina snarled. "My life is in ruins and all anyone can think about are the feelings of some nun's ghost who has caused me misery since I was a little girl! What about what I want? Eh? Did you ever think of that?"

"I certainly think that's all *you* ever think about!" Corrine said, her voice rising. "You talk about your life being in ruins! Do you think mine is any better? Do you have any idea of the price I paid just to make you well? Do you know what I'll have to pay to keep you safe? I doubt it ever crosses your mind!"

Christina stared with the same flat anger she'd held when she'd thrown Corrine out of their secret Society at Falston long ago. Corrine stared back, refusing to break eye contact. Then Christina's face twisted, and she flounced into her room. Ilona followed her, closing the door on Corrine with an apologetic look and a whispered, "Later."

Corrine turned and went to her room with leaden feet. She paced in agitation for a while, waiting for either Mara or Siobhan to come and help unlace her corset. After all that had been done to save Christina, Corrine couldn't believe that her friend had turned toward Rory again. Even though Christina knew that Rory had stolen, lied, manipulated, and possibly killed, none of that mattered. Christina was blinded by Unhallowed promises.

Corrine wondered if Christina would still be in the townhouse by morning. It was likely that she wouldn't, but Corrine hoped that Ilona would keep Christina from escaping if it came to it. Ilona had seen firsthand the type of people they were dealing with; surely she understood now, if she hadn't before, that the Unhallowed must be kept at bay. Corrine heard sobbing on the other side of the wall and murmured hushing. She took a few steps toward the wall, then stopped. Christina wouldn't listen to her. Somehow, she had been convinced that Corrine had barred her entry into paradise.

Corrine bent, unlaced her boots, and then removed them and set them by the bed. Still, neither Siobhan nor Mara came up to help her undress. She guessed at last that Mara wouldn't—perhaps she was waiting downstairs in the parlor even now. Corrine decided to read the last of Father Joe's letters while she waited a few moments more, just to be assured that Miss Brown was asleep.

But this letter was different than the others, folded in an envelope addressed to Miss Brown and obviously much more recent.

17 June 1864

Dear Miss Brown:

My name is Richard Jameson and I am a lieutenant in the Army of the Potomac. Only God knows whether this letter will reach you, but I felt it only right under the circumstances that I try to reach you however possible.

Your sister, Alexandra Brown, or Alex, as she prefers to be called, was captured by our forces during heavy fire at Petersburg. Though the Confederate Army has taken possession of the town, all prisoners of war were to be immediately transported. However, in light of her wounds and her delicate position, I begged that she be allowed to remain under my care until she is fit to travel. I am in no wise certain that my commanding officer will not soon commute her to prison. Her sharp tongue wins her no friends amongst my soldiers.

Yet I have a daughter of my own at home of similar age, Corinne, and it hurts my heart to think of a girl of her age and gentle rearing brought to such a pass as your sister. From what I can gather, your sister left home to serve in the Army of Northern Virginia early this year. I take it that she has written to you seldom, if at all, and I can imagine the terrible anxiety you must feel on her behalf. I felt it best that you should know of her condition, that she is alive and receiving what care can be given her.

I pray that she will soon be well enough to travel, for the Confederate Army has redoubled its efforts against us, and retreat may be called. I pray that somehow I may send her soon to you, that she may once more know the comfort of her family's embrace.

With warmest regards in the midst of great trial,
Lt. Richard Curtis Jameson, Army of the Potomac

Corrine dropped the letter in shock. Her father had written Miss Brown. Why had Miss Brown never told her? She didn't know if it would have mattered, but just the fact of it. Both her father and Alex had been lost at Petersburg? Had they been together when they died? Why had Miss Brown kept silent about this?

Corrine stood and went to the window in her stocking feet. Rain had come again, tapping its chill fingers against the panes. The moist spring air flowed through the old windows, cooling the heat in her cheeks. She looked down at the mostly empty lane and the darkened hill. Beneath the flickering gaslights, a shadow moved. Corrine froze. She wanted to step back from the window, but she couldn't. The shadow resolved into a cloaked figure. He turned and raised his bloody hand to her in a greeting she'd mercifully almost forgotten. She felt the power of him in her knees, the queer trembling that rushed up through the earth, as if he tried to summon her with the sheer force of his will. Then he lowered his hand and dissipated into darkness.

As soon as she could move, she snatched up the signet ring from the vanity and raced downstairs to the parlor, where Mara waited with candles already burning.

"Wondered if you was coming at all," Mara said, looking up from the circle she'd laid out with white stones on the floor.

Corrine heaved a breath. She couldn't tell Mara about the letter from her father. It cut far too close to the bone. "The Captain," Corrine said. "I just saw him. Out there." She pointed.

Mara went to the window. "Hmm. Don't see him now. But I felt something a minute ago. Probably that spell I

216

did on him finally wearing off," she said.

Corrine tried to calm her galloping heart. She couldn't get her father's letter out of her mind. And the Captain's presence, much as she had come to pity him, only heightened her anxiety.

"What does the Captain want?" Corrine asked.

"Only to watch and wait now, I'd reckon," Mara said. "We both of us have scared him pretty good the past few months." She went back to carefully placing the remaining stones in a pentagram on the floor. "He just wants to make sure we don't run now."

Corrine thought of her visions of Jeanette and of Alex, holding out her hand to the Captain as the trees blazed and cracked above them. She remembered watching helplessly as the Captain took little Penelope from Falston what seemed ages ago. "Are you certain?"

Mara looked up at her. "When have I been wrong?"

Corrine swallowed.

"What I thought," Mara said standing up and dusting off her scullery-roughened hands. "Now, bring me that ring."

Corrine stepped toward her and dropped the signet ring in Mara's waiting palm.

"You go sit over there," Mara said, gesturing toward the most northerly point of the pentagram. Corrine did as she bid, settling herself uncomfortably on the floor. The corset imprisoned her spine stiffly upright; she couldn't have slouched if she'd wanted to. But the way she sat, with crushed crinoline and hoop, made breathing difficult. She repositioned herself and folded a portion of her skirt under her knees so she could kneel.

Mara nodded, took up her position across from

Corrine, and began the chant. Her low, guttural words wrapped around the circle. A silence heavy as wet cotton filled Corrine's ears.

"The circle is protected," Mara whispered. She leaned over the pentagram and set the silver ring in the center.

She looked up at Corrine. "I want you to fix your eyes on that, and think about the Prince. Think about visiting him like you'd visit your grandma on a Sunday afternoon, talking to him like you would your neighbor. Like slipping down into the domains, but not quite. More like stepping into a dream."

Corrine nodded and took a breath. The dying fire in the room carved the patterns on the seal into deeper relief. Corrine almost imagined they were canyons, a labyrinth she could wander through.

She was astride the kelpie, though she didn't know how he had come to be with her.

We are bound, *the kelpie said into the stillness.* Though a summoning would have been easier than this.

Fog receded, and as the kelpie's hooves ground gravel, she recognized the gazebo from Fearnan's labyrinth. Only it was shaped differently. It arched like a giant canopy over a stone altar or four-poster bed. A stone man lay there, shrouded in stone leaves, sprouting stone death angels. A stone man with the Prince's face.

The kelpie walked to the bed, reared up, and brought his forefeet down by the man's head. His finned hooves struck sparks from the stone. Corrine gasped and clutched at the reins and realized oddly that she had no name for the kelpie, no way of calling out to him to make him stop.

The stone man's eyelids flew open, and Corrine looked down into the Prince's ever-changing eyes.

Say what you will, *the kelpie said to Corrine.*

She hadn't rehearsed anything, and suddenly she longed to ask him about her father, as she'd once asked the hawthorn people. But it was Father Joe who was at issue here. She sat as straight and tall on the kelpie's back as she could.

I have come to assure myself that you will keep your part of the bargain, *she said. The eyes followed her. Whether they were amused or angered, Corrine couldn't tell.*

Show me that Father Joe is alive, *she said. Her gaze strayed to his chest where the rathstone glimmered and throbbed between the stone leaves. Her eardrums vibrated with its irregular rhythm. If she had a weapon, could she bear to cut out the rathstone this time?*

Images of Father Joe subsumed the stone Prince. The priest was alive, though badly beaten, secured to an earthen wall by gnarled roots in some Unhallowed dungeon. He looked as though he had not slept or eaten for weeks.

You will bring him to me whole and undamaged at Beltane, *Corrine said.* Or our bargain is forfeit. *She felt silly, but tried to make her face as hard as she could.*

She nudged the kelpie with her heels then, and he sailed over the stone bed. As the mist closed around them, she thought she heard the Prince whisper, Traitor. *But whether he spoke to her or the kelpie, she was uncertain.*

Corrine's sight gradually cleared until she saw the candle flames, the white stones, and Mara looking at her expectantly across the circle.

"Well?" Mara said.

"I delivered the message," Corrine said. Her body ached as though she'd been riding a horse down a rocky path for days. "Whether he'll heed it or not, I've no idea."

"Did he seem surprised?" Mara asked.

Corrine thought. It had felt as though she had stumbled into something she wasn't supposed to see. She had never seen him so weak and vulnerable, except in the dreams he'd used as lures to ensnare her. In fact, she remembered early dreams when *she* had turned to stone and he had taunted her with her immobility. What had actually been true? Was it all a question of what he made her believe?

"I think he might have been surprised," Corrine said. "And I would guess that he's unhappy about my having seen him in such a fashion." She described his stone tomb as she reached forward and took the signet ring from the center of the circle.

Mara grinned. "I'm sure he was. That's his natural state. He must have drained himself pretty badly with trying to help Rory steal Christina and everything else he's been up to lately."

"Which means—" Corrine began.

"Somebody gonna die soon," Mara said.

Corrine shivered and thought of the Captain's hand slick with blood in the gaslight. Once again, Alex stood with him under the trees as battle raged all around them.

"If he's weak now, why don't we go into the rath and defeat him?" Corrine asked.

"The Council?" Mara said. She slowly began gathering the stones and blowing out the candles.

"No, you and me," Corrine said.

Mara opened her mouth to respond, but a movement at the doorway made them both turn.

Miss Brown emerged from the shadows. Corrine stiffened.

"Because neither of you are ready for that kind of battle yet," Miss Brown said. "No matter what you might think." She leveled a stern gaze at them.

Mara looked as though she would very much like to argue.

Corrine longed to say something about the letter to Miss Brown from her father, but said instead, "You sent me before—"

"And it was very foolish of us. We'll not risk either of you like that again. You're both far too precious."

Mara shook her head in silence.

"Now to bed with both of you," Miss Brown said. "And next time you want to practice your magic, make sure you do it under a room where no one's attempting to sleep."

Corrine blushed and slid past Miss Brown. She met Mara's eyes briefly and hoped the maid deciphered her expression as one of gratitude. She was glad they'd done something, however trivial. The illusion of control was better than none at all.

~Thirteen~

April 30, 1866

A WEEK HAD PASSED SINCE MR. ADAMOU HAD BEEN
thwarted at the door and the message had been sent
to the Prince. Corrine had re-read the letter from her
father so many times she'd lost count. She gritted her
teeth every time she thought of asking Miss Brown
why she had withheld knowledge of this letter. The
Unhallowed hadn't planted it to bring peace and
harmony within the Council, Corrine knew. She tried
to stay focused on the fact that Father Joe was alive
for the moment, that the bargain she'd made would
be upheld. She didn't want to think about what she
would do after the exchange was made. Every time
she considered living with the Prince in his rath, she
forced the thought aside.

Mara's voice came from down the hall, presumably
helping Miss Brown to get dressed. Ilona and Christina
usually helped each other, unless Christina required
more. Corrine threw off the covers in a huff. She needn't
have worried about Christina running away, apparently.
Christina barely managed to get out of bed in the last
week and still refused to speak to Corrine.

Enough, Corrine thought, as the bed creaked and released her. *I have too much else to think about. Tomorrow is the day.* Moments after she'd changed into her chemise, Mara arrived to help her with the rest of it.

"Are you ready for all this?" Mara asked, as if reading her thoughts.

Corrine looked in her eyes and saw what she always did—the swamp, the trailing lianas, the swirling black water. It had become almost comforting. She would miss it.

"I suppose," Corrine said looking down at the buttons on her jacket.

"Wait," Mara said. She put a hand on Corrine's arm. Corrine couldn't ever remember Mara touching her except in the line of service. "What are you up to?" Mara said, her eyes narrowing.

Corrine heard Miss Brown coming down the hall, heard her pause at the door to Christina's room before continuing on downstairs.

"Nothing," Corrine said.

Mara let go of her, and put her hands on her hips. "You done crazy things before. Why do I get the feeling this is no different?"

Corrine looked her in the eyes as well as she could. "We need Father Joe back. I'm doing what I must to make sure that happens."

"Even at the risk of yourself?" Mara asked.

"Do you want to take my place?" Corrine was surprised to see Mara's cheeks flush.

Mara stepped back and looked down at the floor. "There's a reason he wants you in particular, you know. A reason he courts you and not me."

The gainisg's words echoed. *He wants you for his bride.*

"And why I must go into the raths but you won't?" Corrine said, ignoring the bait.

"Because . . ." Mara's gaze rose, and her eyes pleaded with Corrine not to ask. "I just can't. My power is better used here," she muttered.

Was Mara afraid? The thought struck Corrine as odd.

"But what if you have to go into the raths someday?" Corrine asked. "Would you?"

"Only if I have to," Mara said, regaining her usual self-possession. "Don't you be the reason for it."

But Corrine couldn't make that promise.

They heard a commotion of voices downstairs and went toward it. On the way down, Corrine realized that Madame DuBois had come to visit. Siobhan met them halfway up the stairs, frantic for Mara's help, and Mara hurried down to assist her in setting another place for breakfast.

Everyone else was already assembled. Christina talked softly with Madame, and Corrine guessed from the few words she picked up that Madame said something soothing. Miss Brown looked a little pale as she folded a newspaper on the table and dusted the newsprint from her hands.

Madame broke off her conversation with Christina to say, "You saw it, eh?"

"Yes," Miss Brown said.

Ilona's eyes rose from her porridge bowl.

"Two girls murdered in Whitechapel."

"And?" Madame prompted.

"They were drained of all blood," Miss Brown said reluctantly.

"The Prince strikes again," Madame said, as she seated herself.

Mara and Siobhan entered with breakfast. Mara carried a steaming kettle of porridge, and Siobhan set a plate of boiled eggs on the table. Siobhan ladled the porridge out while Mara held the kettle steady.

Corrine felt too sickened to eat. Had they rescued Phyllida and Elizabeth only for two other girls who were less likely to be missed to be taken in their places? Mara certainly had anticipated it. The Prince was strengthening himself for the confrontation to come.

Ilona gave her a dark glance. Corrine guessed she was still suspicious of what had transpired with the Prince in the alley, though Ilona hadn't questioned her about it again. Corrine dropped her eyes to her teacup and the few leaves that floated there. There was only one more day before it was all done. What future could be read in these tea leaves? What would she count as success?

"We must think about tomorrow," Madame said, reaching for a boiled egg and cracking it indelicately on the table. "But more importantly, we must think about tonight." She looked at Corrine as she rolled the egg between her thick fingers before peeling off the skin in a long, segmented curl.

Corrine swallowed. "Tonight?" she squeaked. She cleared her throat.

"Thea and I are of the opinion that we must carry on Father Joe's directive to bring the battle to the Fey. They have very foolishly allowed us right into the heart of their game, counting on ultimate victory, I'm sure. They know we have a rathstone and haven't bothered to try and take it. They're counting on us to be honorable and to keep our word."

Corrine frowned.

"Madame means that perhaps a more . . . aggressive approach to the situation would assure us greater success," Miss Brown said.

"What does that mean?" Ilona asked.

"That we take the Stone tonight, and leave a false stone in its place," Madame said. "So that when we take it to them tomorrow to exchange for Father Joe, they won't know that we've given them a fake until after the fact."

"But—" Corrine started to protest. Madame interrupted her, turning to Mara, who stood listening near the doorway.

"You have the necessary ingredients for the spell?"

Mara nodded slowly. "But it's going to be hard, making an illusion for a three hundred pound rock last that long."

"Surely, with Corrine's powers unbound . . ." Madame said, digging the egg apart and popping the yolk in her mouth.

"I—" Corrine tried again and failed.

Mara met her eyes. "Maybe, if we do it just right." Corrine didn't miss the implicit challenge, or the warning.

"But how are we to carry the stone out of the abbey by ourselves?" Ilona asked.

Christina pushed the dregs of her porridge around with her spoon and sighed.

"That is a problem," Miss Brown owned. "We thought perhaps you could hire some men with a cart to help us, Ilona. Men who know how to be discreet."

"Or . . ." Madame began, turning finally to Corrine, "we could use the kelpie. Maybe he would consent to carry it for us? In that way, we wouldn't have to run the risk of spies by involving other people in our plans. What do you say?"

Corrine felt uncomfortable. "I suppose I could ask. Though I'm not really sure how."

China shattered. Silverware scattered across the table. Christina convulsed and swept her place setting off the table as she fell onto the floor. Ilona leaped toward her, pulling a chair out of the way.

Corrine ran with the others around the table, though it was like running through molasses to get there. Christina shuddered, her eyes rolling back.

"They're getting worse," Madame whispered.

Christina's face shifted, took on lines familiar to Corrine.

"Brighde," Corrine breathed.

"You are all fools," the ghost said through Christina's mouth. "You will fall into his trap because you did not heed my warnings. He is coming. And you sit here like a bunch of clucking hens . . ." Her voice trailed into unintelligible Gaelic.

"What do you *expect* us to do?" Corrine asked, gripping Christina's shoulders. "Tell me a better way!"

Christina bucked and groaned. Ilona held her down as well as she could until the shudders ceased.

"Take her upstairs and put her to bed," Miss Brown said. Corrine shied from the look in the headmistress's eyes.

Mara and Ilona struggled to manage Christina and all

227

her skirts between them as they carried her from the room. Siobhan scurried to pick up the broken china and scattered silverware. Spilled tea dripped from the tablecloth.

Miss Brown turned to Madame who stood with her hands curled around the back of a chair, staring into the middle distance. "What are we to do, Maud?"

"I still say we strike first. They stand to gain two stones! This way, it's to be hoped they'll only gain one. And perhaps not even that, eh?" She said, forcing a smile and wink at Corrine.

Corrine nodded, but Brighde's warning had set her insides fluttering. She had seen Brighde agitated, but not so angry, not so terribly disturbed that she would cause Christina such harm. It was no wonder that Christina wanted to flee with Rory, especially if he had promised her freedom from these horrible fits.

"And how will they know the difference until it's too late?" Madame said, clearly enlivened by her own cleverness. "They can't feel the stones as the Half-Born or the Hallowed can. To them it's just another stone unless someone tells them differently."

Or the magic works, Corrine thought. But she kept silent. The more she spoke, the more she felt in danger of losing her control, a precious control she'd built since the alley encounter. The letter from her father had set her dangerously on edge, but she wouldn't rise to the goad. She walked an edge fine as a sword. She feared to tip too far one way or the other.

"Don't you think they'll expect this sort of thing from us now?" Miss Brown said. "We did send Corrine into the rath in disguise. Surely, they'll suspect us of similar trickery."

Madame waved a hand at her. "Pish tosh. They will expect us to be chagrined over the last time and do it properly."

Miss Brown's expression hardened.

"Look," Madame said, moving to take Miss Brown's hand, "let us just go tonight and see how things go. Consider it a trial run, no? If it doesn't work out, we'll do things by the book tomorrow." She patted Miss Brown's hand.

Miss Brown looked at her dubiously. "I suppose it couldn't hurt to just see . . ."

"There you are," Madame said, smiling. She released Miss Brown's hand and turned to Corrine. "Now, Thea and I will go to see how Christina is faring. You should make ready to play your part tonight, if it comes to that."

Corrine nodded. From the look in Miss Brown's eyes, Corrine gathered that she was not to further upset Christina by going to see her.

She went into the morning room instead. As she opened the writing case, she wished again that she still had the Unhallowed book. Miss Brown hadn't said anything about finding it, so Corrine guessed it wasn't to be found, and she wasn't about to press any issues with Miss Brown under the circumstances. But she couldn't help thinking that the book could perhaps hold some spell or charm that would free Brighde. Or perhaps she might be able to understand why Brighde was so terrified of the Prince. What else could the Unhallowed do to souls besides keeping them from moving on?

Corrine sat back as far as the stiff chair would allow her and closed her eyes. She took the five summoning breaths and glided over the ocean into the sun. She found the kelpie in the garden, wandering among the hollyhocks, lipping at them disconsolately. He turned a milky eye on her as she approached. The reins were knotted on his withers; she grasped the nearest one.

He snorted. "Nothing to eat," he said. "Except flowers and grass. Give me bones and blood. Give me skin and teeth and hair." The magic in the garden gathered around him in pulsing green waves.

Corrine pulled the rein tighter until he was forced to look her in the eye. "None of that," she said firmly, trying to keep her voice even. The magic drained away.

The kelpie sighed. "You starve me unto death, Half-Born. Tempting me with your pretty flesh and fairy eye."

Corrine yanked the rein. "Behave. Or I'll give you to the Prince. And I don't think you want that, do you?"

The kelpie's eye went red, a bloody, angry red that made Corrine wonder if she'd overestimated her ability to hold him. The sky darkened; clouds boiled over a scarlet sun. She pulled the rein as hard as she could, until his head was pulled all the way around. She concentrated on the clouds, turning them soft and gray as cygnets. Rain slicked the kelpie's clammy sides and ran in silver rivulets down Corrine's face.

The kelpie's eye dimmed, and his lips drew back in what passed for a smile.

"Very good," he said.

"You were testing me." Corrine released the rein, and he shook water out of his mane.

"Of course. The Treasures must know their choice is well-made. They have failed before, you know."

Corrine shook her head. She hadn't known that. She led him over to a convenient rock and climbed onto his back, her wet dress crawling up her calf. The kelpie gazed hungrily at her bare flesh, and she tried to hitch her chemise as far down as she could.

"Sorry," she murmured. "Shall we?"

Without a word, he went straight into a trot. He didn't slow when they reached the well and leaped straight in. Corrine dissolved into raindrops, raindrops that fell up instead of down. At last, they were swimming upwards toward the surface of the tropical sea, and the kelpie hauled them out on white shore.

The mountain brooded before them, its crown ringed by cloud. Its sides were white with snow.

Corrine sighed. "I don't know if I can do that yet."

The kelpie extended his foreleg and rubbed his head along it as if the bridle itched. "You must try. Time flees."

"Why is it so important?" Corrine asked.

"Because you cannot open Hallowmere until you've mastered all the domains," the kelpie said, lifting his head. "The gate to Hallowmere is beyond the last domain—the domain of spirit. We who are without souls cannot enter the domain of spirit, but you can. My brethren know this. That is why the Prince hopes to win you to his side before your skills are at their sharpest. The Treas Ulaidh know this too."

Three gulls flew overhead, wailing as they went. Corrine was reminded of the three ravens at Fearnan.

"Then why did they try to keep me from learning the magic?" Corrine asked.

The kelpie grinned. "They were in the midst of a bargain. Until they could be sure of it, they couldn't be sure of you. So they watched and they tested. It is their way."

I'm not so sure I like their way, Corrine thought.

She urged him onward, up the silver dune trail. She half-expected to see Brunel and the other ghosts, but she imagined they had long since departed, released by the expiation of her guilt.

"Why do the Hallowed not make bargains or attempt to aid us very often?" This had often bothered Corrine, but she had been afraid to ask Father Joe or Miss Brown. The Council perceived any questioning of its motives as an attempt to undermine it. However, Corrine couldn't help wondering about the mysterious Elaphe and the Hallowed who allied with him.

The kelpie wheezed with laughter. It was an unpleasant sound, like overworked rusty springs. "The Hallowed are far too weak. Many of them have faded into nothing. Many are mad. The few who remain keep to themselves, waiting for salvation."

Corrine detected derision in his voice.

"But," he said, "ask for what you came to ask."

The mountain loomed closer than it had seemed on the shore. They were already in the foothills. Corrine tried to guess at its height, but the mountain's shoulders were lost in cloud.

Fear stiffened Corrine's spine, but she distracted herself by talking. "You know what we need," she said. "Will you help us with the Stone of Destiny? Can you carry it and hide it until I call for you again?"

"I can," the kelpie said. "But how do you know I will not betray you and take it to the Prince?"

"Because you won't," Corrine said. "You helped

us of your own accord when Rory would have taken Christina."

"Might I not have done that just to win your trust?" the kelpie asked.

Corrine gritted her teeth. The kelpie's hooves struck sparks from the strange mountain stones. Corrine tried to ignore a low, distant rumble.

"You must learn to decipher who is false and who is not. You must learn to anticipate your enemy's moves, as in a chess game," the kelpie said. "Otherwise, you will never win."

"Mm," Corrine grunted. She didn't know what he wanted her to say.

"There is one . . . difficulty, though," the kelpie said, pausing at cliff's edge to catch his breath. The sea beckoned with its blue depths. The breath of the mountain was cold. Corrine shivered in her wet clothes.

"Yes?" she said.

"I cannot enter the church. It is Hallowed ground."

Corrine remembered the Prince's anger when she suggested that he take the Stone of Destiny for himself.

"So what should we do?" she asked.

"Bring it outside. If you can get it out of the gate and summon me, then I can help you."

Corrine sighed. She had no idea how they would carry such a heavy stone between all of them. Unless she somehow developed the ability to render things weightless.

The rumbling increased, followed by tremors that crept up the kelpie's legs and into Corrine's limbs. The kelpie's hooves rang on the rocks.

"What is that?" she whispered.

"The earth spirits are offended by my presence," the

kelpie said. "I am a child of water, after all."

He walked a little farther before he snorted and stopped, bowing his head. "You must dismount and go to the peak alone," he said.

Corrine looked up the trail. Jagged boulders leered along the path, and the end, she was certain, was white with snow. She waited, hoping perhaps the kelpie was wrong.

But the rumbling grew stronger. The kelpie stomped his foot, and Corrine slid off. The mountain air sliced through her wet clothes.

"I will wait for you at the shore," the kelpie said. "Take a bit of my mane and think of me. It will return you to me, whatever befalls."

Corrine put her fingers in one of the knots, careful to avoid any bones, and tugged. She clenched her teeth against hurting him, but the knot came into her hand easily. She closed her fist around the curl of horsehair.

She wished for shoes or boy's clothes but though Father Joe had always said the domains were in her mind, she couldn't seem to wish just anything she wanted into being. She turned. The kelpie was gone.

Corrine wasn't sure how long she walked or when the stone became snow. She refused to think of the terrifying dream of the Prince finding her on the mountainside, of the Three Treasures urging her to silence. Soon, though, it was night, and she stood at the summit, her feet torn and frozen, the hem of her dress heavy with ice.

The stars led her between echoing pylons of rock until she came to a ring of stones surrounding a cave. She waited a long while, listening to the starlight chiming against granite, wondering if the fanged entrance with its glittering pool would appear. Rocks tumbled and echoed behind her. Corrine turned to see a great black shadow stretching behind her, drinking the stars. As it boiled toward her, instinct forced her into the cave like a rabbit diving for cover.

Outside, the black storm swallowed the mountain. Corrine sat in a lodge made of earth before a pit of crackling stones. Someone tossed water on them, and the stones sizzled and sparked. The light revealed his face for a moment. Only when she recoiled did she realize that her clothes had disappeared. All that she possessed was the knot of kelpie hair, which she bound tightly around her shaking wrist.

She scrabbled toward an entrance, but there was no door.

"Go away," she said.

"I have watched you since your birth," the Prince said. "The skin is the dress of your spirit. You must accept it, if you are to pass to the next domain."

"You should not be here," Corrine said. She dug against the walls of the lodge frantically, but they shrank, until she was forced to sit toe to toe with the Prince. She tried to cover herself with her hair as best she could.

The Prince threw more water on the rocks, wreathing them both in steam.

"Now," he said. "It is time."

He leaned forward, as if to kiss. There was nowhere to go. A thicket of thorns erupted from his mouth.

Corrine felt her body dividing itself in a scream of pain. She touched her wrist with her fingers before they melted away, and suddenly, she was gasping in the blue tide with the kelpie standing over her.

She looked down quickly and saw to her relief that she was not only whole but clothed.

The kelpie looked at her, worms of witch-light flaring in his eyes. "You failed," he said.

"The Prince——" she began.

A dark cloud careened toward them across the dunes. The kelpie scented the breeze that swept ahead of it.

"Let us be away," the kelpie said. "Put your hand in my mane." Corrine struggled to stand, and almost before she'd gotten a good hold, her vision blurred silver, blue, green, and gold. The next moment, she sat alone in the chair in the morning room, inhaling deeply as though she hadn't breathed for the last hour. Dizziness drowned her such that she feared to move. The kelpie, of course, was nowhere to be seen. The thought of the Prince and the domain of earth nearly shuddered her flesh from her bones.

That evening, Corrine, Mara, Madame, and Miss Brown sat through the vespers service at Westminster Abbey. Corrine only half-listened to the Anglican priest droning out the service. She was more concerned with the veil that hung over her face and the too-loose mourning dress that Mara had attempted to cinch together with pins. It had belonged to Madame, the mourning clothes she'd worn for the year after her husband died. She thought queasily of how she had looked in the mirror before they'd left the townhouse—like one of the Three Treasures in their long veils and trailing dresses. Corrine had wanted to tear off the veil and dress and run away somewhere to hide. But she couldn't. The strictures of her bargain with the Prince were tighter than her corset. And there was nowhere to hide from him, not even, apparently, in her own mind.

Everyone else was scattered among the pews around the quire. Madame had thought it better if they entered and stayed separate from one another. Madame and Miss Brown were at opposite ends of a pew, and Mara was higher up, wearing mourning like Corrine. Ilona and Siobhan had stayed at the townhouse with Christina, and Corrine hoped that nothing would befall them as they waited alone.

This is just the rehearsal, Corrine kept trying to tell herself. But if they were caught, not just by the Unhallowed but by the priests of the abbey . . . Corrine shook her head. Originally, Father Joe had planned to pose as an Anglican priest and infiltrate Westminster, smoothing the way for their eventual theft of the Stone of Destiny. He had never had the chance. Corrine looked at the stained glass windows through the shadows of her veil, wondering how they would fare without him. Madame seemed too boldly confident in their ability to outwit the Unhallowed. Soon, none of it would matter.

After the service, everyone slowly wandered off to find a hiding place. "Nap, if you can," Miss Brown had said. "And at the stroke of midnight, meet in St. Edward's Chapel by the Coronation Chair. You'll see it. But you'll probably feel it first."

The problem was, though, that she had felt and heard nothing since entering the abbey. Generally, if a rathstone was present, she could hear its song, feel the vibration of its power. Not this time. She wondered if that had anything to do with the heavy parure pendant that was clasped over the locket and signet ring. Perhaps two rathstones in the same space cancelled one another out? Corrine wasn't sure.

She wandered out of the quire into the south ambulatory. The great rose window threw fading rainbows across her dark-clad arms. She wanted to push back the veil and look more closely at the incredible artistry in the abbey—every surface, it seemed, was covered with paintings, frescos, or mosaic work. Statues, memorials, and ornately built tombs were shoved into every possible crevice. The memorial to Lord and Lady Fane, with its gilded columns and ornately-carved angels particularly entranced her. She wished that she were here not on pretense, but truly to study and learn. She had forgotten that there was even such a thing as normal existence, a life which did not involve magic or the Unhallowed or the battle for Hallowmere.

Corrine paused in the Chapel of St. Faith, where the masculine-looking saint held a bible in one hand and what looked like a grill in the other.

"That is the gridiron on which the saint was roasted alive," a voice said beside her.

Corrine started. She was more shocked to see a priest beside her than she would have been to see some Fey creature. He wore the white collar and black shirt and trousers of a priest, but he didn't look familiar from the service.

"Oh," she said.

"It takes great faith and courage to undergo such trials," the priest said, looking at the painting.

"Yes," Corrine said.

"Whatever trials you suffer, my child, be assured that

God will see you through," the priest said. "Even as St. Faith suffered and entered Paradise."

"Yes," Corrine said. She suppressed a shudder. *I hope it doesn't come to that.*

"May your prayers be answered," the priest said, bowing his head. He moved on before she could thank him.

As daylight was replaced by candlelight, Corrine knew she needed to find a hiding place before the abbey closed. She had only briefly seen the others from a distance, walking down the nave or kneeling in a side chapel. She didn't know if they were already hiding or where they might be.

As she crossed into the north transept, she searched in earnest, sure at any moment a priest or acolyte would catch her and escort her out. There were many tombs and monuments here, and Edward the Confessor's chapel was close. She halted. Many of the tombs she'd seen were morbid, but this was the most gruesome she'd ever seen. In a corner behind the monument to General James Wolfe, skeletal Death crept out of the tomb, poised to strike a woman whose husband attempted vainly to protect her. Corrine went closer. The tomb belonged to Lady Elizabeth Nightingale, and just beside it was another tomb with a gap big enough for Corrine to hide unnoticed between the tomb and the wall.

She looked around, then crept between tomb and wall, rustling a little due to her bulky dress. But no one came to investigate. The cramped conditions reminded her a little of the domain of earth, and she pressed her face against the marble to keep from remembering. Her stomach growled, and she wished she had considered bringing something to eat. It would be a long wait.

Corrine woke, not to the sounds of a bell tolling, but to screaming. The screams were indecipherable, but they echoed from the quire, accompanied by the pounding of feet and drawing of swords. She pushed her veil back and crawled toward the edge of the tomb. She peered around the corner toward the quire. Ghostly forms flickered across the entrance. A lone voice pleaded and babbled in a tongue she could barely decipher. Another, sterner voice joined in. "This is the House of the Lord!" the second voice cried. Then there was a deep, liquid thwack and an ominous silence. Corrine shrank behind the tomb. The bell tolled; her insides vibrated in time with its deep voice.

She was about to creep out from her hiding place when a creaking noise drew her attention to Lady Nightingale's tomb. She would have sworn for a moment that she saw Death reposition his fingers on his spear. She shook her head. "Stop imagining things," she muttered to herself.

Then, Death turned his head entirely and grinned at her.

Corrine gasped and shuffled backwards until she crawled out from behind the tomb on the other side. She could see the skeleton peering into the shadows behind the tomb after her.

She hauled herself to her feet and ran. The thin moonlight and few glowing candles guided her through the transept. The eyes of sleeping kings and queens flew open as she passed, their stone lips whispering, *Fairy girl.*

Some of the statues began climbing down from their pedestals after her. She looked back and saw that Death still stalked her, sometimes crawling on all fours like a dog, his spear clenched in his skeletal teeth.

She touched the heavy rathstone about her neck, wishing she could open a gate and escape, wondering what would happen when she finally reached the chapel. She looked over her shoulder and just barely looked ahead in time to avoid crashing into Madame.

"Corrine," she whispered, taking her by the elbows, "it is all right. The chapel is here."

"But, they're coming!" Corrine gasped. "The statues, Death—"

Madame frowned, peering behind Corrine. "I see nothing," she said.

Corrine swiveled. The corridor behind her was empty. The statues were still. Only shadows cast by the sparse candlelight moved.

"Come," Madame said, pulling her firmly into the chapel.

Madame ushered her past the tombs of kings and queens with barely a glance in their direction. Corrine saw flaking gilt, handless statues, chipped mosaic. Everything here was older and more disheveled than the rest of the abbey, ravaged by the hands of relic seekers and time.

Mara and Miss Brown waited by a scarred wooden throne—Edward the Confessor's coronation chair. Beneath the seat rested a square slab of unremarkable stone, its placement obvious proof of the English monarch's disdain for his Scottish enemies.

"Well," Madame said, as she huffed up to them,

"let's begin. Summon the kelpie and let's get this back to Fearnan!" Echoes of her voice flitted like bats around the chapel.

Corrine opened her mouth to speak, but Mara beat her to the punch.

"No use," Mara said.

"What do you mean?" Madame said, her brows knitting.

Mara gestured. "That isn't the real Stone of Destiny."

So. Corrine thought. And then she shuddered. Did the Prince have it already?

"What do you mean?" Madame said. She stepped forward and put her hand on the stone, as if she could determine its authenticity.

Mara turned to Corrine. "Do you feel it?" she asked, as if she hadn't heard Madame's question.

Corrine shook her head. "I thought it was just because of the stone I'm wearing," she said.

"No," Mara said. "You'd feel a real stone, no matter how many you had on you. This one ain't it."

Madame and Miss Brown exchanged glances. Corrine could almost hear their thoughts echoing her own. *Does he already have it?* and *What shall we do?*

Something rattled at the chapel entrance. Corrine glanced back.

Death grinned and shook his spear.

Corrine stepped closer to the others, who didn't seem to notice the skeleton at all.

"All that way for nothing," Miss Brown said. "And Joseph—" She covered her mouth with her hand. But instead of Father Joe, Corrine saw in her mind's eye the photo that had once rested on Miss Brown's desk at Falston. The photo that she had once thought was Miss Brown's brother, Alex. But her father's letter had confirmed her suspicions. Not Alex, but Alexandra, who had met the Captain at the edge of the battlefield.

Miss Brown looked at her sharply as though she knew what she'd seen and dropped her hand. "Well," she said. "There is nothing more we can do here. We may as well return to Primrose Hill. Either we give them the stone Corrine is carrying tomorrow night or we risk angering them by handing them an illusion of the Stone of Destiny." She sighed. "Then, it's back to the drawing board at Fearnan, I suppose."

Nods went round the circle in agreement.

A shock vibrated the air, like the concussion of a cannonball exploding far away.

"What the . . ." Miss Brown stepped forward.

A wall of sound froze Corrine's heart. The statues and tombs crumbled; the stained glass rained like blood from its casements. The walls rippled.

Corrine blinked. Everything was still in place, but the chorus of sound, like a thousand wailing bobcats, went on unabated.

"Haints," Mara said through stiff lips. "He's brought haints."

"The *Bean Sidhe*," Miss Brown said.

"Banshees," Madame said.

Corrine could barely hear. Before she could ask what they meant, the horror of the name crept through her body. Every muscle contorted, jerking her toward the entrance to the chapel, but she resisted it. The others walked forward in painful, involuntary spasms.

Mara clutched at her vainly as she passed. "Corrine," she said with gritted teeth. The sound drowned her voice. Corrine clutched at Mara but the strong girl pulled away even while she tried to resist the wail of the banshees.

Corrine watched them jig and stutter out of the chapel, out of sight. Death grinned as they passed.

She heard the great doors crash open.

And then she heard him whispering, just as she had in the alley, his lips like butterfly feet against her ear. "You made a bargain with me, Corrine. And if you do not come to me now, I will fulfill my promise."

Visions flashed, not only of Miss Brown, Mara, and Madame struggling to stop themselves from leaving the abbey, but of the townhouse—Siobhan, Ilona, and Christina huddling in a circle of weak candlelight while the Unhallowed crept ever closer. No banshees wailed there, but Corrine knew they would not be far behind if she didn't accept her fate.

Corrine walked. She walked past grinning Death, through the swirling ghosts of the quire, past the kings and poets who whispered through their marble lips, *Fairy girl.*

No one—not a night watchman or priest, statue or ghost—impeded her progress. Even the candle flames went tall and still as she strode past.

Outside on the portico, Mara, Miss Brown, and Madame huddled in a sweating heap, trying desperately to hold to something, anything that would save them from leaving the abbey's sacred ground.

The Unhallowed waited beyond the iron gate in the shadows. Something heavy constricted Corrine's throat. The banshee song ceased. Corrine surveyed all of them assembled there under the thin fingernail of the moon.

"For love is strong as death, and jealousy is cruel as the grave," the Prince said. His voice carried up the rise to her, all velvet assurance.

Corrine went to the gate. She saw the Unhallowed faces, each wooden bow, each masked smile.

"Corrine, don't!" Father Joe's voice was faint; he spoke through bruised lips. "Corrine, don't come out of the gate. You're safe there. Don't give him anything. Don't . . ." A satyr guard cuffed him across the face.

Corrine looked at the Prince, anger warring with defeat in her heart. She refused to think of her failure in the domain of earth.

"Corrine, come to me," he said.

Corrine's fingers loitered on the gate, the sting of iron subsuming her feelings. She opened the gate and stepped through, putting her hand in his. "I have fulfilled my part," she said, anger grinding her voice almost to a whisper. "Now fulfill yours."

The Unhallowed roared. The satyr guards unbound Father Joe and pitched him high over the fence.

Then the Prince enfolded her in his arms. His kiss sealed her lips like a brand.

~Fourteen~

Beltane 1866

THEY HAD BEEN ON THE WOLF-DRAWN SLEDGE FOR DAYS. The snow chimed like crystalline bells as it fell. Corrine listened as she snuggled under the warm, heavy furs with her Prince. He held her, the fur drawn up almost over her face to keep her warm. She listened to the irregular thud of his heart through his jacket. He smelled of leather and fur, but there were fainter scents—myrrh, blood, the whiff of the grave.

She sat up straighter so that she could see the backs of the white wolves as they leaped in their traces.

"We'll soon be home, my love," he murmured.

She looked into his face. Visions flashed—a beaten man, a murdered girl, a boy torn apart by wolves, and then a series of faces that she was sure she had once known and loved—but he touched her cheek and they stopped. She smiled. He always knew how to take the pain away.

"Tell me again how I came here," she said. She loved hearing how her Prince had found her.

"For a long time, I spoke to you in dreams." He brushed her hair from her face. "I was very ill and weak,

246

but I knew you were alone and frightened. I tried to soothe you, but you could not hear me."

She sighed. She admitted to herself that she didn't really like this first part. But the end made it all worth it.

"It became even worse when you fell in with some evil witches who wanted to keep you from me. They were keeping the stone that would heal me."

"Why?" she asked, as she always did.

"I don't know, my love." He slitted his eyes against the snow. "For some reason, they didn't want me to have it."

"That was unkind," she said.

"And?" he said, raising a brow.

"I felt their unkindness and I brought the stone to you to make you well." She smiled up at him. His hazel eyes reflected the whirling snowflakes. She saw herself dancing there among them—her golden hair unbound, her eyes greener than spring.

"Yes," he said. "But you still feared me; you still believed what the naughty witches had said. You continued to listen to them and for a while you even shut me out of your dreams. So, I came to you in disguise. I protected you on a voyage across the sea and kept you from harm under the eyes of the witches. And on your birth-night, I came and danced with you. And still you would not come to me."

The thought that he had done so much while she had done so little saddened her.

"You closed the rathgate against me, and the witches fled with you to that horrible city they call London. And you and your friends fought me—all because the witches had made you believe that I wanted to hurt you or use you for some horrible purpose. At last, I decided that the only way to rescue you was to force you to come with me. I stole one of the witches who had most carefully enspelled you, and told you that to have him back, you must bring me another stone in exchange. But when you came to the gate of the place where you were hiding, you saw me. And, at last, you knew me. You came to me of your own sweet will, and in your deep kindness, despite all he'd done to you, you released the witch back to his coven."

"And now?" Corrine said.

"And now we are traveling to my old palace to meet my aunt, who is a most gifted physician. She will help speed your recovery far better than I can alone. And I hope, when you are fully mended that you will at last say yes."

She ducked and hid her face against his shirt before he could force her to look in his eyes. Her face burned despite the cold. He always ended the story with the same hope, the same question. She had never yet found the courage to answer him. *Why would he want me?* she wondered. There were many other beautiful, more accomplished women in his court. They all sought his favor. But he had eyes only for her.

She pretended to drowse against him, burying herself in his embrace so she could push away the darker questions that lurked at the corners of her mind. The witches were bad; they had made her very ill and had made her believe horrible things. The Prince had said so. He had rescued her. There was no reason for her to ever have to go back to the witches again. But the visions, insubstantial as they were, haunted her.

He stroked her hair until the visions receded again. He was ever gentle, her Prince. He never forced or pushed. That was not his way.

Corrine woke just as they arrived at the palace in the eternal twilight of the Prince's rath. She shook off shreds of disturbing dreams as the Prince helped her down and the hob seneschal swept his long fingers before her in a courtly bow. She leaned on the Prince, her legs trembling with the effort of standing on her own. The witches had made her very ill, and she could still feel it in her bones.

The Prince's aunt came toward them through the snow, surrounded by bird-footed courtiers in green robes. Her hair flamed golden above her ermine-trimmed cape. She held out a welcoming cup of jet and ivory in her long fingers. Corrine looked into the lady's amber eyes and trembled. There was something about her that Corrine knew she should remember, but she wasn't sure what.

"Aunt," the Prince said. "I thank you for this welcome." He looked at Corrine and gestured toward her. "Corrine, I present my aunt and the court's best physician, Lady Thornvane."

Corrine smiled hesitantly at Lady Thornvane.

The woman looked at Corrine and frowned. "What have you done, my lord?"

The world wavered and blackened at the corners. Lady Thornvane became a mass of gnarled thorns constricting around a rotting heart.

Corrine recoiled, reeling on her feet. The Prince steadied her with his arm around her waist.

"All is well, Aunt," he said. A glance flashed between them that Corrine couldn't read. "Do you not wish to welcome your future niece?"

The lady's brow raised. "She has accepted you, has she?"

The amber eyes swung to Corrine, and Corrine clutched at the Prince's hand.

"Not yet," the Prince said. "But perhaps in time, when you have made her well."

Corrine blushed furiously.

The Prince's aunt grunted and pushed the cup against Corrine's lips so that it knocked against her teeth. Corrine glanced up as she drank the dark, spiced wine. Lady Thornvane's mouth curved into a vicious smile.

When Corrine was done, the lady drank.

"Perhaps you are right," she said. "Welcome to both of you." She bowed then, and turned back to the castle.

Corrine took a few wobbly steps forward and nearly fell.

"Shall I carry you?" the Prince asked.

Corrine shook her head and walked forward, hoping she looked more steady than she felt.

Corrine and the Prince followed his aunt and her entourage through many corridors, up curving flights of stairs beneath frescoed domes. Holly and ivy grew along the banisters, and mistletoe hung from the tiled ceilings. Corrine remembered something about mistletoe, something nice from that horrible London place. She caught her breath under a great swatch of it. She stopped the Prince while he was on the step below her. She took his face between her hands and kissed him.

His lips were cool and soft. His skin prickled under her fingertips. She drew back, smiling.

He swept her into his arms and carried her up the stairs. "Why," he whispered in her ear, "did you never come to me before?"

She tried to answer, but the reason escaped her. There was no reason. The witches must have kept her from it. Like witches in a fairytale, keeping the princess locked in their tower for no good reason except that it made a story. Now she was free. And she would never go back again.

Though the rest of the rath was gripped in winter, the Prince's gardens were green and warm. A black wall girdled the garden in a great circle, and the wind and snow howled against it in vain. The Prince's guards carried Corrine to the garden and laid her in a bower of hellebore and nightshade. The bell-shaped flowers hung over her and breathed their soporific scent on her cheeks. She was half asleep when she realized her Prince stood over her. A brush of those horrid dreams eclipsed her joy for only a moment. But when she opened her eyes fully, he stood waiting, bearing a tray like a serving man. Blushing, she pushed herself upright, bending the hellebore stems in her haste.

"Your medicine, with my aunt's compliments," the Prince said. He set the tray at her side. A thick, dark smell rose from one of the clay cups.

"My lord, you should not have—" she said.

He put a hand over her lips. "It is mine to do. I would have you well before I must leave you."

"Leave me?" Her fingers halted on the cover of the clay pot. She looked into his eyes and felt she might weep.

"I am sorry," he said, casting his gaze down onto the crushed flowers at her feet. "I should have waited to tell you." He plucked a bit of vine from a nearby bush, and Corrine watched a dark rose blossom between his fingertips. He held it toward her, and its petals gave off a mysterious spice more compelling even than the nightshade. "Do not be troubled. Take your medicine, my dear, and we will talk."

Corrine reached for the bowl, but a movement off among some blossoming trees caught her attention. A woman stood watching her, a woman whose feline smile looked so familiar that Corrine gasped. She knew she had seen that heavy golden chignon before, that dark, compelling gaze.

"Corrine," the Prince said. His voice had gained an edge. The black petals caressed her cheek. "Drink up now. I hear on good authority that it's quite awful when it's cold."

Corrine dropped her gaze to the bowl brimming with dark fluid. She drank as quickly as she could bear, trying to ignore the congealing texture and metallic taste. She wiped her mouth with linen.

The Prince smiled. He took her hand and helped her to rise. The medicine sent new vitality through her limbs, but it couldn't quell her sadness at the thought of his going.

"You're leaving me?" she said. Tears filled her eyes and rushed down her cheeks, making dark stains on her dress and the ground.

Dark tears fell from his eyes like smoke. "My dearest, would that I did not have to! But the witches, they will stop at nothing to have you back. They fear your power."

"You are leaving to protect me?" Corrine asked, watching his tears wreathe him in mist. She reached forward to dry them with an edge of her sleeve and he clasped her wrist, entwining his fingers with hers.

"You know I don't want to leave you," he said. "But perhaps when I return, you will at last be well enough."

"Well enough?" she said. She knew she was being coy and she didn't care.

"Well enough to say yes," he said, drawing her into his arms. "I have been so lonely, Corrine. I have waited so long for you. Surely now that we are together . . ."

She put her head against his chest and listened to the faint singing of his heart. Before now, she had always put him off. It was not because she was shy or even because she didn't love him. Sometimes her heart seemed near to bursting with love for him; sometimes it seemed her heart would tear itself into pieces. But there was something not quite right, something not . . . She looked past his shoulder. The woman was there again, gathering herbs under the blossoming trees. She glanced up at Corrine and the Prince and shook her head. Corrine remembered where she'd seen her face—a portrait, a metal-embossed trunk. The woman moved away.

Corrine started and broke the Prince's hold. "Wait!" she said.

The Prince's grip tightened on her wrist and he pulled her back to him. "Forget about her," he said, his eyes darkening. He put a palm over her forehead and frowned. "Your fever is rising again. Let us get you back to your bed." He called a cloak out of the air and wrapped it around her, then lifted her and carried her from the

253

garden. She looked back over his shoulder, searching for the strange woman, until he cradled her head against his chest to shield her from the cold.

A black girl stood in her room. Corrine didn't find her skin color particularly perplexing—many of the Prince's subjects had dark skin—but it was the fact that she had suddenly appeared during the sleeping time at the foot of Corrine's bed. And now, she was standing next to Corrine, with her hands on her hips and her eyes full of lightning.

"What the hell are you doing?" the girl said. She drifted, as if her image were a bit of paper blowing in the wind.

"Sleeping," Corrine said. "Why are you in my room?"

"Listen," the girl said more urgently, "do you know who you are?"

Corrine frowned. "I'm Corrine. Who are you?"

"Mara. Don't you remember me?" The girl came closer as if to touch her, but Corrine shrank deeper into the furs and silks.

"I don't know who you are. And if the Prince knew you were bothering me . . ." She looked toward the door where the satyr guards lurked outside.

"Corrine, he took you from us. He's got you under a powerful spell. Father Joe says whatever you do, you *must not* marry him, do you hear?" The girl's expression was strained, as though any moment she might be forced to vanish.

"Who is Father Joe? And why would he care who I marry?" Corrine said.

"You know damn well who Father Joe is!" Mara said in exasperation. "Get your head out of your—" She stopped and sighed. "Look, I can't stay much longer. Just try to remember. We're trying to get you out, but you can also use the rathstone to come back to us, you know."

"I don't know what you mean," Corrine said.

"The one you got from . . . Oh, there's no time to explain. Just try to come back to us. And we'll keep trying to help you, all right?" The girl flickered, and then her image faded like a stain on the air.

"I don't need help," Corrine said to no one.

But she was disturbed, nonetheless, and couldn't go back to sleep. She threw off the bedclothes and stood barefoot beside the bed. The palace wasn't particularly hot or cold, and the shades were drawn over all the windows to keep out the eternal gloom. Usually one of the nixes or bird-footed women came to wake her and help her dress, but she guessed by the clock it was still far too early. It was only the thirteenth hour.

The Prince sent her to bed around the tenth hour, often with a cup of warm, spiced wine to help her sleep. Everything always had the same metallic taste for which he apologized. "My vineyards have suffered in your absence," he said, "but now with your presence they will find renewed vigor." So sweet he was that he thought even the vineyards of his rath would adore her as he did.

She stood at the door, disturbed. She wanted to speak to him and tell him what the black girl had said. She wanted to be comforted by him, to let him take away the peculiar familiarity that crawled across her scalp when the girl spoke. She had said she didn't know the girl, but she did. She just didn't know how.

The Prince would probably tell her it was just a disturbing memory of the witches. They had tormented her and her mind still hadn't quite let go of being under their spell, he had said once. But the way Mara spoke hadn't felt like the words of a tormenter. It had felt like someone who had known her a long time. Someone who was maybe a little *too* familiar with her. The room fragmented, and this time she saw a great tree-lord moving through the marsh, walking until he saw the giant bud of a water lily pushing through the black water. The bud was swollen and almost painfully scarlet, so brilliant it seared Corrine's inner sight. The tree-lord lingered over the bud for several moments before he moved on.

Shaking, Corrine leaned against the wall near the door. Who were these people? What did all these visions mean?

She banged on the door. One of the satyrs opened it. His goat-lipped smile looked more like a sneer; his horns curved backwards into his shaggy hair.

"Mistress wishes?" His little tail twitched as he bowed.

Distant music trailed up the stairs, music that Corrine hadn't heard when the door was closed.

"I need to see my Prince," Corrine said.

"I'm afraid you mustn't leave your room now, Mistress," the other guard said.

"But I want to see him," Corrine said. She felt like a child asking for her father, and it made her angry.

The first guard moved toward her, shifting his spear to his other hand.

She ducked under him and ran. The guards shouted,

but she sprinted down the holly- and ivy-hung steps, pushing through the clinging fingers of mistletoe. The frescoes and mosaic work were almost indistinguishable now for all the greenery. The satyrs bounded after her, but she was quicker than them somehow. She followed the music down the vaulted corridor.

As she drew closer, she heard the shrieks and laughter of the Prince's court. Pain speared into her side, as though someone was sewing her lungs together with a fine needle. The satyr guards' hooves clicked behind her. A few more strides and they would see her. She slipped through the ballroom door, and slid along a wall of dark columns. She doubted her linen gown would hide her much, but maybe if she made it over to those shadows . . .

Then she looked at the dais and froze. Her Prince was there, surrounded by his courtiers—adoring nixes and leering phookas, hairy satyrs and long-fingered hobs. A hollow-eyed kelpie reminded her of something she couldn't quite place.

The Prince sat on his gnarled throne. Around his throat glimmered a golden serpent that held a dark star sapphire between its golden jaws. Lady Thornvane entered, wearing a crimson gown embroidered with horned animals that moved and leaped with every step she took. The Prince stood as she approached, watching as she knelt at his feet. He removed the pendant from his neck and clasped it on his aunt.

"For your bravery and loyal service, dear aunt," he said. He kissed her on her forehead and helped her to rise. "Safeguard this stone, and use it to further our aims in this our reclaimed rath."

Lady Thornvane's amber eyes flared.

"Let the banquet begin!" the Prince called.

Phookas with their poisonous blue skin and cleft lips drew twisted tables up from the floor, while a bevy of nixes fluttered about laying out spidersilk cloths and onyx plates. Wicked crystal sparked like fire along the table, and the hob seneschal came behind, filling the glasses with the Prince's favorite dark wine. Though dishes and trays of various foods were brought out, a great vacant space was left before the Prince and his aunt. Everyone seated themselves, with the Prince and his aunt at the head of the table in carved ebony chairs. Corrine longed to join them, but forced herself to remain in the shadows. She thought of going back to her room, but was afraid now that she would be seen, and perhaps punished like a wanton child. She didn't want the Prince to think of her that way.

Then, the ballroom doors swung open, and the Prince's hobgoblin guard bore in an elaborately worked tray. On top of it lay a beautiful girl, smiling in her sleep. She clasped bunches of sugared grapes in her hands, and violets, nasturtiums, and other edible flowers festooned her body. The hobgoblins sat the tray before the Prince and Lady Thornvane and departed. Corrine stared, while the Prince's courtiers whispered in anticipation.

The Prince bent over the girl. Her eyes opened and her smile grew. He passed his hand tenderly over her cheek, and jealousy stabbed Corrine forward. Then the Prince sank thorny teeth into the girl's throat. Her breath stopped, and her skin went paler than hot ash. Corrine gasped. The girl's eyes glazed as Lady Thornvane leaned and bit into her wrist. Her skin withered and crumpled around her bones, blackened at the fingertips as though frostbitten.

Corrine put her hands over her mouth, trying not to scream. She remembered a hand like that once, reaching out from under a blanket in a rain-soaked alley. A hand with a silver ring. A girl who had been lost that she had to find . . . But she couldn't remember who it had belonged to or why the memory of it came now.

The phooka and his companions removed the girl from the tray when the Prince and his aunt had had their fill. They carried her over to a corner where bones had already been piled and finished the work the Prince and his aunt had begun. Corrine shrank against the living wall, her stomach revolting against what she'd seen.

Hands seized and dragged her from behind the column where she crouched. The satyrs forced her to her knees before the Prince. The phooka stared, his tongue darting from blue lips.

"Corrine," the Prince said, getting up from his chair and coming to stand over her. The miasma of blood was heavy about him. "Why are you here?" He signaled to the satyr guards and they released her.

She stood slowly. The top of her head came just to his chest. She couldn't look at his face. She glimpsed Lady Thornvane staring at her with such hatred that she looked down at her feet. "I had a bad dream," she mumbled.

"Look at me, dear one," he said. When she wouldn't, he put his hand under her chin and raised it so she was forced to look in his eyes. "What you saw was a bad dream sent by the witches. Only now—this moment that you are here with me—is real. When you wake, you will remember only this moment."

He slid his hands across her shoulders and into her hair. Then he pulled her head back and kissed her deeply on the mouth. *Sleep*, his lips whispered into her mouth. She melted into liquid fire in his arms, and for the rest of the night she dreamed that she and her Prince were two flames melding and drifting, dancing with one another all through the sleeping time.

Her Prince had gone as he had said he would, leaving her in the care of his aunt. Corrine had begged to go with him. She had cried and taken fistfuls of his cloak in her hands.

"Say you'll be my bride," he'd said. "And then I will not have to go alone."

She wanted to say yes, wanted to say she'd marry him, only that she couldn't. Something was not quite right. But all that came out were dark-stained tears.

And then she'd said, "But I've been there before, in your city." She didn't know how this could be true, but she knew somehow that it was.

He had frowned then, his eyes growing stormy and dark.

"Take care of her," he'd said to Lady Thornvane. "The Turning is not yet complete. Do not fail with it this time." Then he'd looked again at Corrine. "She must be ready when I return."

She'd watched one of the bird-footed women hunch over then, shrieking and stretching until she became a large, green crow. The Prince mounted her and she lifted heavily off over the wintry plain.

The snow threatened to turn pink at Corrine's feet before the golden-haired physician took her roughly by the arm and said, "Come. You are mine, now."

Since then, Lady Thornvane hadn't been very nice. In addition to the warm, spiced wine every night there were other nasty-tasting draughts that the Prince's aunt forced her to drink from a gilded skull cup. Corrine didn't like the cup and fought it whenever she could.

The Prince's aunt never left Corrine alone in her room, but didn't like having to see her, either. So, while the physician consulted with her bird-women in tongues Corrine couldn't quite understand, Corrine was forced to sit in an adjacent library. The satyr guards crouched outside. Corrine sensed their boredom for whenever anyone walked by—a lissome nix or a blue-skinned phooka—they stood to attention, their short, furry tales wagging in eagerness. The rest of the time they just crouched, spears held listlessly, murmuring in their sharp, lilting language.

She embroidered for a while, until she pricked her finger and bled black on the fine linen. She seemed to remember once liking books, so she began perusing the shelves and pulling down those that looked most interesting.

Some of them prickled her fingers when she touched them. Others refused to be read; their letters squiggling away from her until she got a headache from trying to read them and gave up. One, however, was readable— *History of the War of Mortal Aggression, or Customs of the Conquerors.*

Corrine read all afternoon of the mortals after that—their filthy habits, bizarre social conventions, and base ability to breed seemingly unto infinity. She read of their discovery of cursed iron, shrinking as she thought of the horrid metal touching her flesh. She read of how they aged and saw the horrifying depictions of their old men and women, as well as drawings of their delicious-looking children. Everything about the mortal locusts was peculiarly fascinating, as if she'd picked up a faint thread of memory and any moment might tug and spill out the source in its entirety. She supposed she had been raised among them, though the Prince had never discussed much with her beyond his attempts at rescuing her from the witches. She supposed at one time she must have thought herself one of them.

Visions flashed. A black-robed priest was speaking to her before a fire, holding out a locket made of moss and bone. A woman with eyes blue as larkspur helped her up from the dirt. There was a great iron beast that rolled on the waves and made her ill, a little church high on a hill . . .

Corrine shook her head and shuddered. They weren't real. *This* was real. This chair and table, the satyrs outside, the low clucks and singing voices of the bird-women in the next room.

She looked into the next room, hoping to glimpse something, someone, a face to prove that it was all true. She glimpsed a woman bearing a kerchief-covered tray, a woman who glanced into the library. She met Corrine's eyes, and her lips quirked in a half-smile. There was a feline tilt to her eyes that Corrine recognized, something in her smile. The woman in the garden. Then, memory hit her like a wave. A trunk. And under the trunk's lid a portrait of this woman, a portrait that smiled at her sadly even after it had been torn . . .

The name whispered to her. *Mary Rose.*

She was about to leap up after her, but then she heard the Prince's aunt say, "How dare you? Remove your presence from my sight at once."

Something clattered, and Corrine saw the woman leave in a flurry of green silk. She didn't look at Corrine again, but she didn't have to. Corrine knew her.

Lady Thornvane came to the door of the library and looked in on her, her amber eyes almost molten gold in her fury. Corrine stared hard at her book and heard the twisted doors slide shut between the rooms. The door to the outer hall slammed and locked itself.

She spent the rest of the afternoon trying to recover more of the memory, trying to understand who Mary Rose was or how she knew her or why the name gave her such a secret, sad delight. What had her old life been before the witches, before the Prince found her? What did Mary Rose have to do with it? As she moved along the shelves, a golden-spined book tingled when she touched it. She drew it out, and was delighted by the two serpents that coiled on its cover beneath her hands. She opened it and thick clots of ink swam onto the pages. They resolved into a single message. *Take me with you.*

Corrine looked around the closed room before slipping it in her pocket.

When the sleeping time finally came, instead of sleeping, Corrine looked out of her window across the green garden and cold towers of the Prince's palace. The walls trembled and groaned around her. Sometimes, the palace shifted, like a living thing forced into the same eternal position. It was often restless and mercurial—she had woken sometimes to a very different view than the one to which she'd fallen asleep, but this sleeping time, the palace seemed unable to settle.

She looked out over the pearly-gray twilight. It was wrong. She knew it was, but she couldn't remember what should be in its place.

There was a click and a sigh in the wall near her bed.

Corrine turned.

Mary Rose. She opened her mouth to say the woman's name, but Mary Rose put a finger over her lips and shook her head.

She gestured for Corrine to follow her into the quickly-shrinking door by the bed.

Corrine came and the woman seized her wrist and dragged her into the hole before it snicked shut behind them.

The woman put her mouth against Corrine's ear. The scent of cloves and lilies swirled around her. "Come with me," the woman said.

Corrine followed her through rock-lined tunnels and colonnaded halls, crept down corridors lined with sleeping doors, until at last they wormed their way through a giant rabbit warren and came out into a chamber that appeared to be a root cellar. What little light there was came from the phosphorescent lichen and glowing worms that wriggled through the walls.

Mary Rose listened at the warren entrance for a moment before pronouncing, "I think we'll be safe here. I think we're far enough underground that Leanan won't hear."

Leanan. Lady Thornvane. More memories. The amber-eyed witch trapping the priest on a frozen lake . . .

"His name is Father Josephus," Mary Rose said. "Or, in your time, Father Joe."

Then came his shouting at her at the ball when she'd danced with the Prince, the morning when he'd climbed into the dory on the sinking ship, the argument before he'd disappeared . . . Corrine drew in a deep, gasping breath.

"I don't know—" she began.

"Your memories will sort themselves out in time," Mary Rose said. "It is fortunate you still have them, though I know it feels quite unfortunate now. At this moment, though, time is very short. My father will soon return and he will expect . . . Do you understand what is happening to you, Corrine?"

Corrine shook her head. Tears stung like biting flies. "The Prince said—"

"That you were a changeling stolen from us by witches? That he rescued you to be his bride? That the visions that trouble you are sent by the witches to torment you?" Mary Rose's tone was sharp.

Corrine nodded.

"Tell me, Corrine, do you remember your childhood among us? Surely, if you were meant to be the bride of a prince, your parents must have been very important."

"I've been trying," Corrine said. "He said—"

"That the witches had taken it from you and it would all be returned in time? And that all those terrible visions of him drinking mortal blood are just dreams sent by the witches to haunt you?"

Corrine twisted her hands together in her gown. "Yes," she said.

"And this time, I'd hoped he'd become a better liar," Mary Rose said. Her eyes glinted in the half-darkness.

"What?" Corrine whispered.

Mary Rose grasped her hand. "Come."

The wall yawned in front of her, and they were burrowing again through the glimmering earth. Things passed in Corrine's peripheral vision—pocket watches, doll heads, twisted spoons—all the detritus she'd ascribed to a life that had never belonged to her.

At last they came to a tiny, ornately carved door. Mary Rose opened it and pressed her face against it to peer outside.

Then she tugged Corrine and they were through the door in a vast cavern, lit by floating balls of witch-light. The cavern was filled with human girls in filthy conditions—girls ranging from five to eighteen. All of them wandered smiling and glassy-eyed, as if they walked in a waking dream. Satyr and hobgoblin guards stood high above the pit.

Mary Rose pulled Corrine quickly beneath an over-hang. Corrine felt indignant at being hauled around. She looked behind her just in time to see the tiny door melt into the wall.

"What are you doing? Why have you brought me here?" she said.

Mary Rose dug her fingers into her shoulders.

"This is what happens to all those precious girls, Corrine. They're not dreams spun by evil witches to taunt you. They are *food.*"

Corrine jerked around as best she could so she could look in Mary Rose's eyes. There was a vague memory or a dream—something about a girl and the Prince biting into her as easily as if she were a slice of cake. "What do you mean?"

"Every night you drink strange-tasting, spiced wine, do you not? You have seen the Prince drink from the throat of a girl and the phooka eat her remains. You don't want to believe, but . . ."

Something moved above them and Mary Rose fell silent. Someone had come out onto the cliff edge above the pit with the guards.

"Watch," Mary Rose whispered into Corrine's ear.

The witch-light lanterns floated close enough that Corrine could discern Leanan's features. Corrine shrank back as far as she could.

Leanan sent the lanterns floating out over the pit. Their light grazed a shoulder or a cheek here and there, briefly exposing faces lost in the stupor of dreams.

All the lights at last circled one young girl, who looked to be perhaps eleven. Leanan extended her hand and lifted it, and the globes raised the girl from the floor in a ring of pulsing witch-light until she was standing on the cliff edge next to the witch.

Leanan examined the girl coolly, avoiding touching her directly, but looking into her ears, her eyes, her mouth as if she was searching for something. She lifted the edge of the girl's dirty shift with her thumb and index finger and peered at the girl's toes. She nodded to one of the satyrs and he came forward and drew a shallow cut across the girl's arm with his dagger. The girl didn't flinch. Leanan touched the very tip of her tongue to the girl's arm.

The Prince's aunt sighed. "This one's merely meant for eating, I'm afraid," she said to the satyr. "Take her to my rooms. I shall dine on her later."

The satyrs carried the girl off. Throughout the entire

ordeal, she had never said a word or once cried out. Corrine bit her lip to hold in a sob.

Leanan stood for a moment looking out over the edge of the pit. "Surely there must be at least one other," she said aloud. "He cannot have killed or Turned them all. Surely they are not all locusts and cattle." At last, she turned, sweeping the train of her gown behind her, and disappeared from the cliff's edge.

Corrine sat hard against the rock, weeping.

"Do you know it to be true now?" Mary Rose asked. "Do you understand that you have come among the Unhallowed? That your beloved Prince and all his kin are no more than vampires, scavenging off of mortal blood?"

Corrine nodded.

"And," Mary Rose pressed further, "do you understand that they wish to make you one of them?"

But Corrine wasn't looking at her. The roaming witch-light tricked out a familiar face, a face she had seen in a photograph on Miss Brown's desk seemingly ages ago.

She made to lunge, but Mary Rose caught her. "What are you doing?" the woman hissed.

"Alex," Corrine said, "Miss Brown's sister—she went away to war—with my father." She remembered her father's letter to Miss Brown. It came back in such hard, heavy waves that she could barely breathe.

And then the witch-light revealed another face—dark blonde hair, green, dreaming eyes . . .

"Penelope!" Corrine shouted.

There was a great moaning sound as the palace shifted above them. Dust sifted down through from the cavern ceiling.

"He is coming," Mary Rose said. "He knows that something is happening to you. Corrine, listen!" She gripped Corrine by the shoulders and forced her eyes away from the little girl drifting through the crowd. "I am going to do something and it will hurt quite a bit, but you must trust what happens, yes?"

Corrine nodded and Mary Rose released her.

"I am sending you back out of this rath and into the mortal world. You and Alex and . . . Penelope will be very sick for a time, but Josephus will help you. Give him my greetings and take these with you." Mary Rose pressed something into her hand—a golden chain with a little golden book and a packet that smelled rather like camphor. "Take the medicine in the packet. It will speed your recovery. The Prince will come after you, and he will be all the more powerful because he can access the power of two stones now. When you find the Stone of Destiny, you must use it as soon as possible to send you to another rath where he cannot find you, do you understand? One day the mortal world will be safe for you again, but not now."

"But what about you?" Corrine said.

Mary Rose smiled. "I learned long ago that this is my place. But it is clearly not yours."

"Will the Prince . . ." Corrine couldn't bear to say it. Just thinking of him, the loss of him, made her body ache as though someone had cut off a limb. She suddenly understood Christina and how she must have felt to lose Rory again. And there was another memory—Christina, Rory, Brighde and Angus . . .

"He will be angry, but he dare not hurt me." Mary Rose tilted her head, as though she saw Corrine's memories. "Brighde was very special to him, for as much as he punished her for her betrayal. And he still has hope of me."

Corrine stared. "You are their child."

Mary Rose inclined her head and smiled. "The last child to be born of human and Fey."

"But Mara . . ."

Mary Rose's brow wrinkled. "That one still eludes us."

The palace heaved.

Mary Rose looked up toward where the hobgoblin guards patrolled. The witch-light globes dimmed and wobbled before resuming their circuits around the cavern.

"We mustn't chatter more," Mary Rose said. "You must go now, before he arrives and finds you gone. Are you ready?"

Corrine nodded.

"Then go with my blessing. And may Elaphe heal us all," Mary Rose said. She clasped Corrine to her in what Corrine thought was an embrace, but as Mary Rose's grip tightened over her shoulder, she wasn't certain. Her shoulder began to burn as though a fire had been set on it, and she tried to cry out, but Mary Rose held her head against her so that she couldn't. The burning intensified until Corrine thought she would faint from the pain. An algal, slimy taste coated her tongue and a feverish sweat broke out across her body. She struggled, wondering if she was dying.

Then, Mary Rose released her and Corrine swiveled to see a tall, dark horse standing outside the entrance, reins dangling toward his finned fetlocks.

"I wondered if you were going to leave me trapped in there for eternity," the kelpie said. He looked hungrily around at all the bewitched girls. "Paradise," he sighed.

Mary Rose looked at him sternly as she drew Corrine out from the overhang. "Not now, kelpie. You must take her back to the mortal world. She has work to do."

Corrine eyed the guards as she knotted the reins. She went over to Alex, who drifted nearby, and steered her toward the kelpie. The girl struggled a little as Mary Rose tried to get her aboard, but she didn't cry out.

Corrine went to where she'd seen Penelope last and tracked her down through the crowd, trying to avoid the witch-light globe as much as possible.

"Penelope," she whispered in the girl's ear. But the little girl didn't hear her. She was lost in some dream that Corrine couldn't breach. Corrine grabbed her hand, and when Penelope didn't seem inclined to follow, Corrine hauled her up into her arms. Penelope was so thin that she seemed not to weigh much more than a four-year-old.

"There is one more thing you must know," Mary Rose said, as Corrine struggled to lift Penelope and then haul herself up behind them both. The kelpie looked back as if to protest carrying so many people.

Mary Rose took Corrine's hand and Corrine looked down at her. "Your father is still alive, Corrine. And if you succeed in all of this, I have no doubt you'll save him too."

A witch-light globe dipped close to them. Everyone went still, looking at one another in the harsh glow. The globe shrieked like a hawk and dived toward them, drawing several others in its wake.

"Corrine, go!" Mary Rose said. She held up something silver in her hand. Corrine saw it was the Prince's signet ring that she'd taken from him so long ago, the ring that had meant she had promised herself to him.

Mary Rose threw it against the cave wall and a latticework frame raced in silver fire across the rock. The gates swung open. Corrine clamped her knees around the kelpie as he leaped toward the gate, trying to hold onto both girls and the reins at the same time. She glanced back and saw Mary Rose encircled in a ring of pulsing witch-light globes. And then Corrine saw, sweeping down toward Mary Rose, the changeable eyes of a great raven, a dark wolf, a wooden death mask with searching eyes—the face of the Prince himself.

"Go!" Mary Rose shouted, even as the kelpie leaped.

The palace walls crumbled around her and she swallowed dirt and darkness until all was light and air.

~Fifteen~

June 15, 1866

Corrine raised her head from the other girls' shoulders only when she heard the kelpie's hoof knocking stone. She wiped dust from her eyes, and tried to sit straighter. But before she could the door opened and people called her name.

"My God, Corrine! Penelope!" She struggled against the hands on her waist, then found herself looking up into Father Joe's dark eyes. He smelled terrible to her. Everything did. She tried to hold her hand over her mouth to keep from being ill. Penelope spilled from her arms into a heap on the front steps of Fearnan. They hadn't returned to London.

And then Miss Brown came around the kelpie and saw the girl hunched over his withers.

"Alexandra!" Miss Brown put her hands to her mouth and bit at her knuckles as though the pain would keep her from fainting. "Alex?" she said again, in disbelief. She rushed forward to the girl and dragged her off of the kelpie's back almost before Ilona could help her.

"Mama," the girl moaned, still caught in her dream. "Mama, don't think bad of me, Mama."

Corrine had wondered if Alex ever felt guilt for leaving her family. She guessed from Alex's protestations that she did.

Miss Brown sank down on her knees with her, sobs tearing from her in great gasps. She patted Alex's dirty face with her handkerchief. "No, darling, I swear, Mama won't think bad of you. Not at all."

Alex didn't say anything more, and Miss Brown held her for long moments, smoothing away the dirt and the grime with her tears and handkerchief. Then Ilona helped her to rise, and Mr. Turnbull came to help carry Alex inside. Siobhan and Mara bent over Penelope, helping her to stumble to her feet.

Miss Brown came to Corrine, though Corrine could hardly see her through the dust and dirt that still seemed to clog her eyes. Miss Brown also had a harsh, perfumed smell—lye and lavender, moth balls and sweat.

"Corrine, thank you," she said, tears making ugly red tracks down her face. "Thank you for bringing my Alex back to me."

Corrine nodded and sighed, thinking of the letter written by her father. He was still lost to her. The kelpie snorted and stomped, then disappeared.

"May I go to sleep now?" Corrine asked.

"Yes," Father Joe said, half-laughing.

His outline went gray as twilight. She looked away and thought she saw perhaps ten or twenty girls all in various stages of dishevelment wandering in confusion around the front steps of Fearnan. Then she was being carried up to bed, and the rough cloth of Father Joe's cassock abraded her cheek such that she almost cried out in pain. When she landed in the hard bed, the thought came that she had lost her Prince forever, and sleep chased him far beyond her reach.

Mortal food made Corrine deathly ill. She vomited blood for what seemed days, then stared listlessly at boiled mutton and potatoes. She looked on the pale or rosy limbs of her nurses with greater hunger than anything offered her on bowl or plate, but the thought was revolting. Nothing felt right. The sheets were too rough, the wood too solid, the fire too smoky and dim. Coal stank, but the burning of wood made her both enraged and ill, especially when someone laid what she knew was a bit of rowan on the hearth. That time, she had gone into a rage and perched in her drafty window seat, threatening to leap out of the window if someone didn't remove the log from the fire. Coal was better, at least.

Everything was wrong. Everything. She remembered clearly what had happened. She remembered what the Prince had said and done, and the truth that Mary Rose had revealed to her. She remembered Leanan's cruelty. And yet, she pined for those moments when she had been with the Prince, when they had stood together in his poisonous garden or when he had told her the story that she now knew was a lie over and over again. She knew what had happened, and yet her emotions veered as wildly as a bucking kelpie.

In one moment, when Christina came to visit her, looking pale and unhappy as she always did now, Corrine took her hand. "I know now," she said. "I know how you feel." And the confession pulled tears from both of them, though Corrine's were still tinged a little with blood.

Father Joe sat with her most often, except of course

when necessity dictated she bathe or change her clothes. Often, he didn't speak, but glanced at her occasionally, as if he waited for something to come—some realization, some change—about which she wasn't fully aware.

Each night, he and Mara renewed the wards over her, trying to ensure that the Prince would not visit her in her dreams. Corrine sensed him hunting for her and she could not admit how often she reached for him, but there was a dark veil between them that neither of them could cross. All she heard when she stood against the curtain were whispers and curses.

But one night, she heard him weeping. She heard the Prince's tears. And the black blood welled underneath the curtain and pooled at her feet.

Then, Father Joe was shaking her awake. "Corrine," he said. "You mustn't. Don't let him cross the veil. Keep the borders closed to him."

She dug her fingers into his coarse cassock. "I can't; I don't want to anymore!" He held her as the sorrow shook her body, the sorrow for the world she had lost and the horror of the truth.

"I know," he said, rocking her and holding her close. "Believe me, my child, how well I know it." He stroked her head gently, but the touch still felt harsh compared to the Prince's and she sobbed all the harder for want of him.

"The Turning is an evil, evil spell," Father Joe whispered. "It takes all your brightest dreams, all your deepest hopes for love and twists them around your heart in a great, thorny tangle. You feel you will die before you ever get free of it."

Corrine knew now what he had experienced at the

hands of Leanan, and just as she now felt greater compassion for Christina, she also understood Father Joe's sorrow, his barely leashed rage.

"But it worked on you, didn't it?" she said, resting her cheek against his chest. "You are . . . like them now. I can feel it."

"Yes," he said. "I am the only one with whom they have both gloriously succeeded and failed at once."

"But . . . if you are like them, how do you . . . ?" It felt rude to ask the questions.

He sighed. "Ever notice the ready quantity of piglets and calves at Falston?" he said. "I've trained myself not to feed as often as they do, and not to live off human blood." He trembled a little, and Corrine caught the edges of some memory that he quickly hid away. A little boy, a palm-strewn alley . . .

"Will I . . . also have to do that?" The thought was more revolting than it would have been a few days ago.

"I don't believe so," Father Joe said. "I think the Turning was not very advanced in you. You didn't feed willingly off anyone?"

The image of the girl at the banquet hovered in her mind. She pulled away and looked into Father Joe's face. "No," she said. "Not that I remember."

He squeezed her upper arm. "Good. You had not progressed with it as much as I feared. If you had, you would be Unhallowed now, but with all the powers and attributes of the Half-Born. There would be nothing the Council could do to aid you."

And you would have to die. She nodded, understanding the bitter truth of those unspoken words.

"You will be well again," he said. "But life will never

feel quite as it did. There will be a dullness about it, a roughness that will grate on you at times." He stood and began pacing before the low-burning fire. "There will be times when you feel you would give everything to be with him and to live again in the joy of his presence."

Corrine wound her fingers into the rough sheets. To deal with that every day . . . How could she do it? How could she live without him?

Father Joe turned. "But I have done it. For centuries. I have lived every day cut off from her love. I have lived every day in this hard, fetid, ugly world, scavenging on pig's blood, and I will keep doing it. Until I know that Hallowmere is safe from them and the Hallowed have been returned to their natural state. Until I know that the Unhallowed are no more, I cannot rest. No one should endure what we have, Corrine. No one."

That she could not argue. But she ached to hear the Prince's voice say again, *Why did you not come to me sooner?*

Father Joe returned to her bedside. "In the beginning, I must admit I feared for you. I feared you were too weak for the battle. Your mother, bless her, hid behind the iron cross and refused to believe the Unhallowed were anything but nightmares sent to punish her for some unknown offense. And your father . . ."

"My father!" Corrine interrupted. She would have leaped out of bed if he hadn't stood in the way. "My father is alive!" she said.

In all the desolation, she had nearly forgotten this one small fact, this little gem that had carried her on the kelpie's back out of darkness and witch-light and back into the mortal world.

Father Joe looked at her a little dubiously.

"Mary Rose told me so," Corrine said. "She said—"

Father Joe stopped her. "Mary Rose? You are certain you saw her?"

"It was she who saved us. She sent us back. She sends her greetings and . . . medicine that you're to give us to help us get well." Corrine looked at the darkened nightstand, searching for the little leather pouch. It was there, along with the Unhallowed book that had ridden safely back in her pocket.

Father Joe closed his eyes and bowed his head. "Mary Rose," he whispered. She heard all the secret sorrow in his voice, but its origins were too distant to track.

"She's the daughter of Brighde and the Prince, isn't she?" Corrine said.

Father Joe nodded. "And your foremother, five centuries distant." He looked as though he wanted to put his head in his hands, but he gazed at her in the semi-darkness, little flames catching dark glints in his eyes.

"My foremother?" Corrine frowned. "But that would mean . . ."

"The Prince is also your ancestor."

She put her hands over her mouth and shook in wordless denial. "But he said . . . I kissed . . . We were to be *married* . . ."

"He needs your blood, Corrine. Or he believes he does. It has always been the custom of the Fey to marry only within the circles of the nobility. Several of the noble clans were exterminated when the war began between Hallowed and Unhallowed and the rest were sealed away in several closed raths. To add insult to injury, I cursed all the Unhallowed with barrenness *except that the Prince get a child from Brighde* again. I said this out of malice, for I had just watched Brighde die in childbirth in my arms, and I was angry that she had been lost. And I was still terribly bitter over the harm done me by Leanan."

Corrine's stomach heaved. She leaned over the side of the bed and vomited into the pan that stood there waiting should she need it. She hadn't vomited for days, but her stomach was still so tender that she clutched it in agony.

Father Joe dipped a cloth in the nightstand pitcher and patted it across her forehead and mouth when she sat back in the bed.

"You must know all this," he said. "I never wanted to tell you any of it; I had hoped that you would never become this involved. But you see now why I sent Mara with that message. I was terrified that you would marry him, that you would become one of them, that he would, for the first time in centuries, spawn an Unhallowed child who might be even more powerful than his father. And that you would suffer for the knowledge of your kinship, however many centuries gone."

Corrine stared. Was this true? Had he only wanted her for that reason? It was so awful, so like one of the old Gothic romances she had once loved, that it seemed too fantastical to contemplate. But had he not truly loved her? If it had only been about a child, would he not have simply . . . She swallowed.

Father Joe followed her thoughts. "I know, my dear. I know how awful this must be for you. And it pains me greatly to be at the very heart of it. But I think you see the truth now and why we must keep the Prince from you and from Hallowmere. If he regains either, there is no telling what he will be able to do with the other. And if you recall, he has taken the Iron Oath as his pledge that he will have both you and Hallowmere. We must stop him before that happens. We must get to Hallowmere. Do you understand?"

Corrine's stomach ached as though it wanted to send her over the bed again, but there was nothing left. She was hollow and empty as a shell. If what Father Joe said was true, and she felt deep in her heart that it must be, then he was also right.

"Which means we need the rathstones," she said dully.

"As quickly as we can assemble them," he said.

"But how will I find all of them by myself?" Corrine asked. "Mary Rose said something about using the Stone of Destiny, but—"

"You can't," Father Joe said. "You'll need help. And you won't be able to go into the Prince's rath again. The desire to stay would be overwhelming. If he captures you there, I'm quite certain you'll never want to leave. No," he said, pacing again, "I think we must find a way to lure him out, make him come to you. We must send you into another rath where he is less powerful."

"But he has two rathstones now," Corrine said. She held an arm over her knotted stomach and eased back against the pillows.

Father Joe saw her and said, "Perhaps this should wait. Miss Brown wouldn't like to know that I'm keeping you from your rest."

"No," she said, "Mary Rose said the same thing. She said it would be too easy for him to find me here, that we needed to use the Stone of Destiny for me to escape him. But how can I travel to all the raths to find all the stones?" she asked.

"We send those who are willing to go after the stones. It's a terrible risk, but I think it's our only choice."

"Whom do you mean?"

"Ilona, Christina, Mara, Siobhan, and you, of course."

"But . . . no one else has magic besides me and Mara," Corrine said. "How would they ever find the stone, much less survive?"

Father Joe's smile was forced. "This is always the way of it, Corrine. We work with whatever broken bits we have and make use of them. Siobhan has magic, though she won't use it. Ilona can fight better than any man. And Christina has a magic all her own when it comes down to all that."

"But how can we do this alone?"

"You won't be. We will do everything we can to guide you, to keep up the illusion that you are all still with us, and to strew deception and mayhem in the Unhallowed ranks whenever we can. There are also a few Hallowed left in the raths, some of whom guard the rathstones. We will send out word to them, and they will help you, if they can. The Council can't promise complete safety. It never could. But we are running out of alternatives, Corrine. Don't you agree?"

Corrine nodded. It certainly wasn't the best way, but when she thought of going entirely alone, rath by rath, of having to crawl back into the Prince's rath and try to take the stones from him, she understood the wisdom of doing things this way.

"This is a last desperate measure," Father Joe said.

"But it's entirely voluntary. We will not ask you to do something you don't wish to do. If we have to, we will find another way."

Corrine thought of all the girls trapped alone in the dark pit. She didn't know how many hundreds, how many thousands, waited either to be used in pursuit of Hallowmere or to be slaughtered like cattle at the Unhallowed table.

"No," she said. "We'll do it this way. And I know how."

She looked up at him as he came and patted her shoulder. His touch was still too rough and clumsy, but she felt the prickle of his Half-Born power.

"May I sleep now?" she said.

"Yes," he said. "And a good rest to you. I'll be by the fire if you wake again."

He went back to his chair and she turned away from him on her side. She could still smell her blood-rich vomit, but the smell of the terrible truth about the Prince's kinship to her was even worse. Yet, through it all, she had remembered. Her father was alive. And somehow she would find him and bring him home.

Sixteen

June 20, 1866

THE KIRK OF ST. FILLAN HUDDLED AGAINST THE GROUND, its roof open to the sky, the headstones of its grave-yard broken and overturned on the heather. It had been a long time since anyone had worshiped here, and even longer since Father Joe had been a young monk freshly inducted into the monastery. A great tree grew through the sanctuary, spreading its arms above the rotten pews. Father Joe walked around out-side alone, pacing the foundations of the place he'd once known as a bustling collective of his brethren, while everyone else poked around the silent church. Alex and Miss Brown stayed close to one another, whispering over the crumbling knotwork masonry under one of the windowsills. Penelope stayed with Ilona. It had taken Alex and Penelope nearly as long as Corrine to come out from under the Unhallowed spell. Between the three of them, Mara had been nearly exhausted.

Corrine had been surprised to learn that several girls had also somehow been caught in their magical wake and were also recovering at Fearnan. She had seen them just before Father Joe had carried her upstairs, but had dismissed them as a vision or a fever dream. Most of them were still abed at Fearnan, as there really hadn't been enough medicine to go around, but they were slowly recovering their strength. Miss Brown had been learning their names and families, trying to find ways to explain how they'd been found in Scotland and to send them home as soon as they were well.

Corrine smiled when Miss Brown's eyes sparkled as she touched Alex's sleeve. Of all the things worth giving up life in the Unhallowed rath, rescuing the girls was certainly one of the greatest. Ilona settled Penelope in one of the sturdiest pews and came to Corrine as she searched among the broken stones by the baptismal font.

"Corrine, do you really want this?" Ilona was dressed in her boy's clothes, her cap pulled low over her face. Christina wandered nearby, looking without interest at the decrepit church, passing her hands thoughtfully over the tree's trunk. "Can we not all go together and protect each other?" Ilona asked.

Corrine shook her head. Comforting as this would have been, she knew that it would also be too obvious. The Unhallowed would expect something like that.

"It would be like throwing all our eggs in one basket," Corrine said. "Too easy for them to find us. If we force them to spread themselves thinly, maybe we have a chance of slipping through the net."

"But we're spreading ourselves thinly too!" Ilona said. Her whispers echoed off the mossy stones.

Corrine patted her arm. "I know. Believe me. But I think this will be much better. He would not expect this." And as she said it, she knew it was true. The Prince would expect them all to come at him. He would expect her to come back to his rath with a knife to cut his heart out when she realized what he had known all along. His soft kiss burned her mouth again.

"Corrine?" Ilona said.

Corrine focused on her friend and tried to smile. Ilona had only asked one thing of her, and it had been a question she was sadly unable to answer. She had asked, looking sidelong at Penelope as she slept, if Corrine had seen Jeanette, the girl who had disappeared from Falston before Corrine had arrived. It had hurt Corrine to admit that she hadn't seen Jeanette in the pit. Ilona had swallowed and nodded then, and that had been the end of it. But Corrine knew that nearly all of them—Christina, Father Joe, and, once, Miss Brown—missed someone. And though she didn't know everything that had happened to Siobhan and Mara before they arrived at Falston, Corrine wouldn't have been surprised to learn that they had lost someone to the Unhallowed too.

"Yes," Corrine said, "we should get started. Wait here and I'll fetch Father Joe."

She went out into the warm evening, where Father Joe stood by the foundation stones, looking down across the village and toward the loch. The highland mountains rolled off behind them, their stony heads seeking the first stars.

"Father," she said, "we should begin."

He gestured down the hillside toward a cluster of ancient trees swaying over a knoll. "It was there I first saw her, when I was little more than your age, walking in the sunlight, her golden hair aflame."

Corrine reached for his hand and squeezed it. He looked down at her.

"And it is here I hope to end what never should have begun so long ago," he said.

Corrine nodded.

Together they went inside the church. Mara had already begun laying the pentagram out near the baptismal font. Miss Brown and Alex lit candles near the circle. The rest of the church was thrown into shadow.

"Now," Father Joe said, "Mara and Corrine will begin the visualization and establish contact. If the Hallowed here chooses to grace us with her presence and, as we hope, the Stone, the rest of you will move into position for the spell. Everyone else will stay outside the church." He eyed Miss Brown, Alex, and Penelope. "Hold to those warding stones, else you might be swept in the magic's wake."

There was a little gasp and a sob. Corrine turned to see Siobhan backing away.

"This is bad," she said, shaking her head. "Bad, bad, bad . . ."

But before she could continue, Ilona collared her and smacked her hard across the mouth.

"Listen, you," Ilona growled, "you'll not ruin this. Corrine and Father Joe—we've *all* been through too much to quit now. It's time to pay your debt. It's time to learn to fight for yourself. You'll not be a victim on my watch, do you hear?" She shook the maid just a little until Siobhan nodded.

"Ilona, Ilona!" Penelope stood from her pew and came to where Ilona held Siobhan. "I can go in her place. I can find the stone!" Penelope wasn't quite as energetic as she

287

had been in the old days, but Corrine guessed in a few weeks, she'd be back to it.

Ilona half-smiled. "Little one, I wish you could, but you're far too young. Now go outside with Miss Brown and Alex and hold tight to that wardstone, understand? We'll be back as soon as we can."

Penelope pouted, but when Ilona looked at her, she turned and went to where Miss Brown and Alex waited.

Ilona turned to Siobhan. "I hope that little girl shames you into doing your duty, if nothing else does!" She pushed Siobhan over to her place and the maid cowered there. Corrine shivered to think of Siobhan in the hands of the Unhallowed. If they found her, they would make short work of her. She prayed that Siobhan's rath would be simple and quick, that perhaps, like this, it was only a matter of going into a church and asking the Hallowed for help.

She and Mara sat in the circle holding hands. Father Joe came and gave them a quick blessing. "You all know what to do when you find the stones, yes?" Everyone nodded, even Siobhan. "I wish that you had been able to finish all of the domains," he said to Corrine. "But never fear, we'll continue with earth when you return."

Corrine nodded. She had never told him of her failure with earth, though she had mentioned that she had passed through water with the kelpie's help. He seemed to speak too lightly now, and Corrine knew that he wondered whether he would ever see her again if the spell worked as they hoped.

Don't think that, please, Corrine thought at him. She had to believe that she would return, that there was a world beyond the one that hung in the balance. Otherwise, it all seemed as fruitless as the Prince would have her believe.

Mara settled the cakes and half an old bottle of rum she'd brought. "Sir James drank all the scotch, damn him. This was all I had," she whispered. Corrine smiled.

She took Mara's hands and was almost immediately flying with her over the towers and into the garden of the sun. Without shifting form, they dove into the well. Only this time, when they emerged, it wasn't on a white beach, but somewhere dank and dark and so cramped that neither Corrine nor Mara could stand.

Mara made a little witch-light, and Corrine recognized the type of place they'd entered.

"A springhouse," she said.

Mara nodded and looked around. She hummed a soft, low chant, and the cakes and bottle of rum appeared in her hand. She left the cakes on a rock by the little spring and poured a little rum nearby, but not so that it would pollute the water.

Then she sat.

"What do we do now?" Corrine asked.

"We wait and see if she comes," Mara said.

It seemed like hours before tiny, slick fingers crept over the edge of the rock, feeling for the cake. Bit by bit, the cake disappeared. And then a loud moan nearly startled Corrine out of her very skin. Dry rushes rattled and then a curious creature like a bundle of sticks with withered limbs and tiny fingers hauled itself onto the rock. Its head peeped up out of the rushes like a turtle.

"Are you Nephri?" Mara said quietly.

"Scared you, did I?" the gainisg asked. Its voice was tremulous and fluting, like a lost shorebird.

Corrine nodded.

"Do you know why we're here?" Mara asked.

"Aye," Nephri said.

"And? We have made you offerings, and if you are inclined to aid us—" Mara said, shifting forward.

Nephi shook her head so that her reedy body rustled. "Nay, nothing doing, little witchlet. Lots of your sort poking around here trying to take what I got. Elaphe made me the rightful keeper of it long ago and so I shall remain."

"Listen here now," Mara said, but Corrine put her hand on her arm.

"Nephri," she said, "If you won't help us, we understand. But before we leave, I was told to give you a message."

The turtle head poked out further, and Nephri's large eyes glowed in Mara's witch-light. "Message?" she whistled.

"From your cousin Sedge on the River Thames," Corrine said. "He said to tell you he's living in a bucket on a mudbank now. But he misses the days you used to go moaning about the river banks in search of the dead together. He misses it very much. And he says to tell you that he will see you again if you will allow us to use the Stone of Destiny just this once. All of you will see one another again, if we can do this small thing."

There was a fluting wheeze that sounded at first like the gainisg was choking or gasping. Then Corrine realized that the creature was laughing.

"Old Sedge, eh?" Nephri said finally. "That's the best message I've had in centuries, little witchlet. Certainly worth the Stone of Destiny. But mind you don't tell

290

Elaphe—he's awful particular about oaths and guardians and all that sort."

Corrine smiled while Mara looked at her incredulously.

Nephri hopped off her rock and back into the spring.

"How did you—" Mara began.

"You just have to know the right people," Corrine said.

Mara looked as though she might be angry, but then she grinned.

Nephri came huffing and puffing up out of the water, dragging a strange stone after her.

"But . . . we thought—" Corrine said.

Nephri's fluting laugh rattled her reeds. "Oh, that old story about Loch Tay was just a rumor to throw off treasure seekers. The river doesn't know where it is anymore than the priests in that church do."

Corrine nodded. They would never have found it if she had not tried to pull up a bucket on the bank of the Thames and found Nephri's cousin under it. That such chance played so great a role in all of this chilled her.

"In any case, return it when you're done and don't tell Elaphe. And"—Nephri shook her tiny forefinger in Mara's face—"next time, bring scotch, young witchlet. Giving rum to a Highland Fey—shameful, I tell you, shameful!"

Mara's cheeks went dark crimson, but before she could apologize, Nephri hopped back into her spring.

They each took hold of the kidney-shaped stone, worn smooth with the waters of time, with a deeper indention in its center. They rose with it through water, fire, and air until they faced one another again across the circle, the stone held between them. Witch-light emanated and twined all around them, Mara's darker than Corrine's. Their power looped and knotted together, flooding the pentagram and braiding it with light, while the Stone of Destiny hovered darkly between them.

Corrine held the Falston stone in one hand and Mara held the Fearnan stone in the other. Slowly, as they had practiced, Corrine built the power within herself, up through the domain of water. She felt the kelpie's power buried inside her like a clamped oyster, and she pried the dark pearl from it and supplemented her own with it. She watched Mara rise through the last two elements she had not yet mastered, her skin crackling with the colors of every domain—gold, green, blue, black, and violet.

The gates of the raths hovered just at the edges of her consciousness. The stones sang just beyond them. She sensed a gate to the Prince's rath close by, the stone in his chest and Leanan's pendant singing their siren songs, but Mara drew her away.

Here, she said.

And all at once she saw them, saw all the gates where the rathstones hid, waiting for the Half-Born to find them again. And she saw, too, that Hallowmere and the Three Treasures were closer than anyone dared believe and yet so much farther than she had ever imagined. She saw the golden gate, the jaws of Elaphe, opening wide.

"Christina!" Ilona screamed a thousand miles away.

Corrine turned halfway in the gate, and saw Rory run through the circle, scooping Christina into his arms, before the two of them disappeared. In the hole they left, she saw something even more horrifying. Magic pulsed in waves of witch-light from the church. Miss Brown, Father Joe, Alex, and Penelope huddled together, holding tight to their wardstones behind some boulders. Barreling down the loch road toward the church at top speed was a man on a horse. Corrine recognized his dark curls and wild eyes just as the light swallowed him. Mr. Dimitrios Adamou. Come from London, she presumed, to save her.

Then he too was gone, and the golden jaws closed over her.

AFTERWORD

There seems to be some sort of novelistic faux pas in writing about places one has never visited. As a writer of nonfiction as well as fiction, I understand the urge for historical and physical accuracy and I have tried here as much as possible to be as accurate as I can with limited time and resources. One of the reasons I love fantasy is because it transports us to places we've never been. Pockets of Victorian London still exist, of course, but only as memories, monuments, or ephemera. It's not a country you can travel to, except in books. I hope here, whether I've visited London or no, that readers are nevertheless transported to the truth of the time and vision, depicted as accurately as possible. Here are a few books that inspired me along the way:

Inside the Victorian Home, Judith Flanders
Fairies, Brian Froud and Alan Lee
Everyday Life in the 1800s: A Guide for Writers, Students, and Historians, Marc McCutcheon
What Jane Austen Ate and Charles Dickens Knew, Daniel Pool
The London Underworld in the Victorian Period: Authentic First-Person Accounts by Beggars, Thieves, and Prostitutes, Henry Mayhew
Victorian London Street Life in Historic Photographs, John Thomson